Satisfy Me Again

Books by Renee Luke

MAKING HIM WANT IT

Books by Sydney Molare

SATISFY ME
(with Renee Alexis and Fiona Zedde)

Books by Fiona Zedde

BLISS

A TASTE OF SIN

EVERY DARK DESIRE

SATISFY ME
(with Renee Alexis and Sydney Molare)

Published by Kensington Publishing Corporation

Satisfy Me Again

Renee Luke
Sydney Molare
Fiona Zedde

APHRODISIA
KENSINGTON BOOKS
http://www.kensingtonbooks.com

All characters, companies, and products in this book have no existence outside of the imagination of the author. Events depicted are purely fictional and are not inspired by any person living or dead.

APHRODISIA BOOKS are published by

Kensington Publishing Corp.
850 Third Avenue
New York, NY 10022

"Kiss and Tell" copyright © 2008 by Renee Luke
"Matinee" copyright © 2008 by Sydney Molare
"Going Wild" copyright © 2008 by Fiona Zedde

All rights reserved. No part of this book may be reproduced in any form or by any means without the prior written consent of the Publisher, excepting brief quotes used in reviews.

All Kensington Titles, Imprints, and Distributed Lines are available at special quantity discounts for bulk purchases for sales promotions, premiums, fund-raising, and educational or institutional use.

Special book excerpts or customized printings can also be created to fit specific needs. For details, write or phone the office of the Kensington special sales manager: Kensington Publishing Corp., 850 Third Avenue, New York, NY 10022, attn: Special Sales Department, Phone: 1-800-221-2647.

Aphrodisia and the A logo Reg. U.S. Pat & TM Off.

ISBN-13: 978-0-7582-2191-9
ISBN-10: 0-7582-2191-6

First Kensington Trade Paperback Printing: January 2008

10 9 8 7 6 5 4 3 2 1

Printed in the United States of America

Contents

Kiss and Tell

Renee Luke

1

Malik Drew wrapped his fingers around his hard dick and stroked from the base all the way to the head, drawing up a bead of precum to the tip. Clenching his jaw tightly, he dragged a deep breath into his lungs, need clawing sharply at his gut.

Though he was tempted to close his eyes so he could imagine he was buried deep in the silken wet heat of a woman, he kept his gaze fixed on the television instead, on the sweet sexiness of *her*, the reason he was throbbing. The reason he was alone in his hotel room working his body when it should've been her doing it for him.

Should've been her soft hand stroking his flesh, her lush mouth moving against him, her tight body he fit himself within. Damn, he ached for relief, pulsed for the woman on the screen to become real to him.

Available to him.

Again he worked down his length, blood pulsing hard against his palm, sweat dampening his brow, his shoulders tense, his body primed and eager for her.

Sucking in another whistling breath between his teeth, he

kept his eyes fixed on the innocence of her smile, the shimmer in her green eyes, the curls surrounding her perfect face, curls that begged to be wrapped around his fingers and clinging to his skin.

Aw hell, what was he doing jerking off? Tearing his eyes from the TV set, he glanced at the closet, then the suitcase propped against the wall. He should throw on some shorts and a T-shirt, go down to the hotel bar, and find some fine-looking woman who'd be willing to come upstairs to take care of his needs.

Wouldn't be hard either. They all knew who he was, number 34, star running back for the New Orleans Saints. Sporting black and gold, he'd been the NFL's leading rusher for three years straight, last year's season culminating in a trip to the big-show and a Super Bowl ring.

Hell nah, finding a willing and easy chick to get in his bed for a couple hours to ease up the ache of lust wouldn't be a problem. Screw the bed—what he needed didn't require one, just a little mouth work so he could blow his wad and for a flash forget about what he really wanted.

Who he really needed.

"Shit," he growled, squeezing his lids tight for a second, his hand continuing the rhythmic glide of his fingers wrapped around his dick, slow and steady, the tempo he'd use when he made love to her for the first time.

He didn't want any female, any piece of ass who'd bend it over and offer it up.

He looked back at the television, the commercial break of the prerecorded show coming to an end and the camera flashing back on her.

He wanted *her*. The one woman who'd driven him back to wet dreams and masturbation.

Callie Moore, sex therapist and show hostess of *Kiss & Tell*, the late-night, tell-all television show he was watching now. Where he'd first seen her at least a year ago doing her thing for the camera, drawing in her audience with compassion in her eyes and a voice that caressed his skin in a way that should only be done between lovers.

A year of making a damn fool of himself, a year of fan letters to her show, of phone calls to the network. Hell, he was a *somebody*—didn't they recognize that? And yet he'd been unsuccessful in getting them to give up any personal info on her at all.

Short of becoming a real down-and-dirty stalker, he'd given up and retreated into hand jobs. Ones he gave himself.

Leaning back against the pillows, he kept his focus on the screen as he tried to ignore the feel of the air conditioner blowing against his sweat-dampened skin, tried to ignore the slight movement of the gusts that reminded him of a woman's breath.

Shifting his gaze, Malik shot a look at the digital clock on the bedside table. Damn, the hour was almost over. Curling his fingers tighter, he increased the speed of his strokes, knowing he had only a few minutes left to blow his wad before her show drew to a close, and the hotel lacked TiVo like he had at home.

God, he ached for her. Ached to be buried deep inside her heat. Swiping his thumb over his tip, he spread the ball of pre-cum, smoothing it down his length to lubricate his fingers as they moved rhythmically over his tight skin.

Again, he caressed his thickness, feeling his pulse drum against his palm, tension building heavy in his body. He watched her lips as she spoke, imagined them moving against his, against his skin, his cock. He listened to her voice, absorbed it, allowing her tone to seep into his pores.

Ah, his balls drew up, relief washing through him. Finally he was getting close; finally he'd be able to get a little sleep.

Diddy's "Last Night" started humming from his cell phone, the ring of an unknown caller. "What the hell?" he murmured, glancing from his phone lying next to him on the king-size mattress, then back at the television. The only people who knew his cell number had ring tones of their own.

Not letting up his stroke, the pace picking up the beat of the song, he reached his free hand to the singing phone and read the number. One he didn't recognize. Damn. Could be important.

He flipped it open. "Yeah?"

There was a pause, then a soft voice. "Malik?"

Her soft voice.

Aw, shit! "Yeah," he growled through clenched teeth as cum pumped from the base of his dick, up his length, filling his hand with spurts of hot, thick seed. His body shook, and he nearly dropped the phone as the tremble of release spread through his system.

But he managed to keep the phone pressed to his ear as he lost control and came hard for a woman he'd never met, the woman on the other end of the phone.

She was quiet, but he could hear her delicate breathing between his harsher tugs of air, he could hear her there even as his own groan vibrated in his ear.

Callie clutched her bottom lip between her teeth to keep from laughing. She knew what he was doing—the shuddering growl followed by his low groan was unmistakable.

He'd cum just as she called, and from the sound of his side of the call, he was alone. Or at least whoever he was with hadn't gotten off the way he had. The sound of him, the sound of his jagged breath and raspy voice caused her nipples to bead up tight. Hearing a man like Malik Drew get off was incredibly arousing, and her body was responding quickly.

When his breathing slowed slightly, she swallowed the dryness in her throat and whispered, "Is this a bad time?"

"Nah, your timing's perfect." He chuckled.

The rich huskiness of his laughter sent warm heat straight to her core, her body melting at the vision of him her mind created. Smooth brown skin over the corded muscles of an athlete's body. She knew what he looked like, how he was built. She'd studied every inch of him for months, ever since his letters had been coming in.

Almost every inch. Moisture dampened her pussy.

"You're sure?" She closed her eyes and took a shallow breath as desire shimmied across her skin. "You're not um . . . um . . . in the middle of something?"

He laughed again, his voice low and sated. "I was, but I finished up."

She took a breath. "Do you know who I am?"

"Of course. Callie Moore."

"How'd you know?"

"Dayum, girl, how could I not? I've been fantasizing about hearing your voice whispering to me for a long-ass time." He paused, cleared his throat. "I'm glad you called."

Callie leaned back on her sofa, the plush pillows easing her tired body. Kicking off her heels, she tucked her feet beneath her and glanced at the stack of letters folded beside her. Even in the dim light of her condo, she could see his handwriting scrawled across each page.

The short silence was interrupted by his voice. "I scare you off?"

"Whatcha mean?" she asked, lifting the letter she'd placed at the top of the stack. The letter contained detailed descriptions of one of his many fantasies of being with her. The letter where he'd left his phone number. Dated months ago.

He cleared his throat. "By telling you I fantasize about you?"

Smiling, Callie scooted back on the couch to recline a little farther. "Too late, I already know."

"Yeah? How's that?"

There was some fumbling and muffled sounds coming

across the line, and she could only imagine that he was maybe cleaning up the mess he'd just made. "Mmm . . ." She bit down on her lip again. Lawdy, she hadn't meant her slight moan to escape.

"How'd ya know?" he repeated.

"Your letters."

He barked out a laugh, the fumbling noise picking up for a second. "Right, my letters."

His voice felt like velvet across her skin, like sleep after climax. Her nipples tingled as they beaded up tight beneath the lace of her bra. "I'm not scared off."

"Got dayum, girl, you're going to find yourself in trouble."

"Mmm, really? What sorta trouble, Malik?"

He growled. "The kinda trouble where you'll be saying my name a whole lot more."

"Okay."

"Okay?"

Pressing her hand to her breast, she flicked a thumb across the extended nipple through the material, the touch causing her inner thighs to tremble and her clit to swell. "Yeah, okay. Make me say your name."

He went silent for a moment. Callie flicked her nipple again, then allowed her palm to slide lower, down her ribs, across the slight swell of her tummy, across the silk of her skirt suit. Her hand settled over her tingling and swollen clit. There was something empty inside her, something that ached to be filled by the man who wrote eloquent letters and who had been setting her body on fire with his words.

His voice only added to the desire swirling through her body, pouring liquid heat that now seeped from her pussy.

"When can I see you?"

Now! She clamped her eyes closed and pressed her thighs together, trying to ease the tingling of her clit. "When will you be in Los Angeles?"

She heard some movement from his end of the line, and it was easy to imagine him moving on the bed, repositioning himself against the pillows, getting more comfortable.

"Sorry, baby, but it's on season. Games." He groaned, a rough sound that came from the back of his throat. "Callie, the closest I'll be anytime soon is San Francisco."

"Oh." She tugged in a breath, biting her lip as disappointment clawed to the surface. Sharp and stinging, she hadn't realized she'd pinned so much on their meeting. Her body burned, the thought of waiting longer, when she'd already waited so long already, twisted painfully at her gut. "Oh," she repeated, trying to sound like it didn't matter.

"Will you come to me?"

The breath rushed from her lungs. "Yes." *Right now.* There was no hesitation. She'd spent plenty of lonely nights, months of them, trying to make the decision to call him. To be with him. To follow the plays of lovemaking he'd laid out in his letters. With her body and mind in agreement at last, there was no turning back.

"You will?"

"Yes." She giggled. He played pro ball, and this was the on season. That meant that if she wanted those nights of amazing sex he promised, it'd have to be on his turf. But she'd set the rules. She'd determine the when.

"I'll book you a room in San—"

"No." Her heart bumped hard against her chest. She had a career on television and celebrity clientele. He was one of the NFL's biggest names. This affair was about meeting needs. Only that. And it *must* be kept on the down-low. "Tell me where you'll be staying and I'll get something close."

"You sure?" His voice was husky, relaxed, the tone sweeping across her skin like a caress of his hand.

Moaning slightly, she clamped her lip between her teeth again, her inner thighs trembling. "Yes, Malik. We have to be discreet."

He chuckled. "I love the way my name sounds on your lips."

She swallowed, dampening the dryness in her throat. She was too close to asking him where he was tonight and jumping on a flight. "Tell me where, Malik, and I'll tell you when."

2

Callie swiped her damp palms against her skirt, then gripped the material in her fingertips to keep her hands from shaking. Taking a couple deep breaths, she moved down the corridor toward the visiting team's locker room at San Francisco's 3Com Park.

Using her media credentials, she'd been able to get back into this area, where fans were kept at bay, but reporters mingled at will, gathering postgame information and getting interviews.

She was there to sneak a peek at the man she'd be meeting back at her hotel room later. Just a little peek, she'd told herself after the game had ended.

A game she'd spent watching number 34's every move, the action on the field not nearly as thrilling as how Malik Drew's body moved.

Or how his ass looked in those delicious tight-fitting football pants, which detailed his every muscle. Showed off his strength. And had made sitting still in her seat damn near impossible as the game progressed, her clit swollen with desire, her inner thighs begging for his to press them apart.

"Lawdy," she whispered, sucking in a breath and wetting her lips. Inhaling another sharp breath, she attempted to calm her nerves. She was going to see, not be seen, so she had nothing to be nervous about. Better to save that energy for 10:00 P.M. when they'd planned to meet.

In her room.

Her nipples beaded up all tight, her breasts feeling heavy with need. Moaning, her step faltered and she paused. Her sudden stop caused someone to smack into her from behind.

"Sorry," she said, stepping aside to get out of the flow of pedestrian traffic.

"You lost?" some guy asked, smiling at her, a pass clipped to his Saint's T-shirt. He held a notebook in one hand and a cell phone in the other.

Callie smiled back. "No, I'm just . . ." *Just what? Trying to get a look at the man she'd be sexing later?* "Um . . . I'm looking for someone."

He grinned, flipping open his phone. "A player? Staff?"

Narrowing her eyes, she stared at the cell phone he'd just flipped open. What sort of contact list did this dude have if he actually thought she'd give a name and he'd be able to call the person up? Lifting her gaze, she looked back to his face, taking in the twinkle in his bright blue eyes.

"Well?" he persisted, his shaggy blond hair bouncing as he nodded his head to add emphasis to the question. His eyes were laughing at her, she realized, like he was used to stray women trying to make their way to the players' locker room. This was the pros after all, and no doubt that meant groupies, just the same as if they were musicians.

Maybe he intended to call security rather than the name she offered. It felt like there was something lodged in her throat. She swallowed hard. Woulda been so much easier to just quietly slip into the locker room, find Malik—from a distance—and look her fill.

Then head back to her room and wait for him to arrive.

Since it was likely a test to see if she actually belonged back there, she figured giving a name was better than being hauled off by security. "Malik Drew," she whispered, her voice cracking as she said his name.

The man nodded, then started thumbing through his phone.

"Wait"—she put her hand over his—"he doesn't know I'm coming. I wanted it to be a surprise." Hell, that's probably what all the wanna-have-a-pro-ball-player hoes said when caught getting into the team's official area.

He laughed.

Yep, as she suspected, she wasn't the first. . . .

As he continued chuckling, he looked her up and down, from the tips of her toes to the top of her head. A slow appraisal that she forced herself to stand still for, though it was difficult not to plop a hand on her hip and let him know how insulting his inspection was.

"He know you?"

"Yes." No lie. *Sorta.* He knew who she was.

He nodded, then tilted his head as he started walking, meaning for her to follow. "Right this way."

Resolved to see this through, Callie fell into step behind him, quickly finding herself at the entry where the crowd of reporters thickened. The man put his hand on her back and urged her forward, moving around the people and farther into the room.

Her pulse was drumming loudly in her ears, the thought of this forced introduction making her heart rate go wild. The lights were bright, the room was filled with voices and the scent of sweat, crushed grass, and soap.

Her knees shook slightly, and she was actually a little relieved to have this stranger's hand at her back, to keep her shaking from being so obvious. But her relief was short-lived, because his cell phone rang, and his hand dropped as he stepped away.

Backing up, she eased against the far wall, her gaze roaming slowly through the mix of reporters, staff, and players . . . half—dressed players. Naked players.

She bit her lip, her cheeks feeling warm as her gaze drifted from one man to the next, her hands once again tight in the material of her skirt as she pressed her hands to her thighs.

Her eyes paused on a naked chest, every muscle defined and covered in warm brown skin. Perfectly shaped pecs formed his yummy chest, then his body narrowed at the waist.

Her gaze drifted lower, past his belly button, following the dark trail of hair as it dipped beneath a white terry-cloth towel that was wrapped low around his hips.

Strong arms hung at his side. Large hands with long fingers were relaxed at his side, but as she watched, they tightened into fists, the muscles on his forearms bunching. She stared for a second, realizing his hands weren't the only body part reacting.

The towel shifted. Her breath caught. She went perfectly still, the air frozen in her lungs as she watched his dick harden beneath the cloth. As he got bigger, the cloth dropped lower on his hips.

And her gaze flew to his face. A face she knew. A face that made her pussy drip with want, ready to be filled up. Dark eyes were staring straight back at her, his look intent. Intense. His jaw was tight, his juicy lips pressed into a straight line. His nostrils flared.

But he was motionless, a statue of Malik Drew. Lawdy, he was perfect.

But then the stillness ended, and he was stalking her. Each stride he took in her direction was filled with raw power, blatant determination.

The air burned in her lungs. She trembled, the breath seeping out between narrowly parted lips. Pressing her back to the wall, Callie trapped her hands behind her. Not so he wouldn't see them shaking, but to keep herself from stripping off that towel as soon as he got within reach.

The reaction in her body was immediate. An ache started deep inside, her body calling out to the oh-so-yummy man she'd been longing for. Her clit swelled, and arousal dripped to her panties. Gulping for a breath, she tried to slow her racing heart.

She wanted him. Now.

Ah dayum, she was beautiful. Malik tightened his jaw to keep from groaning, his breath captured in his lungs. His body went still, watching her watch him.

Sweet and fresh, she looked like springtime—alluring skin, eyes that called to him. Lips that were meant to be kissed. Or wrapped around his dick.

Blood throbbed in his cock, pressing hard against the towel he had secured around his waist, threatening the tuck that kept the material from falling to the floor.

He hadn't expected to see her until later tonight, but hell, looking up and finding her here, in the locker room, looking so feminine and out of place, his need for her was immediate. And intense. And then he was in motion, closing the distance between them.

He paused a step away from her, close enough where he could smell the floral of her skin, see the golden flecks dotting her amazing green eyes, and feel the warmth of her breath as it caressed his naked chest.

"Come with me," he said between clenched teeth. Putting a hand on her arm, he drew her closer. She trembled slightly, so he tightened his grip and tried to keep from acting on the driving need to toss her over his shoulder. To run from the locker room and get up inside her quickly.

Turning away from the crowded locker room, he guided them toward the opposite end where treatment rooms would give them a little bit of privacy. Much like a doctor's office, the room was small, maybe ten by ten at most, and had a single exam table where injured players could be checked out and treated before, during, and after games.

He propelled them into the small room, then released Callie, afraid if he didn't he'd turn her into his body and take what he wanted. His mouth on her, his body deep inside the pussy he'd spent the last year fantasizing about.

He closed the door, turned the lock, then tugged in a breath. His pulse was pounding hard at his temples, throbbing in his dick. Squeezing his eyes closed for a second, he tried to slow his libido down. To get himself in check before he turned around.

To at least say hello before he fucked her.

"Malik," she whispered, her delicate fingers touching his back. She was close. Close enough to feel the fan of her words float across his skin.

Her fingertips traced along his shoulder blade. The touch was soft, but he could feel the slight tremble in her movements. Sensed the nervousness. "Malik."

He turned toward her, catching her hand in his as it fell away from his body. He twined their fingers, then pulled so she was forced to step in his direction, closing the already narrow gap between them. The hem of her sundress brushed against his legs, and his dick jumped, pushing against the confines of the towel.

"Whatcha doing here?" He forced the words, his throat tight. She wore no bra beneath the dress, he realized, looking down at her, able to see her puckered brown nipples crowning perfect breasts. His mouth watered.

Her curls were in disarray, probably caused by the winds that blew in off the Pacific Ocean, strong in the 49er's 3Com Park. The sort of wild, untamed look he wanted to see spread across his pillows. Across his chest. To have caught in his fingers.

She tucked her bottom lip between her teeth, but it couldn't contain the seductive smile. "I wanted a peek."

"A peek?"

"Mmm-hmmm . . . a peek." She lifted her free hand and smoothed the tips of her fingers along his abdomen, just above where the towel drooped from his hips. She paused where the end of the towel was tucked and flicked her thumb over it.

His breath caught as the material slipped a little lower. One more flick of her hand and he'd be naked. His body ready to go, his cock hard and reaching for her. Begging for her.

"Or . . . more than a peek." Her gaze slanted down to where her hand was tormenting his skin, teasing along his flesh. She licked her lush bottom lip, then tucked it between her teeth again.

He chuckled. "Baby, keep that up and you're getting a hell of a lot more than a little peek."

She whimpered, then glanced behind him at the door. "That lock?"

"Yeah."

"A lot more, huh?" She brushed against the tuck on his towel, releasing the folds. Her hand was on him, fingers wrapped around his dick before the cloth had touched the floor. She giggled, her thumb swiping across the liquid seeping from his tip. "Lawdy."

Clenching his jaw, he struggled to breathe, struggled to remain still and allow her to touch him as she pleased. Allow it without acting. Without backing her up and lifting her so her legs were wrapped around his waist. So that he was pressed deep into her wet heat.

She caressed him, sliding her fingers from his head to his base, brushing lightly against his balls before she reversed her torment and moved back up his length again. "A lot more?" she whispered, her words humid against his skin.

"You looking for trouble?"

"No."

"Whatcha looking for, then?" he asked, his body tense. Every muscle bunched. Desire pumping through his body with every heartbeat.

"This." She tightened her fingers around his dick, angling him toward her.

He laughed. "Baby, that's trouble."

"Yeah?"

"Mmm-hmm . . . oh, yeah."

She slanted her face upward, her gaze landing on his. The green of her eyes had brightened. Her mouth was plump and moist, and that smile, that sweet seductive smile he'd seen a thousand times on TV and had prayed a million times to have aimed at him lingered on her lips.

"Malik." She leaned toward him, lifting on her toes. She kissed his chest. Touched her tongue to his fevered skin. "I guess I *am* looking for trouble, then."

"Dayum, baby girl." He slid his free hand behind her neck, getting his fingers caught in her hair, the way he wanted since the very first second he saw her. He thrust his hips, working his dick in her grasp. "You sure you want this kinda trouble?"

"Yes."

Groaning, he pulled her head back with a gentle tug on her hair, then lowered his mouth to hers. It was light at first, lip to lip, a mere mingling of skin and breath. She tasted sweet, her mouth honeyed. "*This* kinda trouble?" He touched his tongue to her open mouth.

"Yes . . . please."

Malik deepened the kiss, angling over her, pressing his tongue into the warmth of her. Into the velvety texture of her mouth. Thrust his tongue past luscious lips, into the depth of her where she tasted like sugar and sex.

His dick throbbed against her palm, ached to be inside her. As if she sensed his need, shared it, she stroked him faster, from the tip of his head to the base. Back again.

Hell, he was weak, her touch undoing him. A little more of that and he'd be cumming in her hand.

"This kinda trouble," she said against his mouth, lifting a leg, forcing the hem of her skirt around her waist.

He released her hand and grabbed the back of her thigh, pulling it over his hip. Her skin was smooth, her leg toned as it wrapped around him.

She kissed him back, nibbling his lip between her teeth, then drawing it into her mouth to soothe where her teeth had been. She lifted the other leg, curving it around his back, her thighs gripping him, her pussy damp and hot against his dick even through her panties.

He smoothed his palm over her thigh, up over the slope of her ass, back down, following the shape of her body, skimming his fingertips along her skin. His touch drawn to her center like a bear to honey.

She was wet for him. Dripping. The cloth of her panties was soaked, drenching his rocked-up flesh in arousal. Making his knees weak, even as he bent them so he could ease her panties to the side and thrust hard and fast inside her.

Gripping her hips with both hands, he ground into her, rubbing his hard length against her clit, allowing her to dance along him as she swiveled her hips, finding a rhythm that matched the pulse pumping in his dick.

She was writhing now, whimpering against his mouth, these sweet little sexy sounds of want and need. Soft moans that were driving him damn near crazy.

Wiggling, she slipped a hand between them and shoved the cloth out of the way, like he'd wanted to do, then she took his hard-on, slick with her melted honey, and angled his head toward the pussy he'd been fantasizing about getting gut-deep in.

"Is this one of your fantasies?" she asked, as if she'd read his mind, her voice hushed, each word spoken between gasps. She teased her wet lips open with his head.

"Better."

"Better?"

"Dayum, you didn't know?" He pumped his hips, sinking a couple inches into tight wet heat, all her hand would allow him. "This is real." He thrust again, and she gave him a couple more inches.

Aw hell, he thought, clenching his teeth. Not even all the way up in her and he was about to cum. And hard. He tried to breathe, to slow it down. To keep his balls from drawing up tight. To keep his body in check.

But then Callie removed her hand from his dick and rode down hard on him, taking every inch inside her until her clit was pressed against his base. Arching her back, she used her knees to set the pace, taking him in and out of her body, her cries pouring into his mouth.

He trembled, the ball of cum building heavy now. "Baby, stop." He held her hips, attempting to slow her down, but she worked past his strength, and damn, he didn't try very hard. She felt too good. Fucking her felt too right. "Slow down, Callie," he said against her lips.

"No."

And then he felt it. Her body trembled, and the walls of her pussy clamped down around him, pulsing and shuddering around him, her climax drenching him.

"Malik," she cried, her head falling back, her back so arched that her long curls dusted his arms.

He shot a glance at the door, wondering if anyone had heard, the voices from the locker room seeping into their privacy. But not even the possibility of discovery tempered his need.

And still she rode him, her knees working, her thighs gripping him. Her pussy tight and climaxing around him.

"Dayum, baby . . . dayum." He went still, then shook hard

as the ball of cum sped up his dick and pulsed from his body, filling her up as he emptied inside her.

She collapsed against him, her arms circling his shoulders, her forehead tucking into the curve of his neck, her wild, windswept curls surrounding his face.

And then she giggled, a girlie sound that was so sweet and feminine that he couldn't help but hold her tighter. He wanted to give her more than just a quick fuck. Something about the innocence of her laughter made him want to give her more, offer her more. His chest got tight.

"I like your kinda trouble," she said, kissing his neck, the humor light in her tone.

"I bet you do."

"I do." She leaned away from him, just enough so she was looking into his eyes. "You still coming to my room tonight?"

"Baby girl, of course. I gotta show you the only quick thing about me is my performance on the field. What you got here was just a warm-up."

She smiled. Sassy and sexy and sugar. "Mmm-hmm . . . let the games begin."

3

Callie closed her eyes and flopped back onto the hotel room bed. It'd been a long three weeks of sleepless nights, of flashes of dreams of Malik, of his touch. Of his kiss. Of the taste of his skin. The feel of his dick.

Letting out a breath, she allowed her lids to drift closed. Ever since their first night together in San Francisco, she'd been able to do little else but think about him. To reread his letters, to hear his words, and to see *his* fantasies in her head.

She laughed. Lawdy, his fantasies involved touch and affection, and hot, hot sex, but nothing overly kinky. Nothing outside the realm of ordinary. Not like the kink she heard on *Kiss & Tell* from numerous guests over the years.

Yet Malik's words were the most erotic she'd ever heard. And in her line of work, she'd heard it all. From threesomes to orgies to sex toys and bondage, she'd been on the receiving end of story after story. As a sex therapist and relationship talk show host, hearing it all was her job.

But not a single story, not a single experience she'd ever had personally had prepared her for how Malik Drew made her feel. How he made her body respond.

Everything about the man screamed *fuck me*, like he was made for it. And wow, he was amazing at it. Her nipples beaded up tight and her clit tingled. Memories of sexing him did that to her.

Memories of having his dick hitting walls, stroking against bottom. Laughing, Callie squeezed her legs together, arousal seeping from her core, her inner thighs aching for his weight.

Opening her eyes, she glanced at the digital clock on the bedside table. It'd been three weeks of tormented need, of desire and lust. Of cupcaking hour-long phone calls, just so they could hear each other's voice.

Now here she was, in a hotel room in Philadelphia, waiting for him to finish up his post–Eagles game interviews and get his ass to her room. She may be following him, going to the cities where he had games, but she set it up. She decided when.

She laughed. No, scratch that—her pussy decided when. Three weeks was too damn long when the memory of how he sexed her last time had chased her every second of every day for the last twenty-one days. And it'd been months of reading his letters that had finally led to that initial phone call in the first place.

His letters, his words, created a yearning in her long before they met. She yearned for him now, yearned for the connection she'd felt when she'd been with him. The rightness she felt every time they spoke. The ease of being together.

It was as if his letters had been a courtship, and despite how she tried to keep her emotions in check, to remind herself this was about a booty call, she couldn't help but feel that months and months of his letters had been more than sexual fantasy; they'd been the start of a future.

"Don't do that, girlfriend," she mumbled to herself, putting a hand over her racing heart. He was a pro-ball player, which probably translated into a player, a dog of a man with a different woman in every city. She was just this week's stop.

She swallowed. Her throat was dry. Tight. They'd spoken nightly now, and not a single time during any of their late-night conversations had she ever heard another voice or mention of another woman.

Still, she'd be a fool to become emotionally entangled, she rationalized. She'd enjoy this for what it was. Amazing sex. Fun. A fantasy come true. His, yes, but also hers. She was getting exactly what she needed from him. More.

Mmmm, inches more. Lawdy, inches and thickness and hardness more. She giggled, smoothing a hand down the cotton pajama top she wore. Pink with Care Bears, meant for warmth and comfort. Turning on her side, Callie glanced at the white lacy baby-doll lingerie she'd brought, sexy as hell with a touch of sweet. Meant to entice.

She still had time before he was due to arrive. Time to change from plain cuddly wear into sex-me-good-tonight panties.

A *knock knock* thunked at the door.

Sitting up, she glanced from the clock to the hotel room door. Couldn't be Malik. It was too early. He'd still be in interviews, probably for another hour before he could get to her.

She pushed from the bed and made her way slowly to the door. "Who's there?"

"Room service."

Huh? She hadn't ordered anything. Moving closer to the door, she put an eye to the peephole and peered out, but whoever was standing there was so close, all she could see was a blur. "I didn't call for anything."

She heard a muffled laugh. "Baby, it's me."

"Me, who?" She giggled, trying to focus on the image she was seeing through the tiny glass. "Back up so I can see you. There's weirdos in Philly. Can't be opening the door to just anybody."

There was more laughter, then the blur of color on the other side of the door moved back and came into a sharper image. Yum, room service sure knew how to deliver. She squinted into the glass, trying to see what he was wearing, trying to assess how fast she'd be able to get his clothes off.

"Room service," he repeated, humor thick in his voice, his Southern accent thick and so damn sexy it made her pussy go wet instantly.

"What did I order?" she teased.

He cleared his throat. "Hot chocolate, ma'am, strawberries, whipped cream, some Midori. *Me*."

Callie took a breath, her pulse racing, butterflies fluttering deep in her belly. Yanking the door open, she moved halfway into the hall, grabbed his shirt, and pulled him to her.

"Get your ass in here. I've missed you." Lifting on tiptoes, she pulled him down for a kiss, the feel of his mouth better than any liqueur he could've brought with him.

His tongue smoothed across her lips, pressed between them as he deepened the kiss, angling his muscular body over hers. A strong arm went around her, flattening her to his chest, crushing her breasts between them.

He tucked a bouquet of roses and a bottle of Midori into the crook of his arm; then he smoothed his hands down her back, roaming over the curve of her ass and gripping the backs of her thighs as he lifted and spread them to wrap around his waist. She tightened her knees, rotated her hips so her damp pajama bottoms were pressed against the hard length of his dick through his jeans.

Malik groaned into her mouth. He'd blown off a couple interviews because there was no way in hell he'd have been able to sit through them with a hard-on, knowing the whole damn time Callie was in town and waiting for him.

Sweeping his tongue inside her mouth, he got caught up in the sweetness of her lips, of the warm silken texture of her skin.

She tasted like honey and whimpered with so much need his rocked-up dick was throbbing hard against the fly of his pants.

With his hands beneath her ass, he took a step into the room, thinking about pressing her up against the closest wall and taking her there. It was the chuckles from some people passing by in the hallway that finally had him kicking the door closed, with so much force it rattled in the frame.

Carrying her across the room, he settled her on the writing desk, then ended the kiss as he stood before her. "Surprised to see me?"

She grabbed his shirt and tried to pull him back to her, her lips plump and wet, his kiss lingering on her pink delicious mouth. "Yes, you're early."

"Couldn't stay away."

He handed her the roses and placed the bottle of Midori on the tabletop beside her.

"I'm surprised I'm not dreaming, Malik. How was your game?"

"You dream of me often?" He grinned. He couldn't help it when he was around her. They'd won, but forget the game. He didn't want to think about football right then; he wanted to hear how her dreams brought him to her at night.

"Mmm-hmm." Her cheeks went pink. She lifted the roses to her face and inhaled. "Thank you for the roses, Malik. Pink, my favorite. They smell so good."

"I know. And you're welcome." He kissed her lips but kept it quick, knowing that the texture would entice him to deepen it, and he couldn't get caught up in kisses. Not yet. He had other things planned.

Her amazing eyes lingered on his face, then drifted slowly to the bed. She plucked a petal from a rose and smoothed it between her fingertips as she slowly brought her gaze back to his. "They'll look good spread across the bed . . . smell good crushed between us."

If she only knew . . .

Blood rushed to his dick. Shit, he was already so hard he could barely walk, barely think. "Dayum, baby girl." He grabbed his cock through his pants and shifted it, trying to make room as he thickened further. "Whatcha trying to do to me?" *What the hell has she done?* His heart ached for her damn near as much as the rest of him did.

She reached for him again, trying to wrap her legs around his back. "Reward you for thinking about me."

Her green eyes were sparkling, and her wild curls danced as she moved, the kind of bounce he wanted to see when she was riding him. Hard. Groaning, he squeezed his lids closed and took a breath; those sort of thoughts were torture when tonight he was planning on going slow.

"I don't need rewards. Tonight is about you." He stepped away from her. Moving to the entry, he opened the door, then retrieved the bag of massage oils and candles he'd left just outside.

When he turned back toward her, she was watching him. Smiling. Something more than simple, explainable lust shimmering in her vivid eyes. Something that made his chest feel tight and his hands tremor slightly.

Hell, going slow wasn't going to be easy when what he really wanted was to strip her down quickly and claim her as his own with deep purposeful thrusts. Thrusts that her body would remember, a body that should be his alone.

He went back to stand before her, kissing her again because her damp, full lips called out to him. "You look adorable," he said, looking at the pink pajamas she wore. "Is this what you wear to try to seduce?"

She licked her lips, her gaze drifting lower to settle where his hard-on was outlined beneath cloth. "I don't need to try."

"Nah-ah, baby girl, you're right, you don't." He laughed, bending to kneel before her. "Thoughts of you bring me to my knees without you so much as trying."

"Malik . . ."

"Let me." He lifted her small foot in his hand, gently pulling off the sock. Her toes were adorned with pink nails nearly the exact shade or flowers he'd brought. Hell, he had to be grinning like a damn fool as he turned back to the bag and grabbed a small bottle of massage oil.

He dumped some on his hand, then worked it into the arch of her foot, massaging across her heel, her ankle. Pushing the cotton pajama pants up as he moved his hands, he rubbed across her calf, then leaned forward to taste the edible oil, not sure which was sweeter, the coconut passion oil or the alluring floral of her skin.

Not wanting to be stingy, he moved to the other foot, removing the sock, then taking care of each toe with his strong hand and warming oils.

"Baby, these pajamas are cute as hell, but they've got to go." He stood and scooped her into his arms.

She giggled as her arms went around his shoulders. "I was planning on wearing those." She pointed toward the bed as she whispered against his mouth. "Mmm . . . you taste like coconut." Her lips moved across his skin as she kissed his neck, running her tongue along the sensitive flesh.

"And you. You like?"

Her tongue swiped below his ear. "I like how you taste." She caught the lobe between her teeth, then traced it with the tip of her tongue. "Want me to change?"

"How 'bout you wear nothing." He plopped her down in the center of the bed, then grabbed the waistband of her pants. She worked with him, lifting her hips, and he tugged them off her smooth long legs and tossed them over his shoulder. "No panties? Mmmm . . . you're making this easier for me."

She laughed. "Don't like them."

"And I don't like 'em on you." Malik drew in a breath, trying to get his need in check. His dick was so damn hard, his need so raw it clawed at him to take her. To lean her back on the bed and get up inside her.

Hell, he could see the neatly trimmed dark curls above perfect pussy lips, already shimmering wet. The scent of woman, roses, and honey. His mouth watered. He needed a taste.

Callie reached for him, her hand brushing across the button on his jeans, her nails clicking against the metal. "I need you, Malik. Give me."

He shook his head. "No rush, baby. Tonight I'm pleasing you. All of you. From head to foot."

"Please me here," she said, sliding her fingers across her wetness, spreading her lips so he caught a glimpse of pink.

Shit! She was driving him crazy, making it damn hard to follow *his* plan when his cock was in full agreement with *hers*.

"Baby girl, I *intend* to. But not yet. Not just yet." It took everything he had to turn away from her, to go back to the bag. He retrieved the bag and the bottle of Midori from the desk, placing them both on the floor beside the bed.

He took the massage oil again. "Lay back. Relax."

"Malik, I didn't come all this way for a massage."

He laughed, placing a hand over his dick, hard and ready tucked inside boxers and pants. "Nah, you came a long way for this."

She giggled. "Yes, so give it to me."

"Soon."

"How soon?"

Not soon enough! "Soon, I promise. But first I want a taste."

"A taste?"

"Yeah, baby, a taste." He allowed his gaze to drift from her eyes, lower across her breasts, still covered in her soft top, across the gentle swell of her stomach, to the core of her that was already soaking wet.

"Oh." Her eyes lit up. She plopped back on the bed, her legs spreading as she reclined, the position incredibly inviting.

Callie took a breath and tightened her hands into the bed-
spread. She had to. Otherwise she was going to grab Malik and
pull him down on top of her. He was teasing her, and Lawdy,
she was shaking with what it was doing to her.

A taste, he wanted to taste her. She squeezed her lids closed
for a moment and tucked her lips between her teeth to keep
from telling him to get at it already. Her clit tingled, and her
nipples were so tight they almost hurt.

Touch me, she wanted to demand, her body aching, needing . . . *craving*. But he didn't. Not at first. And when he did, it
was to the bottom of her foot, with the oil again, slowly being
massaged into the ball, then the arch. Strong hands moved up
her calf, across her thigh.

Her body trembled. Arousal dripped from her pussy. She
could feel it running down her inner thighs. He saw it, too.

"You want me." His breath was hot against her skin, and his
lips settled where his fingers had been on her flesh.

"I need you." She could hardly speak, each word a gasp.

He chuckled. "I need you, too." His hands moved to her
hips, his strong grasps firm against her body. He tugged her
forward so her ass was on the edge of the bed; gently he lifted
one foot, bent her knee, and placed her heel up. Then the other
leg joined the first so she was spread and open, her core exposed.

Begging for lips. For tongue. For dick. For Malik. She was
melting now, dripping honey.

"Relax."

"Impossible."

"Try. Feel each touch of my fingertips. Each stroke of my
tongue."

"You're making me crazy."

"I'm supposed to. Supposed to make you hot. Supposed to
make you wet. I'm supposed to make your body beg for mine.
You're what I want, and I need you to want me, too."

"I do," she almost sobbed.

"But I'm going to make you want me more. Make you hotter. Wetter. Going to make your pussy melt, then cum sweetly on my tongue."

"Please, please." She closed her eyes, struggling for composure. Struggling to not cum, but his words alone were nearly taking her there. Lawdy, just the way he said things, with that accent of his, were her undoing.

He laughed again, a throaty sound she adored. "Soon," he repeated, but she heard him move away. Was it possible to die from need? She was about to.

Opening her eyes, she saw that he'd removed his shirt. He was lighting candles around the room, the scent of vanilla drifting into the air. She studied his back as he moved, each muscle defined, chiseled. His brown skin looked dark and rich in the dim room, lit now mostly by the golden flicker of tiny flames.

He had a tattoo on his shoulder, a lion draped over a football helmet, the Saint emblem shaded perfectly against his skin. Callie grinned, feeling his joy over playing for them. She'd read his letters, knew he grew up in New Orleans and had been a lifelong fan. Now he played for them.

She felt *his* joy. Her heart paused, then sped up. She felt it for him, because in such a short time he'd become important to her in a larger way than sex. He completed her. Made her feel whole, and happy.

He was holding the bottle of Midori when he turned back toward her. His chocolate eyes warm but intense. The smile lingered on his lips, but something else, too. Something serious, like he was about to get down to business.

He knelt at the edge of the bed, opened the bottle, and slowly dripped the liquor on her clit so it slid downward between already wet lips. Then his mouth was there. He kissed her swollen clit, her half-open mouth. Mostly full lips, with just a quick tease of the tongue.

"Malik—"

"Shhh . . . let me." He licked from the bottom of her pussy lips upward, sucking away the arousal and Midori as his mouth moved to the top, his breath blowing softly on her clit. He leaned in close, his chest brushing against the oiled skin on her inner thighs. Getting her juices on his skin.

He touched her clit with his fingers, circling. Massaging in more oil and the melon liquor. "Feel good?"

She nodded. "Yes."

Bending in closer, he slid his fingers downward between her pussy lips, parting them, then touched his tongue to where his fingers had been.

Callie trembled, her body spasming. Lifting her hips, she ground them into his face, wanting more. Feeling orgasm so close, but she was still empty. Still needing him moving inside her. Still craving the completeness of having his dick pushing against her walls, stretching her.

He slid a finger inside, two, curling them forward, making her body shake hard. Then his mouth moved back to her clit. He kissed her slowly. Softly. Licking her clit, twirling it with his tongue. Too softly at first, not enough. Not enough.

Again she ground her hips upward, lifting them from the bed, finding a rhythm she was frantic for. The rhythm he used to stroke his fingers inside her. And finally, finally he increased the pressure of his tongue, lapping against her swollen clit, the tingle spreading.

"Malik," she cried out, cumming hard, her body shaking, her pussy walls tightening around his fingers. His movements paused, allowing the spasms, allowing each tremor and shake.

She felt him move away, but she wanted more. Needed more. Another climax lingered; she just needed another stroke or two. She reached down, touching her clit, her fingers getting soaked in oil, in booze, in cum.

Malik laughed, placing a hand over hers. Got-dayum, he'd never seen anything more erotic than her delicate fingers working against her wet skin, her face flushed, her curls damp by her forehead and spread out across the bed. Part of him wanted to sit back and watch; the other part wanted to remain in control.

This was his night, his time to cause her addiction to him, just as he'd been passionate about her for the last year. "You look so pretty touching yourself, Callie. But I got this. This is mine tonight."

"Hurry."

He groaned, his dick throbbing, precum leaking from the tip. "Without a doubt, you're hot. Anxious. Wanting more. So am I." He leaned forward, his abdomen pressing against her body as he pulled off her shirt.

The perfect globes of her breasts were tipped in large brown disks and elongated nipples. His mouth watered, and he tightened his jaw to keep from growling his need. Reaching for the bottle of Midori, he splashed some across her chest, wetting her nipples, allowing the green sticky drink to spill downward, dipping into the indent of her belly button.

Then he licked away every drop, her skin as soft and sweet as the drink. Her skin was satin beneath his lips, warm trembling satin. Skin scented with roses, skin that held the subtle hint of sweat, skin meant to be pressed against his.

Sitting back, he shrugged out of his pants and boxers. He was so rocked up he almost scrapped his plan and headed straight for her pussy. Balling his fists, Malik leaned forward again. "A sip?" he asked, holding the bottle to her lips.

She angled her head back, opening her mouth. He spilled a small amount in, then allowed her to swallow before giving a little more. When she swallowed a second time, he tilted the bottle and filled his mouth, then bent to kiss her, sharing the Midori from his lips.

Placing his knees on the edge of the bed, he settled her inner thighs over his hips, angling his body over hers, deepening the kiss.

He craved more now, had pushed past the limits of his control. She'd cum on his tongue, gripped his fingers. Midori and honey and coconut oil. Rose petals and satin skin. He had to have more.

"I want you," he said between clenched teeth.

"I need you," she whispered back, touching her fingertips to his cheek.

He thrust fully inside her. One stroke. And he was home.

4

Callie awoke slowly, aware first of the weight pressing her body to the bed, of the heat. Her lids fluttered against the morning light, the clear day streaming sunshine through the thin hotel room curtains. Since it'd been dark when she'd arrived, she'd completely forgotten about pulling closed the thicker drapes, but now she wished she had.

Lazily, she opened her eyes, allowing them to become accustomed to the brightness of the sun, golden rays floating vibrantly across the room. But not even the warmth sun was a match for the heat that seeped through her skin, the source, Malik, his body more on her than the mattress.

His cheek was between her breasts, his breath deep and even, streamed across one nipple, tightening it. He had an arm draped over her hips, one leg tossed over her thighs, the thickness of the chiseled cords of muscle heavy on her smaller frame.

Glancing down, Callie gazed at his profile, at long, dark lashes resting on his cheeks, at a nose that was proud and straight, to lips that were full and delicious, and damn, did they know how to give a kiss.

Her body responded, her pussy going damp, her clit swelling. They'd sexed all night, finally falling asleep just hours before with her body relaxed from the massage he'd given, then sated by the way he fucked.

But just that quick, one look at him, and she was wet. Ready again. "Mmm . . ." she bit her bottom lip to stifle her moan, wanting to allow Malik to sleep. He'd played hard on the field, then serviced her good for hours, making her feel incredible. And amazingly valued.

He'd taken his time. Made sure she'd found her release, over and over, before he'd taken his. That kind of lover was rare, and exactly what she'd been missing for all these months. The precise reason his letters had come at the perfect time, had affected her so greatly.

He'd been different in his approach from the start, his words thought out, moving. And from the first line, of the first letter, she'd been intrigued. Admittedly, she'd also been a bit apprehensive.

He was a pro ball player—correction, a fine-as-hell pro ball player—and no doubt able to pull any woman he chose. Yet despite that, he'd been thoughtful and respectful as he laid out his fantasies in detail, letting her know exactly what he wanted to do to her. To her body.

There'd been no '*bitch this*' or '*hoe that*' but he'd been real, and Lawdy, had his words ever affected her.

Closing her eyes, Callie took a deep breath, inhaling the scent of sweat, roses, Midori, coconut massage oil. The scent of sex lingered in the air the same way specs of dust floated in the sunshine.

She grinned. She couldn't help it. Though the sex was amazing, it'd quickly become more than sex. More than the quick fuck she'd anticipated when she'd first said yes to meeting up with him.

"I'm a traveling booty-call," she giggled, then pressed her fingers to her lips to muffle the sound to allow Malik to sleep.

Glancing down, she took in his good looks, but saw deeper into his soul. Saw the man he was. Saw his heart and soul beneath the delicious milk chocolate skin. Rich brown skin, dotted with clinging pink rose petals. Some crushed, their fragrance soft and delicate, in contrast to her man.

Her man?

Her man? Her breath caught in her lungs, then rushed out when it began to burn. There was something comforting about thinking of Malik Drew as hers. Something fuzzy and cuddly. The beat of her heart bumped steady against her ribs. She liked the way it felt. Liked the connotations that settled around *hers.*

Lifting a hand, she touched her fingertips to his skin, traced his lips. The line of his jaw. The shell curve of his ear.

She drew her fingers downward, smoothing along the corded length of his neck, learning each slope of his shoulder, where scrapes from her fingernails had punctured the night before. Farther down, she memorized each chiseled muscle on his upper arm.

When her arm was fully extended, she retraced, moving up his arm, then shifting to his back, drifting her fingertips slowly up his spine.

Though he remained completely still, she knew her touch was affecting him. She could feel his dick grow hard against her hip. Could feel his pulse as he throbbed against her.

Silken liquid dripped from her pussy, wetting her inner thighs. Mingling with the arousal and cum from hours before. Her nipples pebbled. Need poured through her body, a yearning that seemed insatiable. Couldn't get enough of him. Enough of his loving.

Wiggling, she tried to turn, tried to angle her body so she could ease him inside her, but his weight was too great.

"Stop that," he murmured, his breath warm against her skin. His eyes remained closed, every muscle in his body relaxed, except his cock.

The part she wanted inside her.

"Stop what?"

"Wiggling."

"What if I don't want to?"

"I'm tired baby girl, but you're asking for it." He shifted his hips, pressing his rocked-up flesh more firmly against her. Then he went completely still again.

"Malik." she brushed her hand over his shoulder again, the touch so light she felt the warmth radiating from his skin more than she felt the texture. Her fingertips caressing, but not lingering for long.

Wetting her lips, she went on. "Malik, I'm asking. I need you." She wiggled again, a roll of her hips to punctuate just what she meant. "I want you."

"Woman, you tryin' to kill me?"

She giggled. "No, Malik, dead is the last thing I want for you."

She could feel him smile against her chest.

"You're wicked." His hand came up, cupping the breast before his face, his thumb and forefinger tweaking her tight nipple. "What am I going to do with you, baby girl?"

"Fuck me."

"Dayum . . ."

She felt his entire body stiffen, his hard-on firm against her skin. Throbbing in a rhythm equal to the drumming of her pulse.

Fuck me, holy shit, she had a way of asking that made the most vulgar words sound sweet and sugary. Malik's body ached, every muscle strained from the day before, from another hundred plus yard, record-setting, career game.

Yet despite the physical exhaustion of playing nearly an entire game, followed with a night of passion and sex, he was ready. His dick so hard, if he didn't cum soon, the thing was liable to break off. And no matter how tired he felt, the thought of getting up inside Callie had energy coursing through every nerve.

Shifting quickly, he ran a hand up her leg, across her thigh to grab the back; then rotated them on the bed, so she was spread for him, and he was settled between. She moaned, pulling her knees back, allowing them to fall open to the mattress.

"Malik," she whispered, arching her body off the bed, rolling her hips against him.

"Easy." His rocked-up flesh was pressed between them, getting wet from the honey of her lips. His head ached. His balls were pulled up tight against his body, climax right there, and he hadn't even gotten in his pussy yet.

"Easy," he repeated, smoothing his palm up her arm. He laced their fingers, pressing the back of her hand to the bed. Resting his weight on his elbows, he ran his other hand up her other arm, also lacing fingers. Palm to palm, hands above her head.

"Please . . . please." She stalled a whimper by tucking her bottom lips between her teeth. Her long lashes floated downward, her eyes closing as she brought her chin up, her back arching again. Her hips thrusting upward.

Only two options here. Slow or fast. If he didn't go slow, he was going to cum fast and hard. He could feel it already, thick and ready to blow. But despite his need for sleep, his need to sex her, his need to imprint himself within her, was greater and more consuming.

He wanted her to remember how they fit, wanted her body to fit only him. Possessiveness churned in his gut, moving him into unfamiliar territory. He'd never given a damn about a woman this way before. Hadn't cared passed the brains she gave, passed the way she gave it up.

But for Callie, and only for her, everything was different.

She lingered on his mind when miles spanned between them. When she was off doing her thing, hosting her show, living her life. A life he wanted to be a part of.

Permanently.

His body shook. Dragging a deep breath into his chest, he allowed all the emotion to seep away, and returned his concentration to loving Callie right.

He touched his lips to her mouth, stroking his tongue across the lushness of her, but he didn't deepen. Pressing kisses to the corner of her mouth, he trailed them along her jaw, the slender slope of her neck, to the delicate curves of her collarbone.

Lower, he smoothed his tongue across skin that tasted salty, like sweat, sweet like the melon liqueur he'd spilled on her, tropical, like coconut massage oil. Like a piece of hard candy, he closed his lips around the pebbled tip of her breast, elongated and mouth-wateringly tempting.

"Malik," she whispered, her voice and body trembling.

He sucked the puckered flesh deeper into his mouth, rolling the nipple between his lips, lapping at it with his tongue. With a popping sound, he released the first and moved to the second nipple, offering the same attention to the second hardened peak.

She strained beneath him, her arms pushing upward, but he held her, her delicate frame no match for his size and strength. If she'd asked, he'd have let her up, but he knew her response was eagerness rather than a need to be free.

"You need this?" He shifted back, then allowed his head to press against her silken, wet lips. Eased inside, just an inch.

"Yes, please." Her lips quivered, her green eyes on his face, her gaze liquid and needy.

He moved another inch inside her, her walls stretching around him. "You want this?"

"I want you."

"I want you, too." He gave a couple more inches. Dayum, it

was hard not to just thrust inside her fast, with one smooth stroke. One stroke that would put him ball deep in her honeyed heat. But he'd cum if he worked it like that, and he had a little bit of pride left when it came to Callie.

Most of it he'd left on the pages of his letters, when he'd confessed everything to her. Every need. Every desire. All his lust. All his fantasies. And there on the pages he'd left more than just lust and words, but traces of his soul.

Deeper. Another inch. She was shaking beneath him, her pussy clinging to his dick, wet and tight around him. Deeper, until he was hitting bottom, until he was buried deep in her guts. All the way, so his sac was smashed between them, and her clit ground against his base.

"Oh, my, god, Malik," she gasped for breath, "what are you doing to me?"

"Making love." And he was. This wasn't a fuck. Nah-ah, maybe he'd intended their affair to be all about that, but it wasn't any more.

Shifting, he ground into her, then pulled out slowly so she'd feel every bit of his flesh working between her legs. She chased him, raising her hips off the bed, her back arching, her nipples beaded and wet from where his mouth had been.

"Don't leave me," she whispered, her body slick beneath him.

"I'm not." He thrust in again, filling her completely.

Her head turned from side to side, the long curls damp at her temples, so dark against the smooth white cotton sheets. "Mali . . ."

Out again, his ass and hips working, even as he kept his chest pressed to hers, their hands linked above her head. In, a little more quickly. Grinding her clit as he settled deep.

And shit, he could feel it already, could feel the spasms of her body, feel the tightening of her orgasm as it built with each of his strokes.

"Mal . . ."

"I'm here, baby girl." Out. In. Slow and steady, but full and thick. "Cum for me."

She had to cum soon or he was going to lose it. His control was waning fast. He struggled to hold back. Struggled with his need to drive into her and empty his nut inside walls of wet, slick heat.

Sweat slid down his spine. His muscles were taut, fluid in motion, he was an athlete even here.

Against his body, he could feel her inner thighs tremble, felt her body constrict around his dick, saw the way her mouth opened to cry out.

Slanting over her, he closed his lips over hers, capturing her moans, the way she cried out his name, swallowed down her bliss, stroking his tongue across her lips. Into the sweetness of her mouth, in the same slow steady tempo that he fucked.

And when her cum poured over him, he let go. His body jerked. Stiffened. Came. Hard, filling her. Giving over his heart.

She was more than a fantasy come true. She was his reason to breathe. His need to succeed, to prove he was good enough for a woman like Callie.

Malik kissed her. Tender now, reluctant to pull away, their hands clasps, sweat cooling slowly on their bodies, beams of sunshine cascading gold around them. And he'd be a contented man if he never moved.

5

Callie couldn't help smiling as she tucked her bottom lip between her teeth and eased backward through the gathering crowd, allowing people to shift and move around her. She kept her gaze fixed on Malik. On his gorgeous face, dark eyes, rich skin, perfect muscular physique.

He was grinning, his eyes shimmering with excitement as he spoke, his edible lips and full mouth animated as he described what led to his success during the game. He'd had a career high for rushing yards and had led the Saints into the postseason.

He spoke, charisma dripping from each grin, each syllable of every word. And the crowd was held captivated, totally enthralled in the details he gave. Camera flashes popped, and the whirling *click-click-click* of shutters snapping echoed through the room.

Tonight he'd be highlighted on ESPN's SportsCenter and on the NFL Network's postgame shows. All the major networks had mics and reporters scribbling notes, ready to spread his stats across the following sports segments of the nightly news. *Sports Illustrated* and *NFL Today* were planning feature stories.

None of the legitimate news programs bothered her. It was the paparazzi and the tabloid reports that worried Callie. And there were plenty of them. Easing back farther, she pressed her back against the far wall, wrapped her arms around her waist, and tried to catch her breath.

For the last few months, she had been meeting up with Malik in different cities, each time never leaving the hotel room. They'd shared nights of passion, of hushed whispers, low giggles, tender touches, common dreams, goals, and even confided worries and fears.

Swallowing the lump in her throat, Callie kept her gaze on Malik as he spoke, his attention caught up in the interview questions being tossed his way. Even with a crowded room, she enjoyed these moments, where she could observe him, learn his movements and reactions.

She'd learned so much about him already, first from his letters, then from all the time spent in bed, having the most amazing sex and talking. More than lovers, booty calls, and secret encounters, they'd become friends.

Letting a slow sigh seep from deep in her lungs, she shifted her gaze from Malik's smiling face to a couple of men mingling in the crowd. Known paparazzi, the sleaziest, low-down dirt-gathering kind.

So far she and Malik had been able to keep their relationship from the public eye. Aside from their first encounter in the San Francisco locker room, so far they'd met only in hotel rooms, where they'd sexed and ordered room service. Unless Malik was talking about their relationship, there was no way for anyone to know about it. Her lips had been sealed.

Her heart sped. A down-low affair, till now. Tonight Malik had invited her out. Had asked her to meet him at the stadium after the game, to have dinner with him at an actual restaurant rather than sitting on the edge of the bed and eating from roll-away carts.

Tonight he'd said he wanted to put her on his arm, cameras and reporters be damned. Narrowing her eyes, she stared at a few of the worst trash offenders, wondering what sort of lies they'd print, what assumptions would be made when they were seen together for the first time.

Releasing her lip from between her teeth, she steadied her breath and looked back to Malik. It's not like she wasn't used to cameras. She was the host of a nightly late-night talk show, and aside from that, she had a list of celebrity names as clientele. She attracted her own type of paparazzi, but she knew it was nothing compared to the attention her man claimed.

Her man? Her heart rate sped up, and her hands trembled slightly against her sides. When had she started thinking of Malik as her man? Her inner thighs trembled, the memory of his weight pressed between them making her pussy wet, her clit tingle.

Made her nipples bead up hard and desire pour intensely through her body. Sure, he was an amazing fuck, and the only man she was sharing a bed with, intimacy with, but her man?

"Just one more," a man standing next to her shouted, yanking her thoughts back to the crowded room.

"Sorry folks, but . . ." Malik glanced at a gold watch draped around his wrist. "I've got a date. No more questions."

Callie rolled her eyes but couldn't help grinning. After all his time in front of the cameras, he had to know that announcing *a date* wouldn't end the tossing of questions, but only lead to more.

"Who is she?"

"With who?"

"Someone serious?"

The questions flew, and Callie had to force herself to keep still, afraid any movement may draw attention in her direction. Slowly she glanced around the room to see if anyone had noticed her and put two and two together.

When her gaze had roamed over the room, she looked back at Malik, only to find him staring directly at her, a genuine smile curving her yummy-yum mouth. Eyes that caressed her soul. Lips that had kissed her into orgasm.

And Lawdy, the way he was looking at her now had her panties wet, her pussy dripping with need. Aching to be filled up with a dick that knew how to please. Her knees went weak, so she leaned back against the wall to keep from falling.

If he kept looking directly at her like that, every single person in the room would get a clue, and in truth, she was torn between wanting the world to know and keeping intact the secrecy of their affair.

Malik watched Callie, watched the pink blush smear across her cheeks, watched how her green eyes went liquidy as they gazed back at him. She was the purest cross of sugar and spice he'd ever seen.

Sweet and sexy, that was his girl. *His girl.* Hell yeah, felt right. Dressed in a black skirt, a pink top, and the highest damned stilettos he'd ever seen, she was a combo of sex pot and girl next door.

And she had him so hard there was no way in hell he could get up from behind the interview table without the entire room catching a glimpse of wood. He took a breath. Another. Tried to will the blood out of his dick, to get his desire in check.

Reluctantly, he turned away from her. No way in hell was he getting rid of his hard-on if he kept staring into eyes that reminded him of passion and sex, sensuality and femininity.

"All right, a few more questions." It was the only way to get his mind off what he really wanted. To find a room quickly, bend Callie over, lift her skirt, and get his cock into her sweet wet heat.

Groaning, he shoved away his need and returned his mind to football. He replied to a couple of questions, talking about how the offensive line had done well with their blocks, opening up lanes for him to run through; then, moving on, he went over his expectations for the following game.

About fifteen minutes later, he shoved away from the table, ending the interview. He'd given them enough. More than enough. He'd turn the mic over to his coach and slip out with Callie.

As he moved away from the table, he caught her eye and angled his head toward the door. She smiled and nodded, then headed toward the exit.

Malik caught up with her just outside the door, and though he knew they didn't have any real privacy and that cameras and reporters were still following, he caught her up in his arms and kissed her fully on the mouth.

She gasped in surprise, her mouth opening slightly for him. *Got damn*, it was tempting as hell to take advantage, to slip his tongue into her mouth and taste the sugared flavor of her kisses, but he held back.

He had to make sure Callie was ready for this. Ready for something else, something bigger than a hit-it-and-quit-it do-the-do affair. Though they'd already developed something aside from sex, he wasn't sure how she'd react to the step he wanted to take.

Claiming her as his girl.

Groaning, Malik ended the kiss. He was getting hard again, and another few seconds of mouth-to-mouth contact, of her sugared breaths, and he may not be able to walk right. Stepping away, he put his hand to the small of her back. "Ready?"

She laughed. "For what?"

To fuck. His pulse throbbed, and he had to grit his teeth against the rush of blood. "Dinner."

"Oh. Not dessert?"

"Why you sound so disappointed?" he asked, chuckling.

"I like dessert." She licked her lips, already wet from where his mouth had been, her gaze sliding down his body to focus on the growing bulge between his legs.

"Stop that."

She licked her lips again, whimpering. "Stop what, Malik?"

Sliding his palm from her back, he grabbed her hand, twining their fingers. Leaning in close, he whispered in her ear, "You looking for trouble?"

She giggled, her eyelids widening. "What kinda trouble?"

"The kind ya get when you lick ya lips and talk about dessert while looking at my dick."

"Oh."

He laughed. "Yeah, oh."

She was quiet for a moment, her lower lip held between her teeth. "That's a private kinda trouble."

"Yup, and we're in public." He turned and moved down the hall toward the building exit, Callie falling into step beside him.

"You wouldn't."

"You sure?"

"You wouldn't? Come on, Malik, in public?"

He laughed again. Being with her did that to him. Hell, he started writing letters on a crazy whim, because there'd been something about her that had drawn him like a bear to honey, but he'd never guessed when he started that he'd fall for the girl. That he wanted something besides sex.

Ha! Judging by the way he stayed rocked up, he knew damn well sex was part of it. But only part.

Bending low, he whispered in her ear, "I would, so don't try me."

She made a whimpering sound but didn't reply. As they went through the exit leading outside, Callie tried to untwine their fingers and step away from him.

"Nah ah." He tightened his hold.

"But, Malik, you know this will get coverage."

"That bother you?"

She was silent for a moment, her wide eyes sweeping their surroundings, as if she was looking for hidden cameras or reporters waiting to pounce. Only the rhythmic tapping of her heels on the cement echoed through the parking lot. He knew she had her own celebrity status, with *Kiss & Tell* and her clientele. Maybe she wasn't ready for this. She'd been the one in the first place to insist upon discreet.

His gut tightened, disappointment stronger than he'd anticipated. It was also short-lived.

"Malik"—her hand clasped more firmly to his—"I'm okay with this."

"Okay?"

She giggled. The sweet feminine sound constricted his chest and made his heart rate jump. She pulled them to a pause, turning so she was standing in front of him. She reached up, wrapping a hand around the back of his neck, then pulled him down to her.

Her lips were lush against his, her breath warm and scented of honey and springtime. "I'm better than okay." The moister of her tongue swiped across his lip; then she dragged it into her mouth, sucking briefly before releasing it. "I'm good with it."

Malik groaned, his dick throbbing against his boxers, the tip escaping the elastic waistband, pressing painfully against the zipper of his slacks. Hard, and no privacy. Damn, she knew what she was doing to him.

"Baby girl, you're asking for more trouble than you can handle right 'bout now."

She nipped playfully at his lip, then soothed it with the tip of her tongue. A delicate hand crept between their bodies, and her fingers outlined the ridge of him, tracing his length, then stroking across his hard-on through the material.

"Says who?"

Gritting his teeth, he tried to slow his breathing, tried to calm his pulse. Tonight was a date, not a booty call. He wanted her to feel special. Wanted her to know that she was more than sex. Swallowing, he shoved away the lust that was driving him and let out an unsteady breath between his clenched teeth.

"I'm taking you to dinner, baby girl."

She pressed a kiss to his mouth, then stepped away, her beautiful green eyes twinkling mischievously. "Good. I'm starving."

"Oh, yeah? Let's go, then."

She licked her lips, then slanted her gaze toward his crotch. "Fine. You feed me dinner now, later I'll give you dessert."

6

Callie waited by the hotel room door. It felt like she'd been waiting hours, but mostly because she was anxious. Overly anxious. Her body was on fire, her skin felt too tight, her nipples were beaded up, her pussy was wet already. And Malik hadn't even arrived yet.

Instead, she'd spent hours preparing for him, getting the room set up for seduction, even though she knew it wasn't necessary. She wanted things to be special tonight. Memorable. She laughed. Every night, every encounter with Malik was memorable. Burned forever into a scrapbook in her brain, of senses, of taste, of touch. Of emotion.

She swallowed. Things had changed over the last two weeks. Their relationship was now public thanks to the dinner they'd shared at a restaurant, or maybe it'd been all the public kisses. The way he looked at her. His eyes alone melted her to the bone, made her feel like she was going to collapse into a puddle at his feet.

"Malik," she whispered, brushing a palm down her side. Across his Saints T-shirt. Closing her eyes, she gathered her emotions. She was full of passion, filled up with loving Malik. Tonight was about showing him.

Tonight was about admitting it to herself. Taking another slow breath, she thought about the year's worth of letters. Of the stories he'd told, the fantasies he'd shared. And she thought over the last four months of weekend hotel room encounters. Of a down-low affair on and off the player's field.

And now it was time to at least be honest with herself. What had started as a way to find release, satisfaction, had turned into something a lot more serious. Her heart was involved. Deep, head-over-heels crazy for this man.

A noise sounded in the hallway, bringing Callie back to the present. The green light of the keypad lit up; then the door opened silently and Malik stepped inside, dressed in an Armani suit, his fade freshly trimmed.

She smiled, then touched a finger to his lips. "Ssshh . . . come with me." She twined their fingers and led him quietly across the thick carpet to the hotel suite bedroom.

She'd dimmed the lights and lit a half-dozen candles instead, placing them around the room so the shimmering flames cast off enough golden rays to illuminate their movements. The scented candles melted slowly, the erotic scents mingling in the air. Ancient woods, wild fruits.

Across the bed she'd draped black satin sheets trimmed in gold. The flickering flames danced and moved in reflection off the smooth fabric.

Inside the bedroom, Callie released his hand, then turned toward him, her fingers working free the buttons of his shirt. "I've missed you, Malik." Her fingers brushed against the cotton T-shirt he wore beneath.

Lifting on tiptoes, she pressed a kiss to his lips, to the corner of his mouth, traced the line of his jaw with the tip of her tongue. Touched his pulse at the base of his throat just above his collar.

His body responded instantly to the contact. To her touch.

She felt him grow hard against her belly and fought the urge to grind her hips against him. Moisture dripped from her lips; her clit swelled.

"Missed you, too, baby girl," he mumbled, his large hand sliding down her back, then brushing against her bare skin at the hem of his T-shirt. "You smell good." His lips touched her temple; his face pressed against her curls.

He dragged her closer, pressing his hard-on into her softer flesh. Lawdy, she wanted him so much she almost forgot her plans. Almost forgot that tonight was about him. About pleasing him. It'd been a long two weeks to the divisional play-off game. She knew he needed the release. Knew that the adrenalin from winning was still pumping hard through him.

"You want me," she said, smoothing her hand over his muscular shoulders, "and you can have some in a minute."

She laughed, then put two hands between them, pushing back, putting a little distance between them. "First, I want to show you something." Pulling his T-shirt over her head, she allowed it to float to the floor, her gaze focused on his eyes, watching him watch her.

Beneath she wore a tiny push-up bra, her puckered nipples peeking over the top of the black satin. The gold trim contained tiny Saints emblems. The golden thread covered both the bra and the matching panties.

Warmth covered her cheeks as Malik looked her up and down, his appreciation vivid in his dark, appealing eyes. He reached for her. "Don't make me wait. I ain't no Saint."

His voice was rough, thick, the bedroom tone that made Callie wet. Wetter. Her gaze drifted to his crotch where his dick was rocked up, the outline clear beneath his slacks.

She licked her lips. "Okay. Decision made. Come here." Her hand was back in his, and she moved toward the bed. At the edge of the mattress, she turned them slightly, then gave him a gentle push so he sat down on the edge of the bed.

He chuckled. "Girl, what are you about?"

She knelt between the V of his legs.

"Dayum, baby girl." His fingers twisted into her hair, his thumb smoothing across her cheek.

She turned, kissing the pad of his finger as he stroked it softly across her lips. Then she scraped a nail across the button holding his pants closed. Allowed the metal clasp to break free, followed by the jagged teeth of the zipper.

He was so hard his solid dick had the gap opening wider, his head above the elastic band of his cotton boxers, reaching for her, needing her. A pearl-sized bead of precum glistened on the tip.

Bending, Callie touched her tongue to the ball of moisture, swiping it away. He groaned, one hand curling tighter into her hair, the other gripping the black satin sheet.

She touched his skin with her tongue again, then slid her mouth downward, tracing the extended vein that ran his entire length. His hips rotated forward; the hand in her hair urged her down.

"Baby, I know what I'm doing here," she teased, running her tongue along his balls, then smoothing back up across his rock-hard dick. "I like that you're eager, that you want me."

"Very eager." His tone was tense, each syllable pronounced through clenched teeth. His nostrils flared, his hand fisted tighter into the cloth covering the bed. "I want you."

Smiling, Callie eased the cloth out of the way, slowly returning to his cock. Her pussy was dripping now, the small panties she wore were soaking wet. Leaning forward, she rubbed herself along the cloth, her clit tingling. Her body aching to have him inside her. To be filled and stretched around him.

Another pearl of natural lubricant had beaded at his slit, the liquid glistening in the flicker of the candlelight. Lazily she licked it away, moving slowly over him as if learning his feel. As if memorizing it.

Memorizing the touch, the scent, the texture for all the nights they didn't share. He swelled farther against her lips, his pulse drumming in his cock.

Callie used one hand to push his pants down farther, needing them to be completely out of the way, but he was sitting and she couldn't get the cloth off the way she wanted.

She kept a hand around his erection, feeling him throb beneath her fingers, against the palm of her hand. The same tempo vibrating in her clit.

"Malik, help me. I can't get 'em off." She pushed at his pants, then closed her lips around his tip, taking him a few inches into her mouth. Pressing his head to the back of her throat.

Malik held his breath, his hands trembling. Butterflies going wild in his gut. Him, a grown-ass man, with butterflies. *What the hell . . . what the hell was she doing to him?*

The air burned in his lungs till he released it to whistle out between his teeth. "I want to, baby. I want the rest of you." He struggled with another breath. Struggled to keep still while she worked his dick, to keep from grabbing the back of her head and shoving it downward. But I can't move."

God damn, her mouth was so hot and tight around him, her lips gripping, her tongue twirling as her cheeks tightened. It'd been too long since he felt her, since he'd made love to her. Shit, if he could move, he'd remove his pants and throw them hard across the room.

But hell, he couldn't move. Couldn't release the sheets gripped in his fist, couldn't remove his hand from the curls that had wrapped around each finger, around his wrist. He took a breath as he watched the back of her head, fully accepting that she'd paralyzed him.

He'd mastered his body, worked out, knew how to control every muscle, but Callie . . . Callie had him motionless and giving up control with one touch of her mouth. One simple touch of her tongue.

Dayum, if he was honest with himself at all, he'd admit that she controlled with the ease of a seductive smile and the shimmer in her eyes.

His body was rigid, his pulse rapid at his temples, his breathing becoming short and labored. He'd played almost entire football games and not been this winded. And yet he couldn't think, couldn't control a single muscle.

Because she controlled one. His dick. She moved her lips along him, taking him deeper, creating a suction that had his balls pulling up tight against his body, cum building at the base of his cock.

A movement caught his eye. Glancing down, he noticed she had one hand tucked into panties she'd pushed aside, her fingers wet as they dipped into her pussy. Her body melting with arousal.

"Baby, slow it down." Shit, he was going to cum from mouth work alone, when what he really wanted was to get deep inside her.

She whimpered, her eyes coming up to meet his. She eased her mouth off of him, her lips pink and plump and wet. Full and delicious, her lower lip pouted as she removed her hand from her center, then touched his dick with fingers that had been inside her.

His dick bucked hard into her palms, and he bit back climax, breathing hard to keep the ball of cum from working up his dick, to keep from spilling in her hands.

She stood, forcing his grasp from her curls, then straddled his lap, placing a knee on each side of his legs, her ankles on the edge of the mattress so her feet dangled over the edge. His dick was pressed against his gut, eased between honeyed wet lips.

She rotated, arching her back. The movement caused her extended nipples to escape the black satin, the gold Saints emblems sparking as she moved.

"You want me?" She danced her hips along him, wetting

him with her juices from head to base. Silken liquid dripping to his balls.

"Yeah, baby, I want you bad."

She sat on his lap, her ass against his thighs, his feet planted on the floor. It'd be easy to flip them, to grab her up and turn them onto the bed so he was covering her. So he was thrusting his dick all ten inches inside her. Hard and fast. End the tension.

Fuck her right, like her body was begging for. But something about the determined look in her eyes kept him still, his breathing labored as he allowed her to set the pace. Be in control.

As if she sensed his torment, as if she suffered with it, too, she lifted on her knees, holding his dick so the head eased open her dripping lips.

Then in a single, smooth motion, she dropped down; one glide and he was buried deep.

"Malik!" she cried out. "Malik, baby," she whimpered, her breath disappearing as she accepted him within her.

His head pressed against her womb, the walls of her pussy stretching around him, clinging slick and wet and tight to every inch of him.

"Dayum, baby girl, dayum." He put his hands to her hips, ground her down against him as he lifted his body from the bed, his balls tight against her ass, her clit rubbing against his base.

One stroke and already her body was trembling, her nails biting into his shoulders as she lifted up onto her knees and rode down on him a second time. A third. Grinding hard against him with each of her movements.

Oh, shit, he'd already been so damn close, holding back climax with all his might, holding back from cumming between her lips. Now, with her body tight around him, tight and wet and scented sweetly with honey and sex, he knew he wouldn't last long.

Knew when her body clamped down, when he felt her begin to shudder and cling to him, knew he had very little restraint left. If any at all.

He rotated his hips upward, pulling her down, completing the thrust her body had started. "Baby, I love you."

And then he was drenched in honey, her body spasming around his, gripping him in her walls, her nails sinking into his shoulders as she shook hard.

"I love you, too," she moaned, collapsing against his chest, her nipples hard against his skin.

Malik groaned, his jaw tight, every muscle tense, wound up, ready to explode. "This isn't a fantasy." He thrust again, cum working up his length. "This is our future." And then he emptied inside her, filling her up with everything he had.

He smoothed a hand down her spine. "The season's ending soon."

"But we're just beginning," she said between kisses to his neck, to his cheek, to his lips.

"Yeah, baby girl, this is just the beginning."

Matinee

Sydney Molare

1
———

Mina Sinclair had had her share of crazy ideas, but as she gazed at the dilapidated building with peeling paint, a broken and taped glass door, and rotten shingles hanging precariously from the angle of the roof, she knew this had to be her craziest.

If only I'd chosen another night to grocery shop, life would be different.

Two weeks ago, Mina was gathering the contents of her dropped purse off the ground when an SUV squealed across the parking lot, followed by the unmistakable sound of gunshots. Instead of staying low, Mina had made a really bad decision: She rose up and screamed. Of course, the men in the SUV zeroed in on her stricken face. Panicked, she'd somehow fallen into her car, stabbed her keys into the ignition, and zoomed out of the parking lot, losing them in rush-hour traffic. But she'd left her purse—containing all her information—on the ground.

The "visit" came not one day later. The stranger was waiting quietly in her apartment when she returned from work, or rather faking work. Her nerves had been too shot to do more than go through the motions. This stranger sitting in her living room—just like in the movies—validated all her fears.

The man was short, stocky, and had a definite accent. *Italian*, Mina thought. Not that she'd been around many Italians. In all likelihood, it was probably a subliminal Hollywood influence that made her draw that conclusion.

The conversation was succinct: forget what she'd seen, don't go to the police, and a suggestion that leaving town was in her best interest. He'd shoved the case sitting at his feet toward her, making his point. It contained one hundred thousand dollars. The point was taken: "they"—whoever they were—needed no complications, and if that much money was being slung around so easily, Mina was dispensable.

Mina spent a frazzled, sleepless night peeking out of windows, pacing the floor, and jumping at the slightest sound before she formulated a plan. The next morning, she stuffed the money in a duffel bag along with a change of clothes. She'd left for work like normal, ridden the elevator to her floor, changed into a jogging suit, then taken the stairs back down and out the back. Mina caught a taxi to the nearest bus station and jumped on the first bus out of town. She'd switched to trains then taxis then back to buses—anything cash with no ID—to ferry her farther and farther south to a new life.

When the bus had pulled into St. Paulus, Mina, sick of running and watching over her shoulder, had felt a peace descend on her. Without a thought, she'd exited and checked into the small St. Paulus Inn. After purchasing a used car from Paulus Motors—a cheap Ford Focus—Mina had spent the rest of the night formulating a plan. She was still praying it worked.

With a hearty sigh, Mina opened her car door and stood on the sidewalk. The realtor, Charlotte Charles, had proclaimed the building a "fixer-upper" as she'd thrown the keys onto her desk before urging Mina, "Open it up. See if you like it." But as

Mina caught sight of squirrels frolicking on an upper window-sill, of the *TH* and the crooked, broken remaining *RE* of *theatre*, she wondered if there could be any fixing up for this one. Still, she had seen few choices meeting her building renovation and living expenses budget.

Keep your mind open and find some place you can both work and live, her mind chided. After looking at a dozen buildings—loving the ones she couldn't afford and cringing as the list dwindled to this last one—her initial optimism was fading fast but was not gone completely. With a survivor's resolve, she lifted her chin and unlocked the fragile glass door.

Here goes everything.

They heard the car stop in front of the building at the same time. Cal pricked his ears momentarily before mentally turning over the playing card. "My book, old friend." He slapped his hands together.

"Just lucky, you old goat," John grumbled as the cards slid across the table.

A door shut.

"Wonder who it is this time? That realtor lady again?" John couldn't stand the realtor showing his beloved property. In his opinion, Charlotte Charles had misrepresented, misspoke about, and just missed the beauty of the place altogether. Just hearing her voice grated on his nerves. John floated a card in the air before flipping it over and dropping it to the table. King of spades. "Beat that, chump!"

Cal rubbed his hand across his whiskers as he studied the levitating cards before shooting one on top of the table. "You forgot we were playing joker, joker, deuce, ace, *then* king spades?"

John mumbled something incoherent, brown eyes flicking between his suspended cards and the table.

Steps were heard coming up the stairs.

Cal let out a sigh. "Guess we need to postpone this one."

"Yeah. Let me get the chains together. I'll bet we can get rid of this one within ten minutes." John's eyes twinkled.

Cal chuckled and countered with, "I say six and a half, tops."

"You're on!" They gave an airy high five, and then dissolved into laughter.

The cards dropped to the table, some to the floor, as the door squealed on its hinges as it was pushed open.

A step into the room.

"Hello?"

The voice was feminine, husky, and definitely *not* the realtor lady. Cal and John held their chains silent as the body hesitantly followed the voice into the room. A shapely hose-covered leg attached to wide hips and, as their eyes traveled upward, a nipped waist and ample chest. The face was feline, the black hair curling and spiking in total contradiction to the business suit she wore. But in short, the woman was breathtaking.

Mina was surprised and elated that the first floor of the building was in pretty good shape. The old seats had long ago been ferreted away, leaving a nice-sized cavernous space. Yes, there were mountains of trash to be removed, but she could tell the building still had good bones.

She had second thoughts as she stepped into the room at the top of the stairs. The realtor had said the place needed serious work, but as she surveyed the interior, she wondered if she wanted this large of a challenge. Old posters lay curling, disarrayed, covered in layers of dust. It was obvious no one had set foot in here in years. Her eyes shifted to a table in the corner. There appeared to be cards scattered on and around it. She walked closer, leaving a trail of footprints in the layers of powder. Undusty cards.

Mina shivered as thoughts of who else might inhabit the

building flitted into her head. She pulled her canister of Mace from her purse and held it in front of her. It might just be a harmless vagrant, but then again, it might not.

She pushed the thought down as she noticed the walls. Mina ran her hands over them—real knotty-pine-wood paneling. She sniffed. The scent was faint but still present.

Why would they have a knotty-pine-paneled room in a theater?

The thought was pushed down as a smile played over her face and refurbishing ideas popped into her mind. This could be a library. A knotty-pine-paneled library. The smile widened, making it appear that the cat had definitely swallowed the canary.

"Damn, that is a fine-looking woman right there," John stated, eyes focused on Mina's bosom. Today, yesterday, and tomorrow, she was definitely his type.

Cal had to agree with him. He felt a woody forming as her perfume wafted over to him. How long had it been since he'd been only a ghostly voyeur versus an active participant in sex? Nearly thirty years. Thirty years of watching others . . . and getting ghostly blue balls. "Think we should do the chain rattling anyway?"

"Hell no! Did you see how she rubbed the walls? Walls we put up panel by panel ourselves? She knows good details when she sees it. Beats the hell out of that realtor—"

"I know." Cal interrupted John's familiar tirade. "Why don't you just figure out a way to give realtor lady some of your 'good loving' and get that stick out of her butt in the meantime?"

John frowned at the entire concept. "There is no way I would waste my time on a stuck-up, nonfactual woman like that realtor, alive or dead. She is *not* my type, or anybody else's type I know. That's why she is single."

"Sounds like you've been peeking in her windows to know that." Cal smirked.

John waved the comment away. "Whatever. Let's just focus on this little lady right now."

"She definitely has potential," Cal commented as he watched Mina rub her hands over the paneling.

"Shoot, she has more than potential. I can feel it. She's the One."

"Might be. Don't put your chain away just yet." Cal watched Mina's every move.

The air seemed to freshen just from opening the curtain. The late sunlight revealed there was dust everywhere, but it didn't seem as oppressive as it had previously.

As Mina continued to run her hands over the knotted wood and looked at the size of the room, she wondered if the previous occupants had *lived* over the theater. Joy infused her soul as the thought banged around her cranium. Had she already found a place to work and live? Two birds finally killed with one meager stone? She jumped in joy, causing a dirty poster to fall over onto the dusty floor.

Mina sneezed as she lifted the poster from the dust. The title screamed in red ink, *Love on the Run.* A buxom blonde sat astride a Harley, her blouse partially opened and covered by the dark hands of a leather-clad biker. Hmmm. Interesting. The realtor had said it was once a movie theater, but looking at the playbill, she wondered what kind. Mina lifted another poster. This one blatantly proclaimed *Sex Goddess from Venus.* The brunette on this poster wore a sheer white togalike garment, and as she looked closer, Mina realized the shadows she'd taken for smudges were actually the woman's nipples. She shook her head. She'd never heard of either of the movies.

As she leaned to pick up another poster, she felt the unmistakable touch of hands on her butt. She yelped, turned, eyes wide. Nothing but air and the dust she had disrupted as she jumped swirled in front of her.

That felt too real.

Hands cupping the underside of her buttocks, brushing lightly up the sides. She'd had a few men touch her like that, so she was sure. But no one else was in the room.

Snap out of it!

Mina retrieved the can of Mace before turning back to the poster she had been reaching for. Just as she leaned over again, the hands returned, this time squeezing her waist. She yelped, hands clamping onto her midsection and meeting her own body, nothing else.

Get it together!

But she couldn't, as the hand sensation skimmed up past her ribs and rested beneath her bust, clenching and releasing. The sensation, now circular rubbing, seemed to ooze beneath her bra to encompass her full breasts. Breasts that had been denied any other contact but her own hands and a bath towel for too long. A moan escaped as she felt her nipples thickening and elongating, yearning—no, aching—for a touch.

It came.

The impression of fingers tugging at the encased nipples made them turgid, straining to be released into the air. The Mace fell unnoticed to the floor as her hands wrapped around the swollen breasts. Mina couldn't stop her fingers from unbuttoning her blouse, unclasping her bra, and baring her fat nipples into the air.

Phantom hands caressed and pulled at the areolas, stroked and cupped her heavy orbs. Mina pinched her nipples in response, opened her mouth in a gasp as the wetness seemed to enclose around the left nipple and then the right. Bliss.

Mina unconsciously spread her legs and leaned backward as the wetness turned into wet suction. Suckling. Her clit lurched and her panties dampened. Her fingers were beneath her skirt, searching for her stiff button when the phantom lips mirrored her train of thought, flicked across her sensitized nub. She gasped and then screamed as the throes of a monstrous orgasm buckled her knees.

"We shouldn't have done that," John said, hands still stroking the swollen nipples bared to the world. It was those wide squeeze-me-please hips that drove him to touch her again and again.

"Ahuh, but we did," Cal replied, blowing on the panty-clad mons. The sight of those bare nipples had forced him to join in. He hadn't meant to, but seeing John's lips puckered around those dusty berries made him want to suckle also . . . then more.

"We should stop." John kept stroking.

"In a moment." Cal kept blowing.

"We'll drive her away."

Cal looked at Mina's glazed-over eyes and watched her heartbeat thump in her chest. "No. She will definitely be back," he responded with a confidence borne of knowing he knew how to please a woman when he was alive. From the look of things, nothing had changed.

2

"So, did you like the building?" Charlotte Charles asked Mina as she retrieved the keys from her outstretched hand.

Mina gave the matronly woman a hesitant nod. To be honest, she wasn't paying much attention to what Charlotte was saying since she was still so confused by her body's reaction in the building. What in the world possessed her to get herself off in an empty dilapidated building? What if someone else had been there and caught her in the middle of her self-loving?

Her mind zoomed back to the previous hour. Hands stroking and loving her up and down. Twin mouths on her nipples. The culmination of sensations at her clit. She had to admit, it had been the best orgasm she'd had in years.

Smiling, Mina pulled her mind away from the self-tryst and tried to focus on the conversation. Charlotte was now frowning and silent.

"What?" Mina had no idea what she had missed. She prayed she hadn't voiced her thoughts aloud. Now that *would* be embarrassing as hell.

Charlotte cleared her throat. "Did something *happen* at the building?"

Goodness, could she tell? "Ah . . . no."

"You sure?" Charlotte leaned forward, gray eyes piercing Mina's soul.

Mina felt the hairs rising on the back of her neck as she stared at Charlotte. If she had actually voiced her thoughts, Charlotte would have looked shocked, not this in-depth analysis she was doing now. Something else was up. "No. But seems like you think something should have, so spill."

The realtor busied herself with retying the bow on her outdated polka-dot blouse before speaking. "Sometimes people hear chains clanking, see paper flying about, just unusual things."

Well, getting horny and masturbating in an abandoned building was very unusual for Mina, but she didn't plan to reveal that. "No. No paper flying about, just dust. Definitely no chains clanking," she assured Charlotte with a shake of her head.

"Good," Charlotte replied, relief evident on her face.

Mina remembered the posters on the floor. "I do have a question, though."

The frown was back on Charlotte's face. "Go ahead."

"There were movie posters all around, and they were *suggestive*. I was wondering what type of movie theater was there before?"

A glimmer of a smile played on Charlotte's lips before she answered. "It was a triple-X theater."

Did she say triple X? That would explain the pornographic posters. "When did it close down?"

"Oh, around twenty-five, thirty years ago. These young guys, I believe their names were John Whitmore and Cal Tolero or Toledo. I forget. Anyway, it was run by these two guys. But they disappeared one night, and no one has seen them since."

"They were murdered in the building?" No way was she interested in buying Amityville-gone-theater.

Charlotte shrugged. "No one's found their bodies, so it's safe to say, if they were murdered, it probably wasn't in the building."

This was interesting indeed. "Any family?"

"That's what's so fascinating about this case. They showed up one day out of the blue, bought the building, and opened an X-rated movie house. The town was in an uproar, but they had the correct licenses, and truth be told, not enough people protested to have them shut down." Charlotte snorted. "Honestly, I heard that many of our 'upstanding citizens' frequented the place. I know it was rumored they were making a mint. Had to be something to keep them in this small town."

There was much truth in that statement. St. Paulus had one factory that was on its last leg, and the rest of the community depended on logging the forests to survive. According to what the realtor had told her previously, nothing much had changed in forty years. There was a huge warehouse distribution plant being built that should be open within a year. But right now, life was as it had been for many decades, minus an X-rated theater.

"So who owns it now?" Mina inquired.

"The town. No family came forward to claim it after the men left, and then it was condemned and reverted to the town twenty or so years ago."

No family. What kind of men had no family looking for them? Did they return to their families and just forget the town? Or was there something more sinister in the making? Mina's massive curiosity made her suddenly blurt, "I'll take it."

Charlotte didn't blink as she pulled a contract from her desk. "It won't take us but a moment to fill this out. How much are you offering?"

*   *   *

John was having a hard time pushing the lush vision of Mina from his mind. It didn't help that his cock was still hard and throbbing. He wished, for the millionth time, that he could have sex one last time. One last glorious, fulfilling moment of pressing his shaft between warm thighs, tangling between wet bush hairs, and releasing his seed into a deep, dripping cavern of love. Why didn't he follow his first mind thirty years ago?

Cal was having just as rough a time as John. He absently ran his hands over and through his dirty-blond strands, still smelling her oh-so-female scent in his mind. God, she was ripe. And he was dead.

"You think we should follow her?" John finally asked a pensive Cal.

"And be what? Her guardian angels or something?" Yes, they'd visited every home in town and could tell all of their secrets, but this time, it just didn't feel *right*.

"No, just keep an eye on her. She might be upset and not want the building." *And we couldn't enjoy her again.*

Cal heard the thought and echoed the sentiment, but he wouldn't interfere. If it was meant to be, it would be. "Nah, why don't we just let her make up her own mind about the building. Then, whatever happens, happens."

"Think they'll tell her about us?" John knew they'd made too many faces whiten in fear for the townspeople not to gossip about the haunted theater. That didn't keep the vagrants and druggies out. though. For the most part, the addicts just thought they were some of their drug-induced hallucinations.

"Probably."

John knew he was right. No way would they withhold something that juicy from her. If that irritating realtor didn't spill the enchiladas, you could bet the townies would. Resigned to whatever the future held, he asked, "Ready to get back to our game?"

"In a minute," Cal responded, the vision of fat, dusky nipples still on his mind.

3

Mina stood in front of *her* building, the deed clenched in her fist. She couldn't believe the negotiation and sale had taken all of four days. That had to set a record for a commercial real estate closing.

She smiled as she turned the key and opened the door again. The dusty, mildew smell assaulted her nostrils, but she ignored it as she trotted up the stairs to her library.

Try as she might, Mina couldn't get her reaction in the room out of her mind, couldn't understand why this room had made her feel so *sexy*. Twenty years of having sex and she managed to give herself her best orgasm ever. Go figure. The funny part was, she'd tried to duplicate the orgasm, tried to repeat her finger-loving performance again in her hotel room. She'd failed miserably. But she wanted that overwhelming rush of hormones, wanted the gush of juice running down her legs again.

Mina strode into the room, expecting her body to jump to attention. She twirled around, making the dust motes dance as she traced a finger along a wall and pulled a tattered drapery from a window. She finally stopped and grinned at the dirty room. Her new home. That's when she noticed the tall cabinet doors.

The doors reached to the ceiling along the far wall. There were no knobs or handles to use as pulls, so Mina removed a nail file from her purse and wedged one open. She jumped back as it creaked wide. She didn't know if an army of rats would pour out or—she shivered slightly—a dead body. She was more than relieved when neither happened. Instead, inside were round metal canisters from floor to ceiling: celluloid movies. She hadn't seen one in decades.

Excited now, Mina forgot her previous reservations and wedged open the remaining doors, revealing more of the same. As she brushed the grime away and read the titles, an addendum to her plan formed in her head. By her estimate, there were nearly three hundred movies present. And judging from the titles she quickly skimmed, a gold mine of old erotica.

Her head was spinning with more ideas, adrenaline pumping, when she spotted a closed door she'd previously missed. Mina strode over and turned the knob. It squealed on its hinges as it opened little by little. The faint light through an opaque window revealed an old-fashioned bathroom, complete with a claw-foot tub and a wide pedestal basin sink. The spiders had taken up residence, and Mina heard the skitter of small feet behind the wall.

What did she expect?

Mina crossed the floor and stood at the head of the tub. It was stained and the fixtures rusty. She turned the handle, surprised that it moved easily. Of course, no water flowed. She was sure it had been off for decades.

Her hands traveled across the basin sink where spiderwebs covered the faucet head and fixtures. She quickly tangled her hand in the web and pulled them away. An ornate mirror hung above the sink, its silver grimed over. She rubbed some of the grime away and smiled at her image. Winking at her own face, she tugged her shirt from her waistband and opened it wide. Then she perched one hip on the edge of the basin. She was prepared to act on any signals her loins gave her.

Cal groaned as Mina's shirt flapped wide. She wore a scrap of a bra that was so sheer, her nipples were visible through it. He wished he could read her mind, wished he knew if her pulling her shirt open was an act of desire or just hot weather.

John had been elated to see Mina return. His cock rose and saluted as soon as they'd heard the car door shut. It was now a flagstaff waiting for someone to climb upon it. Never one to be a follower while alive, he stayed true to himself in the afterlife as he floated over and hovered in front of Mina.

"John, I don't think we should—" Cal fell silent as John waved him off.

"Hush, man. I just want to feel her again."

"I know. I just don't want us to overwhelm her and she rescinds her transaction."

John chuckled a bit. "You and I both know there isn't a woman alive who would run from a great orgasm, no matter the source."

"True." Cal nodded, eyes peeled to the berries staring back at him. "Do your thing, then. I'll just watch."

"Man, you've been a voyeur for three decades. I can't speak for anybody else, but I plan to see how far I can go with this thing . . ." John's voice faltered as Mina suddenly shifted, placing her breast in the full sunlight. He licked his thick lips, felt his cock grow as he gazed at the golden skin and the fine hairs coating it. They glowed in the warm rays.

John wanted to bite and bruise the tender flesh in pleasure-pain. Wanted to drag his tongue around and around the outtie navel above her waistband. Wanted to turn her around, sink his rod to the hilt, and pinch those hanging tatas as they thrashed into the air. He couldn't help himself: he ran a finger between the exposed spheres.

Cal sighed behind him.

John turned his head to look back at him. "Still gonna watch?"

"I'm thinking," Cal responded, his hand now wrapped around his own stiff cock.

Mina didn't jump as she felt the warmth in the center of her chest. In fact, she welcomed it. Inhaling deeply, she let her head loll backward as the heat radiated beneath and then around her globes. Her nipples hardened and saluted through her sheer bra. Mina ran her finger around her back and unclasped the sheer harness. Her breasts dropped beneath the fabric and into the cool air.

An ethereal touch to the stiff knobs made her moan. She clenched the now-throbbing mounds, held them out for more. A wispy touch flicked back and forth across the tips, setting them on fire and sending sparks downward. Her clit lurched, pulsed. Honey pushed past her pussy lips and wet her thin panties.

Mina lifted from the basin and stood as she pulled her skirt over her ass. She turned and placed one foot on the edge of the tub, her hands headed for her clit.

John stood behind Mina, cupping her breasts in his hands. He knew she'd felt his touch when she'd moaned as he flicked her puckered nipples between his fingers. He pressed his body more fully into her, seating his cock between her thighs. He felt fleeting moments of warmth, nothing more.

Needing more, he closed his eyes, tried his damnedest to telepath his thoughts into Mina's brain. Craved for her to want *him*.

* * *

The image burst into Mina's head—brown skin, cut muscles, hazel eyes, and succulent lips. Mina had had her share of lovers, but one thing she definitely knew: this man had never been one of them.

Let me love you, the man whispered as his hands rubbed up and across her belly, leaving a fiery trail behind.

Mina exhaled noisily as teeth seemed to nip the back of her neck, a tongue following suit. The tongue slowly flicked her earlobe, then swirled into her outer canal. Her entire body tensed as the wet appendage brushed deeper, and then warm, sweet breath was blown around her hot spots. The tongue teased and made promises as it nipped across her shoulders. Oh, the sensations! She was burning at her core. Her body quaked with desire and need as she felt a thick probe seat between her legs.

Feel me.

Her moan was prolonged and guttural. Wisps of heat burned upward as she felt hands move and spread her thighs farther. Mina ached with desire; her clit throbbed with need as unseen fingers tap-danced inward. Her fingers refused to wait; indeed, they mashed and circled her erect clit with abandon.

John pressed himself onto her back, lightly bending her forward. Mina gasped as fingers dipped into her heat, swirled and pumped as she rained honey.

Let me love you.

Mina arched her back in consent, spread her pussy lips in anticipation. The touch was at first fleeting, and then firm as the cock pressed between her lips inch by delicious inch. The thick cock's descent stopped only when her hips were tickled by the man's bush. Then the movement was reversed just as slowly, before the cock was thrust to the hilt.

Damn! Mina's pussy groped and Kegeled around the massive cock. Her fingers slid beneath her pussy to cup a heavy sac. She squeezed and was rewarded with a double pump. Emboldened, she spread her legs wider, arched her back more, pushed backward, and pistoned rapidly, reaching for nirvana.

Mina didn't have to wait long. She felt the pinpricks shoot up her legs, and she clenched her inner walls as hard as she could. Her clit exploded before she slumped to the floor.

John could have cried as he felt the orgasm rumble from his body. He knew it was all in his head, but damn, it *felt* like the real thing, and that was all that mattered. He'd flown from corner to corner, down the stairs and back up in his exuberance. Now he stared at the crumpled Mina, legs sprawled wide, and felt himself harden all over again.

Cal was wheezing, trying to maintain his composure. *Shit!* It had taken every shred of willpower not to join John in tantalizing the woman. His cock was a brick and as he stared at Mina, not getting softer anytime soon.

"That was amazing. Just amazing," John said, eyes full of wonder. "Why hadn't we tried this before now? Just watching and not participating, and all the time we could have been inside of their heads. Could have been enjoying ourselves for three decades."

"I don't know. It might just be you. It might be *this* woman. I may not even be able to telepath my thoughts," Cal responded, though his mind was praying the opposite was true. He so wanted to feel those thighs clenched around his back as he fucked her senseless against a wall. He wanted to be the origin of those sexy coos and sighs.

"You won't know until you try it," John chided him.

Mina groaned, causing Cal's pole to lurch. John might have a point, and what better time than the present to prove it? "Point taken, my friend." Cal gave John a sly grin. "Watch and learn how a master lover works."

John chuckled as Cal floated past him. "I will . . . just as *soon* as he shows up."

4

Cal watched Mina's chest rise and fall erratically. He drifted over her, her scent infusing his nostrils, making his cock throb and swell further. A slight shifting of her legs revealed sheer panties matching the bra, the center darker than the rest.

Good.

He placed himself between the golden thighs and deeply inhaled. Perfume, a natural musky scent . . . *all* woman. Cal blew lightly on the sheer fabric. His lips pressed kisses along her thighs, moving upward slowly but methodically. Mina moaned, twitched.

"You in her head yet?" John asked, floating just behind Mina's head.

"I will be in a minute. Don't rush me," Cal grumbled. John had his chance; now let him do his thing.

"I'm telling you, you've got to—" John shut up as Cal lifted his head and gave him a monstrous stare. "Whatever. Do it like you want to."

"I intend to," Cal replied as his lips touched silken skin

again. He then closed his eyes and let his body fall directly into
Mina's.

Mina felt on fire! Her synapses fired rapidly, her body jerked
and spasmed.

A seizure?

Much as she tried, her eyes wouldn't open, wouldn't allow
her to assess the situation as the burning sensation intensified.
Just as quickly as it had begun, it stopped, leaving only a tingling in her fingertips.

Mina squinted as she tried to focus through the double vision. She patted her chest, then stopped. Her hands seemed different. Mina pulled the hands closer to her face and inspected
them. Long, slender with short nails, they looked like her fingers but *felt* enhanced, like they belonged to another person.
Her hands slid back to her chest, skimmed her breasts. No doubt
about it. The slim hands definitely seemed larger, rougher to
the touch. In fact, it felt like . . . like someone *else* was touching
her.

What the hell is going on?

A dull ache began in her temple. She closed her eyes as now
unfamiliar digits pushed and rubbed the sides of her head to no
avail. Mina tentatively moved her hands lower, across her flat
belly, and stopped again. Not only did the fingers feel different,
but *what* those fingers felt was different!

She looked down, straining to focus, and gasped at what
emerged through her hazed eyes: fine blond hairs coated a toned,
larger arm than she possessed. She flexed her hand—foreign
now—wiggled the thick, stubby fingers attached, and, as she
turned it over, the heavily calloused palm beneath.

Mina needed to see if this was just a mirage or if she was
truly in control of this strange hand, attached to this stranger
arm, which seemed to be attached to her body. She was stunned

as the hand moved back and forth, following the signals her mind fed it.

Mina stared at the dark blond curls imbedded in a wide chest, and as the hair continued lower, hidden beneath a pair of short underpants.

A man?

Her mind tried valiantly to come up with an explanation, tried to mesh the reality of what she was seeing with the impossibility in her mind, but she couldn't.

That's when the bulge in the briefs lurched.

Cal felt his essence osmosing, merging with Mina's cells. A thousand needles prickled him as nerve sensation awakened in his hands, feet, and face. More needles strummed along his back as he settled himself farther into her body.

Cal felt Mina's brain pushing back, trying to eject him. No way was he going to be expelled from this experience without a fight. He held firmly as her brain refused him admittance, shoved him mightily until he was just on the fringe of expulsion. Finally, her mind shifted, allowed him to share space.

His mind swam as he felt the face. Thirty odd years since he'd actually *felt* anything and definitely not from this vantage point. With a hesitant hand, he patted the chest, just wanted to bask in real, live flesh again.

He felt Mina awaken then. Hesitate as she peered at their blended hand. It looked feminine, but Cal guessed from her reaction that the reality she was seeing was way different.

He allowed her mind to lead them both as the hand traversed her face and back across the chest. As he skimmed the beautiful, plump breasts, felt the pointed nipples slide across his palm, he couldn't stop the surge of heat into his loins. In milliseconds, his cock was pointed north.

* * *

The staff rose from her pelvis, curved and stiffening fast. To Mina, it felt like her clit had engorged and needed stroking. Her hands gingerly peeled back the shorts. She stared at the pink crown, the bulging veins conjoining and then separating along the length of the waking organ. Mina could only gawk as the cock stood slowly, as if from slumber, until it was a fleshy totem pole aimed at the heavens.

This can't be real.

Mina wondered if she was dreaming, if maybe the *Twilight Zone* marathon she'd been watching last night was replaying a damnably good rerun in her head. But as the unfamiliar hands inched through the now-coarse pubic hair, circled the base, and then squeezed, Mina confirmed that this cock was indeed real.

Cal groaned as his fingers cupped those luscious lower lips. He sensed transference of sensation as his hands and hot fingers roamed up, down, and around the fat, engorging tissue. He shuddered as he brushed across the stiff clit, his nipples quickening in response. He hastily moved forward, unnerved by the sparks radiating from that brief touch.

Cal pulsed as he slipped within the door to Eden. The membranes he'd only seen, felt, and tasted before were moist, pliable beneath his fingers. He felt a tugging deep within, an innate need to spread wider, allow more access to the fingers. The walls suddenly clenched. As a surge of moisture coated his fingers, he gasped.

This is what a woman feels!

He reveled in the sensations, the body pulsing around his searching digits. He took his time, moving forward centimeter by centimeter as he allowed himself to savor each twinge, each clasp of the muscular tube.

Cal was pushing in and out with relish, hips lifting from the floor with each thrust, when the clitoris sent out a pheromonic

SOS signal. His body trembled as his hand moved tentatively toward the vibrating nub.

Mina's body sizzled as her hands moved slowly up and down the pulsing cock. She couldn't believe how good it felt. The sensations emitted from the friction of the rough, calloused palm forced her to stroke the long member. Tight. Loose. Tight. Loose. Mina's hands moved of their own accord, as if the cock and hand were long-practicing friends. As her fingers pulled at the crown, fluid leaked, lubricating her motions.

This feels too good!

Mina squeezed, pulled, and rubbed the head around and around, her body trembling, more fluid oozing over her fingers. The cock lurched again. She felt unknown sensations below willing her slick fingers to encircle the cock and stroke in earnest. Her hands were blurs of frenetic activity egged on by the pulsations emanating from this cock. Her toes curled; she panted, knowing that a release was near.

When it arrived, it took her by surprise. One moment, she was shagging her cock; the next, a blinding ache hit behind her ear, her nipples flowered, her toes pointed stiffer than any ballerina's, and gizm shot from the cock.

Splattering her stomach.

Fogging her brain.

Bliss.

Cal massaged the bush hair between his fingers before moving higher. He didn't know what to expect, but he knew the mother lode of all sensations lay in the minimountain standing proudly at the top of the sexual cleft. He'd seen it too many times from the opposite position.

With a hearty breath, he plunged ahead. His fingers circled around the base. Cal gasped as zips of electricity radiated outward, enticed him to move higher, touch harder. He followed the hormonal instructions, slipped the stiff button between his index and second finger before he mashed.

Yowza!

It felt like a thousand volts of electricity pulsed from that small piece of tissue. Cal was powerless to remove his fingers, to stop the pushing, mashing, and stroking of the erect nub. He felt the tingling moving up his legs, across his chest, down to his fingertips. The primal need ensnared his fingers, and they continued their herky-jerky dance around the well-lubricated clit. Just as he thought he couldn't stand another sensation, another jolt of pleasure, all the vibrations seemed to triangulate perfectly on the clitoris.

Cal knew this would be a humdinger of a climax. In seconds, his body arched sharply, tendons stretched to the point of tearing as fluid jetted all over his fingers and trailed between his legs.

Nirvana.

5

She was losing her mind.

No two ways about it. Mina was on the road to elevator-doesn't-go-all-the-way-to-the-top, nine-cents-short-of-a-dime, Cheerios-for-brain-cells cuckoo. What else could explain the very real visions of men she'd never seen sexing her, masturbating all over a dust-clogged room, and convincing herself, briefly, that she actually had a cock? That climaxed?

Sure she'd had fantasies. What woman didn't? But these escapades into lust went past mere fantasy. These were surreal, vivid productions complete with lingering memories—rough palms across her nipples, the lemony smell of his breath infusing her nostrils, conjuring up images of hazel eyes and rippling muscles.

Mina wondered if there was an Internet help group full of people happily consoling one another, swapping stories, and offering advice to those also suffering from this same out-of-body, Technicolor, hypersexual malady.

No. She was probably the only nut on the planet with this problem.

Mina struggled to focus as she strung the tape along the downstairs wall for the third time. The first two attempts had dissolved into blurs of stretch, read, and forget. Just as she read the number, an unbelievable idea popped into her head: Maybe those men in her new and improved fantasies were the two dead guys who owned this building. Could she be haunted by two horny ghosts working out three decades of frustrations . . . through her?

Mina giggled at the thought. Yeah, she'd seen movies of ghostly possessions and even one where a woman was impregnated by an ethereal presence, but *this*? This sexual overload of pleasure?

She resolved right then and there to find out more about the previous owners. What they looked like. What their habits were. Surely someone in this town was around in this theater's heyday. If not, the library should have some old newspaper microfiches at least.

Mina smiled as she stretched the tape for the fourth time, this time determined to get the building measured.

Cal and John hovered at the top of the stairs and watched Mina work.

"Doesn't seem like she knows what she's doing, does it?" John remarked as Mina pulled the tape down the wall for the fourth time.

"That or her mind is on something else." Cal had a good idea of what could be occupying her thoughts. His were definitely on the "inner-body" experience he'd had. Nothing could have prepared him for the overwhelming sensations felt from stepping into Mina's shoes for a few minutes. The sudden jump of his cock confirmed this fact.

"Wonder if she's thinking of us."

Cal snorted even though he knew the statement was true. "She doesn't even know we exist." He waved his hand in front of John's face. "Hello? We're invisible."

John cocked his eyebrows. "We might be invisible, but we were inside her head. She had to get an image of us or something."

"Yeah, right." Cal turned to look back at Mina, determined to play devil's advocate. "What makes you think she will put it all together? Not just believe we're some dudes she conjured up out of her subconscious to aid her fantasies?"

"I don't. I just know that when *I* was inside her head, she saw me," John stated with certainty. "And after that orgasm I gave her, I am definitely a face she'll conjure up again and again for future fantasies."

Cal ruminated on this statement. "If that's the case, what do you think she will say when she finds the old albums in the wall?" There were five photo albums hidden in a secret place behind the back bedroom's wall. Most of the photos were of Cal and John, but some were of their patrons and definitely more *interesting*.

"Better yet, what will she say when she discovers the one hundred and fifty thousand in the leather case beside the albums?" John countered. Banks had been a no-no with the kind of cash they'd generated.

"Think we'll be free if she does?" Cal ventured, his mind moving back in time.

Cal and John had grown up together in backwoods Mississippi just outside of Natchez. A tight friendship was forged despite the color line they'd crossed. They'd ignored the sneers, threats, and whispered comments and lived life as they saw fit.

But Cal had pushed that color line too far—according to the small minds in town—when he'd developed a crush on Rev. Leroy Thomas's baby daughter, Katrina. The good reverend and his Baptist congregation made it clear that his time was limited. Cal understood when a threat was a threat and when it was a joke. And Rev. Leroy was *not* joking. Cal decided it was time to go, and John left with him.

They'd worked here and there, in as big of a city as they could find, planning to save and go into business together. Cal wished they could say that all their jobs were on the up-and-up, but he couldn't. They'd gotten involved as mob lookouts in Las Vegas for the usual reasons—young, dumb, and broke. The money was good, and they'd cut a swath through the women—available and taken—they'd come in contact with.

It was fate they got their once-in-a-lifetime chance to get out of "the business" when John hit fifty thousand dollars at a craps game at a casino. They were quickly approached by a mob henchman, Bruno Voroso, who offered them ownership of an X-rated theater his "bosses" needed to unload quickly and quietly.

It wasn't what they had planned. They'd wanted to just take the money and run. But as Bruno explained the profit margin and the fact that they, seeing that Cal and John were partners, had very few options available to them—an explanation punctuated by a very impressive and meaning-filled display of cracking his gigantic knuckles—they'd agreed.

As the train stopped in St. Paulus and they surveyed the little hamlet reminiscent of their hometown, both Cal and John wished they had rethought their idea. But with forty thousand still lining John's suitcase, they'd decided to make the best of it.

They'd withstood the initial protests, the spray-painted graffiti and the broken ticket-booth window. The sheriff applied pressure, but with his officers being some of their best customers—along with incriminating photos proving this—he'd backed down.

The place was mildly filled during the day and packed on the weekend. More than one "upstanding citizen" chose to use the rear exit before the movie ended. And after the jobs began drying up, those out-of-work men boosted business just that much more.

Just as the gravy bowl was filling to the rim, Cal bought The Goose, his private two-seater Cessna. He'd taken the classes, gotten his license, then finagled and begged until John took a ride with him.

Their first and last.

Murphy's Law decided to rear its ugly head. An unscheduled flight, an unrecorded flight plan, and the engine had failed and the plane crashed into an unfamiliar lake, sinking two hundred feet to a watery grave. Their bodies were still inside, their spirits locked within the boundaries of St. Paulus county ever since.

"I don't know, but I sure hope so," John whispered in reply.

"Only one way to find out," Cal assured him.

"And I plan to be here to savor every . . . sweet . . . drop," John confirmed with a nod. "But I hope it's not too soon. Me and that little lady's got some more 'real' coming to do."

6

Mina's resolve to get started on the renovations led her to the local home fix-up store. She'd been an architect's apprentice, so she had some firm ideas of what she wanted and who she'd have to hire to do them.

Cal and John hovered over the Focus as Mina entered the car.

"I sit up front, you in the back," John called as his presence leached through the roof.

"Why do you get front and I get back?" Cal huffed as he settled in the rear seat.

"You can always sit on the gear shift," John countered.

"And have her pushing the gearshift back and forth between my legs?" Cal sniped before growing quiet. An image of Mina shifting gears millimeters from his cock actually sounded like a great idea. As if on cue, his cock woke and began rising. "On second thought, maybe I *will* sit on the gearshift." Cal leaned forward and lifted a leg.

John stopped him with an upheld hand. "Uh-uh. I can tell where your mind just went. The next thing I know, you're inside her head and we've crashed." John shook his head. "No way, buddy, you sit right where you are."

"Well, *you* suggested it," Cal reminded John.

"And I now withdraw the suggestion."

"Be that way," Cal finished, slumping back into the rear seat.

"I plan to."

John looked out the window. He hadn't ridden in an auto since before the accident. It was much different from the "float view" he normally had. The trees seemed taller, the speeding cars more daunting at this level. It didn't help that Mina drove like she was a NASCAR contender. Even though John was already dead, he still flinched as she weaved and bobbed in traffic, barely missing a pulp-wood truck loaded to the gills.

In minutes they pulled into the parking lot of Stark's Lumber and Home Supply. A mobile home, elevated a few stories in the air, beckoned customers at the entrance of the massive store stretched along the intersections of Highways 61 and 52.

Mina slowed to a crawl since the parking lot was a circus. Horns honked incessantly, voices were raised as stopped cars impeded movement behind them, and a line of vehicles snaked nearly back to the entrance from the loading dock. Mina wisely slid into a space near the edge of the roughly paved lot and hiked to the building, Cal and John floating along unnoticed in her wake.

The inside was as expected—floor-to-ceiling home building supplies, tools, nuts, bolts, and appliances for every room. Mina quickly made her way over to the home remodeling section where a dark-haired, balding man sat clicking before a computer.

"Excuse me," Mina said politely.

The man didn't turn around or in any way acknowledge her presence as he clicked away at his keyboard. Not used to this type of treatment, Mina cleared her throat and said more forcefully, "I *said*, excuse me. I need some help."

The man swiveled his chair around, a vacant expression on his face. In seconds, it vanished as his eyes drifted downward, focusing on Mina's chest. "Y-yes?"

Mina's naughty angel whispered in her ear as the man's eyes seemed to X-ray her chest and seat his eyes beneath her bra. She fought down the impulse to act on the lurid dare in her head. Instead, she sighed before stating, "I need some help remodeling a building. Do you have a list of contractors and renovators here?"

The man licked his thin lips and then smacked them in a crude imitation of what Mina guessed was his best "come-hither" come-on. She'd bet her last dollar no one had taken him up on it in the past decade. Mina took a deep breath which, to the man's obvious pleasure, expanded her breasts even more.

"This joker here is being a bit disrespectful, don't you think?" John asked Cal as they watched the man ogle Mina's tits.

"Yup. He has a serious case of Breast Hyperfascination." Cal smirked. "I think he needs an etiquette adjustment."

John laughed. "I've seen no evidence that you even *remember* the etiquette taught at our mama's knees."

"I haven't needed to use it before now."

"Do your thing, then, man. What do you suggest?"

"Just watch and learn. Watch and learn," Cal said as he floated directly behind the gawking man.

I am getting nowhere fast.

Mina bent down until she locked onto the man's magnetized eyes. "Look"—her eyes shifted to his name plate—"Frank, I need some help remodeling a building." She spoke slowly and evenly. "Do you have a list of renovation experts?"

Frank leaned back in his chair and licked his plump lips again. Mina could read his obvious thoughts as he said, "I sure do, little lady."

Little lady? Mina clamped down on her rising temper as she asked, "Could you give me a list, then?" She was tiring of this scenario. Her list was long, the day was short, and the last thing she needed was an undersexed sales clerk trying to pick her up. "Today?"

Frank reluctantly pulled his eyes away from her bosom and stared at his computer screen. With a few clicks, the printer next to Mina came to life. She lifted the sheet from the printer tray, hoping to get away from Frank as quickly as possible. She stifled a laugh as she turned over the sheet of paper and read.

"You sure this is what you meant to give me?" Mina tried to ask with a straight face, but giggles bubbled in her throat and forced themselves out as she handed the paper to Frank. I AM THE WORST LAY IN TOWN! was printed in bold black type.

Frank's face reddened as he read the words. "What is this? This some kind of a joke?"

"It's the paper I removed from the tray. You saw me," Mina assured him as she coughed, covering up the next laugh.

"Must be some sort of malfunction." Frank gave the computer two good raps before he clicked some keys again. The printer spat out another piece of paper.

Frank batted Mina's hand away to lift out the new sheet of paper himself. "What the—" he swore before crumpling the sheet between his fingers. But not before Mina read the words MY COCK IS TWO INCHES LONG. Mina doubled over in laughter this time.

"That was too cold, Cal. I feel ole Frank's pain," John wheezed out between his own laughter.

"Shut up. You can't feel a thing and you know it."

"Continue. This is getting good," John urged Cal.

"I intend to," Cal guaranteed as he leaned closer to the can of strawberry Nehi on the desk.

Frank, beet-red now, scrunched his face and peered at the

computer screen. It was comical how he clicked and then looked at the screen before clicking another key. A Parkinsonian tremble was present as he pushed the PRINT button. Frank wasted no time grabbing the sheet as it exited the printer. It read THE.

"There is definitely something wrong with this computer." Frank banged on the side of the computer again, then leaned over and fiddled with the lines.

In the meantime, the computer silently printed more sheets. Mina couldn't resist pulling the multiple pages from the printer tray. Tears ran down her face as she read each sheet: SHEEP. WORSHIP. ME. She howled when she'd finished, startling Frank. He snatched the pages from Mina's hand, hyperventilating as he shifted through the sheets.

"I—is it true?" Mina yelped around another bout of giggles.

Frank's eyes narrowed, lust evaporating from his demeanor. "I don't know what kind of game you are playing here but—"

Cal chose this particular moment to blow over the can of strawberry Nehi. The soda splattered the front of Frank's crotch, the red screaming against the khakis. Mina hooted and backed up as Frank cussed and brushed at the spreading stain with a limp napkin. After a few futile attempts, he gave Mina one last ugly stare and then stomped away, headed down an aisle of bathroom fixtures, WORSHIP held in front of his crotch.

John gave Cal a wispy high five. "I do believe ole Frank got the message."

They both chuckled.

"Hello, can I help you with something?" a female voice asked behind Mina.

Mina turned to the speaker, a dishwater-blond, slight woman wearing a company shirt and blue jeans. The name tag read "Tracey." Mina nodded. "You sure can."

"I just saw Frank hightailing it down the next aisle and figured he'd pissed off somebody." Tracey's eyes twinkled. "Would you have anything to do with the strange sign he was holding in front of him?"

Mina held her hands in front of her. "Hey, I just came in here to get a list of contractors. That guy, Frank, is the one who went off his rocker. First, he stared at my breasts like they were bare, and the next thing I know, he's printing out all these lewd messages. One stated he was the worst lay in town." Mina rolled her eyes and shook her head. "Why he'd tell anybody, I don't know, but he did. The next proclaimed his *organ* was only two inches long—definitely a needs-to-be-well-kept-secret thing, in my opinion. But the last one was the kicker." Mina tried to keep a straight face but she couldn't. "It said 'The sheep worship me.'" Both women burst into laughter.

"The first two were bad enough, but the last one takes the cake."

"The entire three layers plus the cake stand." Mina laughed so hard, she had to cross her legs to prevent wetting her pants.

Tracey wiped tears from her eyes as their laughter died down. "Frank is a real jerk. I'm sorry I missed it."

Mina had composed herself enough to ask, "Think you could get me a list of contractors and fill this order of supplies I've got?"

"Coming right up," Tracey assured her.

Tracey began clicking on the computer as Mina pulled out her list.

7

Mina was bushed. Ordering supplies had taken more than two hours, and then she'd begun what she'd originally thought would be a simple task of finding a contractor. Wrong. The contractors were already committed, thought the job was too big for their company, or in two instances, refused to work for a woman. Twenty-first-century men still had antiquated ideas about working for women. Mina had finally found one in the next county. He'd agreed to meet her later this afternoon.

The remainder of her morning had been fairly productive. Mina had gotten the electricity and water turned on, swept and mopped the library, and bought a bed. She was tired of the drab motel room and wanted to move into her new home as soon as possible, firetrap or not.

The furniture store had loaded up the massive wooden structure and followed her to her destination. The delivery men had huffed and wheezed as they struggled up the stairs. They had looked so exhausted when they reached the top, she suggested they place it in the first room they came to—the library.

Not her best idea, but she now stood proudly looking at the huge, four-poster structure in the middle of the room.

It's a start.

Mina pulled sheets from a bag and arranged them over the queen-size mattress. By the time she smoothed the last wrinkle from the comforter, her eyes were heavy. Without a thought, she shucked her clothes and slid between the cool sheets, unaware of the reaction her display of immodesty had elicited.

"Goddamn! Did you see that?" John exclaimed to Cal.

"I'd have been blind not to." Cal fingered his whiskers, eyes on the sleeping figure.

John rubbed himself absently. "I feel like I'm about to burst!"

Cal's cock had also risen at the nearly naked display, but he downplayed his reaction. "Thirty years of no sex and now you've become a pervert."

John lifted one eyebrow as his eyes dropped to the tell-tale bulge in Cal's crotch. "Looks like I'm not the only one wanting to get perverted," he responded with meaning.

"Whatever." Cal wasn't ready to admit how much he wanted to be inside those silken folds of Mina's again. He'd prided himself on self-control when he was alive and felt he should uphold that same self-control in death. But damn, he so wanted to be nestled bush to bush, pushing and stroking, muscles straining before he climaxed. What the hell was it about *this* woman?

John floated over the bed, his hand now vigorously stroking his shaft. "I'm going in."

The double entendre tickled Cal. "I can see that."

"Hey"—John tilted his head in Cal's direction—"want to do a threesome?"

"While she's asleep?"

John puffed his chest out. "Believe me, she might be asleep

now, but soon, Ms. Mina will awake. Happily." John aligned his body behind Mina's in the bed.

"Wait a minute. This is wrong. Just wrong to—" Mina's sudden low moan zapped the remainder of Cal's response.

"See what I told you. She is ready and willing for some of my loving." John chuckled while his hands moved over and through Mina's body. "I want to try something. Something I heard about. Watch this."

Cal was silent as John's hand disappeared inside Mina's pelvis. He stared as John's forearm twisted this way and that, guiding his unseen fingers. In seconds, Mina stretched, arched, and moaned again loudly.

"What are you doing?" Cal hissed, fearful John was damaging something internal. Yes, he wanted to have a good time with Mina, but not at the expense of harming her.

"Man, calm down. I'm touching her G-spot. Sweet, isn't it?"

Cal couldn't help but to agree as Mina's legs opened, revealing panties that were rapidly darkening in the seat. He floated down until he was positioned between the spread-eagle legs. John wiggled his arm. Mina moaned and thrashed; moisture leaked through the cloth barrier.

"Still think this is wrong?"

Cal didn't respond as he allowed his hands to travel beneath the skimpy bra and cover a nipple. Once again, there was fleeting warmth, but not *enough*. He met John's eyes. "Ready to get back inside her head?"

"You ain't said nothing but a word. Let's do it." With that, they both closed their eyes and oozed into her body, Cal in front, John in the back.

Mina's dream was a happy one. She frolicked on a white beach, feet kicking in the surf as the foam rolled around her ankles. She giggled as she ran back and forth, jumping in and out of the water in glee. Just as she twirled to escape the oncoming wave, they were there—two men, one dark, the other pale.

Daylight and Dusk, her mind immediately dubbed them.

Dusk she remembered. The hazel eyes, the goatee, and the cut, rippling muscles covering his physique were unforgettable. Daylight was blond, his eyes blue and his frame lanky. Mina knew she didn't know him, but surprisingly, she didn't feel afraid.

Dusk held out a hand. "Let us love you."

Let us love you.

A feeling of déjà vu washed over her as she reached her hand out to take the man's. At the first touch, her body betrayed her—her loins tightened, and her nipples grew erect beneath the bikini top.

Dusk wasted no time slamming his mouth onto hers. Mina's senses were overwhelmed as his tongue darted and swirled inside her mouth. Lips began suckling the back of her neck, along her shoulders. Daylight. She sighed around Dusk's tongue as her breasts were cupped, then squeezed between Daylight's rough, calloused palms.

I've felt these hands before.

The bikini top was untied, and her breasts bounded into the open air. Mina moaned as the bare nipples were trapped between fingers and pinched. She shivered as other hands slid down her belly and tugged her bottoms from her hips.

Dusk released her mouth before latching onto a nipple, pulling it into his hot orifice. Her clit stiffened as he nipped the ripening berries. Daylight trailed kisses down her spine, his lips sucking as he encountered her cheeks, his hands flitting across her now-tingling clit.

Mina moaned loudly as Dusk dipped his head lower, parted her abundant pubic hair, and then covered her clit with his lips. His tongue slid up and down her nub, making her undulate involuntarily. Impulsively, she grabbed his head, guiding his motions as she rotated on his face.

Daylight parted her cheeks, and Mina clenched as she felt his warm breath float over her chocolate hole. The breath left her as a tongue flicked over and around the opening.

A finger crept into her pussy, making her buck. Mina dug her nails into Dusk's skull as her body rolled and jerked. Dusk never acknowledged any pain; instead, another finger was inserted beside the first, pumping rapidly.

The tongue pushed inside her anus, probing and poking before lapping at the entrance. This act was repeated again and again until Mina thought her head would pop with pleasure—her body drenched in sweat, cum running from her canal like a faucet, her nipples about to burst from the sweet agony of an upcoming release.

Suddenly, everything stopped.

Mina opened her eyes, not ready to end this assault of pleasure upon her body. Dusk lay sprawled at her feet, his erect cock held upright in his hand. Daylight stood beside her, cock also in hand.

"Let us love you together," Dusk said, waving his thick stick slowly back and forth.

Hot damn!

"Wha—how should we—" Mina began, excited and confused. She'd never had two men at the same time.

"Ride me, baby," Dusk whispered, egging her on.

"And I'll ride you," Daylight said low in her ear.

Mina wasted no brain cells as she moved over Dusk's prone form. Pussy juice trailed down the inside of her thighs as she positioned herself over the thick shaft. Dusk held her waist as she seated his rod at Eden's door before thrusting downward. Mina showered the cock in honey as it kissed her cervix and caressed every pussy cell in its path. Dusk lifted her high before plunging her back down onto his rigid shaft. Mina squeezed and wiggled in joy at the rough impalement.

Daylight rubbed his cock up and down Mina's back. She grabbed Dusk's waist and bounced on his cock until her thighs screamed for relief. Daylight pushed her lightly forward, slowing her motions as he pulled her ass into the air. Mina quivered as she felt the cock seat itself at the high hole. She moaned as the head was pressed gently forward into her chocolate canal. Inch by inch, she felt her body stretching to accommodate Daylight's member. When she believed she couldn't take the sensation any longer, he retreated, and then returned with short, slow strokes.

Dusk began moving in concert with Daylight's thrusts. Mina felt overfull but fulfilled as the cocks pressed into her body. After a few jerky starts, Mina matched their rhythm, body rotating and undulating up and down between the twin cocks.

Her toes curled, body flushed as the tempo increased. Dusk captured her breasts, bit the nipples. Mina whimpered as electricity shot from her nipples and down to her clit. Dusk's rough bush scratched across her clit, adding fuel to the already smoldering fire in her loins.

"Oh, shit!" Mina couldn't stop her scream as the prickling in her scalp moved down her neck, across her chest, and zeroed in on her stiff button. Her body bucked and pounded the pistoning cocks, strained to get every inch of dick deep within her canals.

The mushrooming of the cock in her ass tossed her over the cliff. Mina held on as her pussy—

"Hello?" The voice was distant.

A voyeur? Who cares?

Mina ignored the voice as she rode the dicks to Xanadu, except the cock, no *both* cocks, were beginning to feel different. Soft. As she watched, Dusk seemed to *waver* before her eyes. His lips no longer felt real on her breasts.

What is going on?

Two loud thumps sounded then. "He-lllloooooo! Anybody home?" the voice boomed, closer now.

Daylight and Dusk dissipated into the air; the beach receded. Mina eyes flipped open. Her library. On the bed. In her underwear . . . and someone was coming up the stairs.

The contractor!

"No! Stop! Wait!" Mina screamed, her mind still jumbled from the dream. She retrieved her clothes and pulled them on, too aware that the only thing stopping the man from spying her through the wide-open door was his manners.

Mina took no time to check her appearance as she bounded through the door. The man was standing at the foot of the stairs, surveying the room, his back to her. She ran nervous fingers through her hair. A stair creaked and the man turned.

His eyes widened before he spoke. "Hi, I'm Joseph Turnbull, the contractor," he said, a smile teasing his lips.

Mina's world tilted at a precarious angle as she took in the hazel eyes, the goatee, the cut, rippling muscles and white teeth.

Dusk.

In the flesh.

8

"**M**y God, we were so close!" Cal glowered as he stroked his still-hard cock.

"You ain't never lied! Get the chains so we can get rid of whoever it is and get back to shagging that delicious pussy!" John urged, hands fisted around his own rod.

"Yeah," Cal responded, visions of Mina's tight ass clenching his shaft still in his head. "Let me see who it is first, though."

Cal pushed his head through the wall. John kept pulling at his pulsing staff, wishing whoever was here would hurry up and leave. Cal suddenly pulled his head back, a strange look now on his face. "Ah, John, I think you'd better come take a look."

"Who is it? That realtor?" John spat.

"No. Please come over here." Cal's voice was tight.

John stopped playing with his cock. He and Cal had been friends long enough to know that strange tone meant something was very, very wrong. John pushed his head through the wall; then his body went rigid.

"What are the odds of there being another person in this

area looking just like you did when you died?" Cal asked, a smirk forming on his face as he watched John's reaction.

"Pretty slim, I'd say," John answered, voice stiff, the answer to this riddle already forming in his mind.

"In that case, I believe congratulations are in order."

John couldn't respond as he stared at his mirror image.

A bazillion thoughts zipped through Mina's head—how can this real, live man be in her dreams? Was he a ghost?

Her eyes perused Joseph from the tip of his head down to his boot-clad feet, stopping momentarily to stare at the slight bulge in his crotch. She'd bet her remaining dollars that his cock would look just like it had in her dreams.

"Ma'am?" Joseph interrupted her thoughts. "I'm the contractor. We had an appointment for four o'clock? Are you all right?" His eyes roamed slowly over her person, face scrunching then straightening, scrunching then straightening.

From his reaction, Mina realized she must look like the village idiot—staring, open-mouthed and not speaking. All she needed was a little drool to complete the picture. Sheesh! She clamped her mouth shut. "Ah, yes, the contractor. You're—" *Just as gorgeous as I remember.*

"—right on time?" Joseph supplied, lips curling at the corner.

"Right. You're right on time."

Get yourself together, girl!

"Did I interrupt something?" Joseph's lip curl had turned into a full smile by this time. His eyes drifted to the level of her chest, then back up.

Goodness! Could he tell?

Mina looked down at her clothes with trepidation, then wished she hadn't. The reality was worse than she could have imagined: Her shirt was buttoned wrong—right side hitched higher than the left—her fly was open, and as she patted her head, she realized her hair was flat on one side and "shocked" on the other. She wanted to run, hide, but she did neither. Instead, she zipped her fly, left the shirt and hair alone, and met his smile with one of her own.

Joseph gave her an admirable nod before removing a card from his notebook and offering it to her. Mina took the card, careful not to brush against Joseph's fingers. She'd remembered her body's reaction from touching similar hands in her dreams. No way could she afford to have her pussy screaming for release as she walked him around.

The white card was simply printed with his name, company, and contact phone numbers. Definitely *not* a ghost. But why would this man, a man she'd never seen before and never sexed, be headlining in her dreams? Maybe it was a sign? Of what, though?

Mina pulled her mind to the present and mustered up all of her manners. "Thank you for coming," she responded cordially.

Joseph turned to survey the room again. "Could you show me all the building, and we could talk about what you want done?"

"Sure."

Mina led the way, bouncing redecorating ideas off Joseph as they walked. They settled into an easy banter as they toured the building and Mina explained her sketches. She'd long ago learned you could get "more bang for your buck" if you got the contractor to "buy into" the renovation ideas. It was a win-win proposition for both. Her building would look great, at a reasonable cost, and Joseph would get priceless advertising and exposure.

"I think I've got all the information I need for down here. Let's head upstairs," Joseph suggested.

Mina's heartbeat suddenly became arrhythmic. *What will happen when we enter the library? Will he also feel what I felt?*

Worry coated her mind as she placed her foot on the first step, a prayer on her lips that she wouldn't be overcome with lust and rape Joseph on the spot.

John followed the couple closely as they roamed from room to room. It was amazing how much this Joseph resembled him. The young man's walk was just like his—a cocky swagger that told the world to fuck off—the way he fingered his goatee, his laugh.

Something about hearing that laugh reminded John of all the parties—orgy-fests, really—they'd had at the theater. Nothing but wall-to-wall women pleasing the men present in every way imaginable. There was no color barrier at these functions. Black, white, red, yellow, all were welcome as long as they were willing to play.

And play they did. There was no question that he and Cal loved the women and they loved them in return. Hell, "irresistible" may as well have been their middle name.

John smiled as the young man joked with Mina. He'd never thought he'd get this chance, dying and all, but it looked like fate had smiled on him in death.

It was undeniable. Joseph was his son.

The real puzzle was: who was his mother?

"I know. It looks like a bordello bed, right?" Mina joked, deciding to head off any comments about the rumpled bed.

"That got recent use, too," Joseph supplied before he gave a hearty laugh.

It did.

"I was taking a nap when you arrived. I just got it today."

Joseph looked around the room, hands running over the pine paneling, before poking his head into the bathroom. "So this will be a bedroom?" he called back.

"No. Actually, I was thinking it would be a library."

His head pulled back as he asked, "You put a bed in your library? That's different." He knocked on something, probably the tub.

"The delivery men gave out when they got this far, so I told them to plunk it in here," she explained, glad Joseph couldn't see the blush she felt rising from her crooked collar.

"Oh."

Mina heard him fiddling with the fixtures. A pinging, clanking noise sounded beneath her, before she heard water gushing. Just as she walked to the door, Joseph yelled, "Watch out!" before he rushed through. A tide of water followed him.

"What happened?" Mina asked, running over to lift the comforter's edges from the floor.

"The faucet sprung a leak. Looks like your plumbing needs some work." *That's an understatement.* "Did you have anyone check it before you had it turned on?"

Mina hadn't given that idea any thought. She just wanted to move in. "No, I didn't. In fact, I used water from the faucet to mop this room." She hoped that he'd do something quickly to stop the free-flowing water before she'd have to replace the floor also.

Joseph seemed to have read her mind. "Let me shut off the main water valve. Then we'll get this mess mopped up." He looked at the bed, then back at her. "I don't think you'll be staying here until we get this fixed."

Damn. "I understand."

Mina grabbed the mop and began the arduous task of cleaning up the floor. Joseph rejoined her in a few minutes, and they took turns swabbing and squeezing. After an hour, the floor was still wet but drying, and Mina was drained.

"I want to apologize for the accident. I knew the pipes were old, so I should have been more careful," Joseph said, remorse tingeing his voice.

"No problem." Hey, accidents happened.

"Great. How about I treat you to dinner and we finish hammering out our contract while we eat?"

Mina was thinking hot shower and clean sheets, but his earnest face changed her mind. Besides, she hadn't enjoyed *live* male company for a bit. "Sure thing."

Cal and John hovered over the couple's table, watching the interplay between the two.

"Sure seems like he's taking an interest in Mina, doesn't it?" Cal commented as the young people laughed and joked like old friends.

"Yeah." The electricity between the two was indisputable. John couldn't miss Joseph's subtle signs of pursuit. Hell, it was like watching himself three decades ago. Amazing.

"I hate to say this, but I sure hope he doesn't get any play anytime soon."

"Me neither."

Cal chuckled. "John, man, you are straddling the fence between decency and incest here."

"Am not!"

"What else would you call it when you're shagging your son's girlfriend? I know it's not official but"—Cal looked back at the smiling couple—"believe me, it's coming."

John was momentarily speechless. He hadn't given it any thought.

"You'd better hope she thinks Joseph was a godsend or something if they hook up and she later finds a photo of us," Cal continued. "Otherwise, Mina's gonna be pretty messed up in the head when she realizes that she's been screwing the father"—he turned to look at Joseph—"as well as the son."

John kept silent as this thought thundered around his skull.

"So, I gather you aren't from St. Paulus?" Mina asked after they'd ordered.

"Nope. Pattersburg. It's the next county over." Joseph sipped his cola. "I can't say I've truly spent much time in St. Paulus. My mother wasn't fond of this town." He wrinkled his nose.

"Why is that?" Mina's curiosity was piqued.

Joseph waved the question away. "Something happened here she won't talk about." His eyes looked at the ceiling, a sad expression on his face. "I think it has to do with my father."

"Was he from here?"

Joseph met Mina's eyes, sorrow etched in his visage. "Honestly, I don't know. He left before I was even born."

That was despicable. No self-respecting man would run off from his pregnant wife. What decent human would allow their child to grow up fatherless? Mina felt her blood beginning to bubble in indignation for Joseph.

"I just know that Mom never wanted me in St. Paulus for anything. Heck, she'll probably blow a gasket when I tell her about this job." Joseph gave a small chuckle.

"That bad, huh?" The man must have been a mutt.

"Yeah. But I'm grown and she'll have to understand it comes with the jobs I do."

Mina knew from the tension in Joseph's voice that it was time to change the subject, at least on the surface. Her mind was churning with thoughts of Joseph's upbringing and his mother's hatred of St. Paulus. "What questions did you have about the plans I've made for the building?"

Joseph visibly relaxed. "Let's see, half the downstairs will be a conference room, the other half something like a coffee shop slash bookstore." Mina nodded her assent. "The upstairs will primarily be living quarters. But the library will be a private club room, right?"

"Correct."

"We'll need to put up a wall separating the living quarters from the library's entrance. I don't think you want folks roaming about your home."

"That would most likely be uncomfortable, to say the least."

"I do have one question." His eyes twinkled in the light of the restaurant. "What will you be doing in the *private* club room?"

Mina had decided she would have the old films converted to DVDs. Then she would allow "members" access to the library to view the erotic movies. Not a return of the triple-X theater per se but in spirit. Anyway, it should spice up the women's lives in this town.

Mina smiled like she'd eaten the entire sugar pie. "It's for members to know," she said slyly.

Joseph quirked an eyebrow before bursting into laughter. "Mina, you are definitely too much."

"Just wait," Mina responded, visions of Joseph, naked as he'd been in her dreams, bouncing around in her mind, "you haven't seen anything yet."

Mina's eyes were heavy as they finished their meal. As much as she'd enjoyed Joseph's company, the only thing she would enjoy more was some sleep. With a promise to meet him mid-morning, Mina exited and rechecked into the St. Paulus Inn. Her eyes closed as soon as her head hit the pillow.

9

John was agitated.

He bounced from wall to wall, murmuring under his breath, stroking his goatee in earnest. Yes, he was glad to find out he had a son, but he honestly wasn't happy about the chemistry developing between Joseph and Mina. The timing was all wrong. He'd just begun his reentry into the joys of sex, and now the object of his sexual satisfaction might very well become his daughter-in-law. It sucked any which way he looked at it.

"Dude, lighten up," Cal commented quietly. He could see John was taking the turn of events hard, but that's how things went. Sometimes you win, sometimes you lose. "Maybe Joseph won't allow himself to get involved with Mina since she's a client."

John gave Cal a stony stare. "As beautiful as that woman is, what man would pass on a chance at her?"

No denying that. Mina was a uniquely beautiful piece of female flesh. "Well, you know what they say: How do you get over one problem?"

John smiled as he answered the old cliché. "Get under another one. And I know just who to work my frustrations out on."

Cal shook his head as he watched John disappear through the wall. Some poor woman was about to get either the scare or thrill of her life.

John passed through the decorative glass door of the two-story Tutor. Bric-a-brac lined multiple curio cabinets, a round country-style table sat in the dining room, and a plaid couch—reminiscent of the wild seventies—sat in what must be the den.

What did I expect?

Still angry, he floated up the stairs, following the sound of light snoring coming from a bedroom. A large antique bed sat in the middle of the room. Matching armoire and dresser were pushed against the walls. A profusion of flowers sprang from the curtains and bedding.

No man has lived here in a while.

From the slice of moonlight, John could see a figure lying twisted in the bedcovers, a bare leg hanging partially over the side. He drifted until he stood in front of the prone person—*l'object de l'irritation.* John took in the nightcap, the frothy frills around the neckline, and as his eyes roamed farther down, the bulbous twin mounds with matching twin points and the thick uncovered thigh.

She's not a spring chicken, but I knew that before I came.

Suddenly, Mina's face sprang into his head. John's cock rose as if on cue. With lusty thoughts filling his head, egging him on, he reached out and covered a fat point. Squeezed.

Charlotte Charles sat up suddenly, hands splayed across her breasts, eyes wide and frightened as they darted about the room, scanning every dark corner. After a few seconds, she slumped backward.

"Goodness, that was strange," she whispered before throwing back the covers and padding into the adjacent bathroom.

John knew from her reaction that it had been sometime since any man had sampled her goodies. Well, tonight would change all that. He sidled up behind her as she ran water into a cup and then sipped from it.

John smiled as he noted the twin points had expanded, lifting her frilly gown from her chest. *Extra long nipples.* He licked his lips as he placed fingers on each nipple and pulled.

The cup dropped into the sink.

John licked the back of Charlotte's neck. She swatted at the area, turning to look behind her as she did so. He could see the confusion on her face.

Wait until you get a load of what else I have in store for you.

John nipped a shoulder. Charlotte yelped, patting the offending area. She swatted and patted as John nipped and licked until he stuck his tongue in her ear. She became paralyzed, chest heaving, as the mouth organ swirled in and out of her ear and around her lobe. A whimper exited her mouth.

John's mind merged with Charlotte's as his tongue danced a tango around her neck.

Show me your tatas.

He knew he was successful as Charlotte's fingers inched upward, untied the frilly concoction around her neck, and pulled the gown over her head. Her breasts hung low, the nipples distended to the length of a pinkie finger.

John pressed himself into her back as he grasped a long nipple in each hand. Charlotte let out a low cat yowl as he milked the long areolas between his fingers. Her head rolled in pleasure, mouth hanging open. John moved to the front, wrapped his lips around a nipple. Charlotte cupped her breasts, held them up as he suckled. Her hips swayed, bumped in the empty air.

John could smell her juice. He wasted no time; instead, his hand drifted beneath the thick cotton panties and parted her thin hairs. Charlotte's pussy was dripping like a faucet. John positioned his thumb on her fat clit and a finger in her pussy, rotating rapidly.

Spread for me.

Charlotte opened her legs, made choking sounds deep in her throat as John's fingers diddled, mashed, and sank into her pussy. Her walls snapped, clutched at his lubricated fingers.

John felt her body tremble and knew it wouldn't be long. He released her, positioned himself behind her again. Charlotte let out a mournful cry, fingers playing with her clit, at this abandonment. John smiled at her discomfort as he took possession of her breasts again.

Let me fuck you.

Charlotte unceremoniously propped a leg onto the toilet. With a hand clutching a breast, John surged into her sopping pussy. Charlotte mewled, back arched, as he pumped her long and hard. Her hips bounced in the air, fingers pulling her own nipples as John's cock rotated within her folds.

John fucked her without mercy. He pounded his cock into her walls, pistoned into her slick orifice. He was pleasantly surprised when she pushed back to meet him, stroke for stroke.

That's it, baby. Just like riding a bicycle.

Charlotte's fingers rubbed and mashed at her clit. John remembered his previous actions with Mina and slid a hand into her pelvis, pressing on her G-spot. He felt her walls clench, knew she was about to come. His cock swelled, balls tightening as she clamped down on his rod.

In seconds, John exploded, ghostly gizm showering her pussy, just as Charlotte's knees buckled.

* * *

Cal stifled a laugh as John drifted back through the wall, whistling off-key. "Feel better?"

"Right as rain, my man. Right as rain," John assured him before returning, midbar, to his scratchy rendition of "Happy Days Are Here Again."

10

The day was a doom-and-gloom one—heavy fog, hair-frizzing drizzle—as Mina set out on her library quest. Thankfully, she found the pubic library with little difficulty. The directions the inn clerk had given her said to travel two blocks over and look for the big gingerbread house. As lightning illuminated the landscape, she gazed at a pink Victorian structure, complete with purple shutters and turrets, and thought the description was aptly appropriate.

Let's hope Hansel and Gretel aren't inside.

Mina parked quickly and strode to the simple wooden door, a lion-head knocker left from a previous life still in place. She opened the door slowly. Cool air rushed to meet her along with the smell of incense.

Unusual.

No one was present at the long counter to her left, and no patrons sat at the tables placed around the room. She waited patiently, hoping the librarian would appear. Nothing happened after a few minutes, so she walked over to the newspaper section, planning to see what she could do by herself.

The racks held newspapers and dailies from around the country—the *Wall Street Journal, Business Daily, National Enquirer, Star*—along with the town newspaper, the *St. Paulus Times Tribune Post.* Someone obviously had illusions of grandeur when they'd named the newspaper.

Walking past the racks, she noticed an object in an out-of-the-way corner, covered with plastic cloth. Mina glanced around, searching for a librarian. Still not seeing one, she pulled the cover off. Just as she'd thought—a microfiche viewer.

Excited now, she searched for the cabinet holding the microfiche. There were a number of wood and metal file cabinets lined along the wall. Mina pulled open the first drawer, halfway down. It squeaked on its grooves as she tugged.

Pay dirt.

The St. Paulus Times Tribune Post 1995–1996 label stared back at her. Right file cabinet, wrong drawer. Mina quickly opened another, then another, before she saw the 1970s labeled files.

"Top of the morning to ya!" a chipper voice said behind her.

Mina turned. The vision in front of her was, in her mind, strongly reminiscent of Hansel and Gretel's grandmother . . . gone Amish. The hair was white and styled into a high beehive, Prince-Nez glasses perched on a pinched nose, and the dress was Confederate gray and billowed outward beneath a white Peter Pan collar, but as Mina's gaze traveled downward to the feet, she had to stifle a laugh. The woman wore black hiking boots with pink laces.

"A glorious day, isn't it?" the woman continued, walking closer.

Mina was mesmerized by her rolling *R*s. Irish? She recovered and found her voice. "Y-yes it is, I guess." *If you think a rainy day is glorious.*

Sharply arched eyebrows raised over the glasses. "I don't

believe I've ever seen you around here before. New lass in town?"

"I believe I am a new lass," Mina admitted, amused at the woman's archaic terminology.

"And on a mission, too." The woman's hand waved at the open drawer in front of Mina. "I'm Gertie Macgregor, the town librarian. Whatever you are looking for, I'm sure to gander upon it forthwith."

Are we still in the twenty-first century?

Mina shook the extended hand. It was soft as melted butter beneath her palm. *I need whatever she's using.* "Thank you. I'm Mina Sinclair. I own the old theater on First Street."

"Extraordinary." Watery silver eyes assessed her thoroughly. "So what assistance do you require?"

"I was looking for information on the two men who owned the theater before me. They disappeared."

"A conundrum of mysterious proportions. This is getting good." Gertie rubbed her palms together.

Mina chuckled at her actions. "Yes, they apparently left one day, and no has seen them since."

"Hmm. Just up and disappeared, you say? Funny, I don't recall any disappearances in these parts recently. The last one I can remember was fifteen years ago when the mayor's teenage daughter went missing for two weeks. But"—Gertie paused for effect—"she wasn't truly missing. She was 'absconded' in a cabin, near the lake, with the high school principal's deadbeat son."

"That must have created quite a stir, I'm sure."

"Like a colony of swarming, rabid bats," Gertie deadpanned. "Of course, the loaded firearm he held at the impromptu nuptials didn't help."

Mina laughed at the colorful description. "Well my disappearance happened maybe thirty years ago. Mid to early 1970s."

Mina held a hopeful breath as Gertie tapped her nose while staring at the floor. Finally, the head lifted, a finger snapped in the air.

"No wonder I don't remember!" Gertie's eyes glittered. "I was a blushing newlywed back then. My Robert, God rest his soul, was the center of my world. A handsome new husband, keeping house for the first time, along with having a bun in the oven, kept me more than busy. I didn't keep up with current events back then. I was just happy being a bairn with a swollen belly."

Mina couldn't even imagine this scenario.

"I wasn't very social; money was tight"—Gertie's face pulled long—"and Robert didn't believe in wasting what little we had on newspapers. So unless he told me, I missed out on it. Amazing how we allow ourselves to be boxed in by bliss, isn't it?" Sad eyes met Mina's.

Mina wasn't sure how to respond, so she remained mute and nodded slightly.

Gertie suddenly cackled, head held back, as the sound escaped from deep within her chest. "Well, that was then. Robert is playing with the angels, the children have flown the nest, and I'm a woman of the world." Gertie twirled in place, arms clasped over her burgeoning chest. Her legs lifted into a series of high kicks before she danced an uneven cadence around the room on the balls of her feet.

Is she dancing a jig? What's next? Clicking her heels and conjuring up some leprechauns?

Gertie screeched to a halt in front of Mina. "So, what be their Christian monikers?"

This changing of gears had Mina momentarily speechless. "W-who?"

"The proprietors of your theater. Really, dear, you must keep up if you hope to avail yourself of the full range of my assistance," Gertie chastised lightly. "Now, their names?"

"Oh. John Whitmore and Cal Toledo or Tolero; the realtor wasn't quite sure."

"No, neither of those names are tweaking my noggin."

I'm wondering if the noggin is completely full.

"Well, I was hoping that I could look through the microfiches and find out more information. You know, what they were like, a photo or something."

"Hmmm. Maybe a photo but I don't imagine that old newspapers would have much personal information."

Mina smiled smugly. "Oh, they might. I failed to mention that their theater was a triple-X theater."

Gertie's eyes twinkled. "Triple X? My gracious, I'll bet the tongues were dragging the roots from the grass at that. Robert definitely would not have mentioned something so . . . sensitive to me. As lusty as I was, he knew I'd want to visit it." She rapidly fanned at her face.

Mina had no problem imagining Gertie as a lusty young thing in her day.

"Well, let's get to it." With a clap of her hands, the librarian pulled open another drawer and dove in.

Mina popped a film beneath the glass cover and began scrolling. Births, weddings, obituaries and football seemed to be the meat of the weekly paper. She found no mention of either of the men on the first few films. This changed with the fourth one.

Her palms were wet as she read about the opening of the town's first theater in the March 1973 paper. A picture showed four grinning men cutting a ribbon in front of the theater. Mina smiled as she saw her building in its heyday. The caption listed the men as Cal Toledo, John Whitmore, Mayor Sam Prichett, and Councilman Rodney Smith. Try as she might, Mina was unable to distinguish any distinct features from the grainy photo.

"Found something, dearie?" Gertie asked just over Mina's shoulder.

"Yes. A photo. I can't make out any features, though."
Mina's face was inches from the screen as she peered intently at
the picture.

"Let me have a look-see." Gertie pulled her Prince Nez's
higher and stared. After a few moments, she shook her head.
"They could be anybody."

"Would you happen to know Sam Prichett and Rodney
Smith?"

"Of course. Sam Prichett was the mayor a long time—he
was the one with the daughter I mentioned earlier—but he died
a few years ago."

Mina groaned at her bad luck.

"Now Rodney Smith is still alive . . . for the most part. He
embezzled a pot of money from the town and now resides in
St. Lucans."

"Is that a town close by?" Hope fanned Mina's heart.

"No. It's the state penitentiary. He's doing a ten-to-twenty
stretch."

Talk about bad luck—one dead, one in prison. "In that case,
I'll keep looking," Mina replied, disappointment lacing her
voice.

"Oh"—Gertie pulled a small table closer and sat a candle on
it—"I thought you'd like a little fragrance to ease your mind
while you worked."

Mina stared at the fat red candle sitting on a cracked saucer.
An open flame in a room full of books. Definitely not the best
idea but she kept her observation to herself.

"It's mulberry aromatherapy. It always helps my mind reach
a higher stratosphere," Gertie stated as she scratched a match
alongside the box and lit the candle.

"Ah . . . thanks." In seconds, Mina was scrolling back through
the microfiche, thoughts of the candle gone.

Though the town apparently embraced the theater initially,

not two papers later, Mina found an editorial blasting the "theater of ill repute." Obviously, the smiles changed to frowns once the true nature of the theater was revealed. From the blistering commentary, the author definitely felt tar and feather would be too good for the men.

Comments about the theater in later newspapers were sporadic—scathing editorials, letters to the publisher—until the April 1975 edition. The headline read THEATER OWNERS MISSING in bold.

According to the report, no one had seen the owners since April 21, 1975. Employees stated that no one let them in for work and they'd had to turn patrons away. Police broke into the building and found no significant clues—clothes were still there, the previous day's till was untouched in the office, and there were no signs of forced entry or a scuffle.

Theories of the disappearance were varied—a mob hit, a murder-suicide, and even one where someone insinuated the sheriff ran them out of town in the middle of the night. Mina chuckled at that one.

Brief mentions of the men were in the following newspapers, but by June 1976, the two were apparently forgotten. The remaining headlines once again told of births, weddings, obituaries, and football.

An ache in her neck forced Mina to stretch and shift position. As she did so, she glanced at the large round-faced clock and panicked. She was already late to meet Joseph at the building.

Mina returned the microfiches to the cabinet and recovered the viewer. Gertie saw her and walked over.

"Find your answer?"

"Not yet," Mina admitted. "But I might have a lead."

"I do hope you are fruitful."

"That makes two of us."

"By the way, I never did ask what you plan to do with that old triple-X theater."

As Mina explained her idea, Gertie burst out laughing and clapped her hands. "Let me get my purse. I want to purchase my membership now."

11

Joseph's work truck was parked in front of her building along with two others parked behind him. Mina could see multiple heads in all vehicles. A work crew . . . and she was late.

Mina parked quickly and jumped over puddles as she rushed to the building. Vehicle doors opened, disgorging passengers, as she ran forward. Mina counted seven men, all wearing work clothes and boots. Joseph met her at the door.

"I apologize for my lateness." Mina's words were rushed.

Joseph grinned. "Actually, we were late. We'd just pulled up when I saw your car coming around the corner."

"Whew. That's a relief." Mina gazed at the men huddling from the drizzle under the narrow awning. "Who did you bring with you?"

"The plumber, the demolition crew, and the floor man." Joseph introduced each person. Mina failed to remember all the names the first time around but knew they would become more than familiar to her in days to come.

"Ready to work?" Mina asked, eager to get this show started.

"That's why we're here."

Joseph ran a well-oiled operation. He gave orders, and the men quickly spread out and began working. In minutes, the sounds of hammering, scraping—along with more than one ribald comment—rang in the building.

Mina watched, fascinated at how fast things were moving. The men had half the downstairs Sheetrock torn away, and she could hear hammering up the stairs. She decided to make sure that no one touched the library walls, since she wanted them to remain as they were.

She heard voices as she stepped onto the landing. Joseph and one of his men appeared from the bathroom of the library area, laughing loudly.

"Want to share the joke?" Mina asked.

The man—Mina thought his name was Mendes, but she wasn't positive—covered his mouth while Joseph continued laughing. "Nope. It's a man thing, and you just might not get it."

Mina knew what a "man thing" most likely entailed—sex jokes. She waved them off and strode down the hallway, following the sound of hammering. Two more men were demolishing the shelves lining the walls, plaster dust flying about the air. Not wanting to stop any progress, she just nodded as they glanced her way, then continued back downstairs.

Looking around at the men, Mina was more than pleased at her choice. Humming to herself, she picked up a maul and slammed it into the old drywall. After all, another hand just meant they'd finish faster.

"Looks like the old theater will ride again!" John gushed as he watched the construction crew tear out the old walls.

"Sure looks like it," Cal agreed. "Hey, John, remember those parties here?"

"How could I forget? Women, liquor . . . do you remember the Double Mint twins?"

"Carrie and Mary. Shit, those twins were unforgettable," Cal barked. "Hell, their mouths sucked my cock like they had vacuum cleaners in their chests."

The twins, dubbed Double Mint after the blond twins in the gum advertisement, were more than adequate sexual partners. Their repertoire of sexual acts was as wide and varied as the Mississippi River. Nothing was off-limits or obscene. Whatever you wanted, they served it up . . . times two.

"Ain't that the truth? Those two drained my ass a few dozen times or more." John laughed, remembering his own escapades with the twin blond pistols.

"Uh-uh. What about that Gypsy girl who did that dance with the castanets?" Cal had been mesmerized by the dark Gypsy named Aria. Her limber movements, her erotic dancing . . . her lack of a gag reflex when he'd fed his dick down her throat. She'd kept him enthralled longer than most.

"Man, I'm getting a boner just thinking about that one. All that lace and long hair . . . you ever seen a woman with hair down to the floor that was real before?" John asked.

"No, and not one since. The way she wrapped that hair around my pole . . . she was something out of a movie."

"When she held that split as you screwed her while she sucked my dick, yeah, she was definitely movie material." John rubbed himself at he spoke. "Shit, I'm horny as hell, talking about old times."

"Me too. It's a shame we can't get Mina to ourselves and have some fun," Cal pouted.

"Speak for yourself." John turned and headed toward the window.

Realizing that John was leaving, Cal asked, "Hey, where are you going?"

"Backup plan, my man." John winked and floated through the glass.

Cal turned and studied Mina working hard on the wall, and then stared at the window John had just exited through. "Wait for me," Cal yelled as he, too, floated through the window.

12

Charlotte Charles was high.

Not on drugs. On life. She was smiling, giggling even. In fact, her secretary, Cynthia, had remarked on the high spirits she was in.

"Wow. Looks like somebody had a great night. Hot date?"

"No, no date. I guess I'm just happy," she'd replied, practically skipping inside her office. Honestly, this was past happy. This was delight. She felt the blood pulsing in her veins, felt the air sliding over and about her skin . . . felt her crotch rubbing across her clit.

Last night had been an awakening of sorts. Her husband, Lester, had been dead ten years, and in those ten years, she'd not sought the comfort of another man's arms. Not that she'd had many arms to choose from. The men her age were either married, had health problems, or most likely couldn't get it up. Besides, with all the diseases out there, she was very reluctant to step back into the dating game. She had suppressed her urges, never acted on them . . . until last night.

She couldn't stop thinking about the previous night. She'd

been aroused enough to imagine a man was there sexing her! Her, a woman who'd never even dabbled in sexual fantasies. She'd been raised in the good-girls-don't-until-you're-married age, and even then, you had all the lights off when you did. Sexy underwear was exclusively for women of the night, and if your husband brought some wild, erotic lingerie home, you had to wonder if he'd been with someone else. There was no such thing as fantasies and kinky sex. It was a missionary-positioned, mute undertaking totally orchestrated by the husband.

But not last night. She'd become an uninhibited wild woman— baring her chest as she imagined hands tugging on her dormant nipples; spreading wide to let fingers mash and rub her nearly atrophied clit, and allowing her hips to move in ways she'd only read of as she fantasized about a thick cock that had prodded her into a blockbuster orgasm.

Sweat broke out along her forehead as snatches of a broad cock attached to a dark body pumping into her flashed in her mind. Funny, she'd always been fond of fair men. Her visualizing this dark dream lover had her stumped. One thing was for sure—no matter how he'd gotten into her mind, he'd thoroughly fulfilled her needs. Her fingers slipped across her clit, and her body constricted in response.

Charlotte rose quickly and walked to her door. "Cynthia, why don't you go to lunch now?"

"So early?" Cynthia—dressed in beads, bell-bottoms, and dashiki like a lost flower child—looked suspicious.

She pushed a facsimile of a smile onto her face. "You work hard, so it's good to take a long lunch sometimes. Besides, I can handle the phones." *Get out.*

"You sure?"

"Positive. You run along and have a good meal. I'll see you back at one, okay?" *Go, please.*

Apparently Charlotte didn't have to tell Cynthia twice, since she grabbed her macramé bag and shot out the door.

Charlotte quickly engaged the suite's lock and hotfooted it back to her office. She wasted no time unzipping her pants and shucking them past her knees. Perching her rump on the top of her desk, she spread wide, her pungent scent wafting up to her nose. With anticipation tripping her heartbeat, her fingers gingerly parted her bush.

John eased into the window of Charles Real Estate, a bit of expectancy in his ghostly heart. Charlotte Charles may have been "long in the tooth," but as an outlet for his frustration, he had to admit, he'd more than enjoyed himself.

He watched in interest as Charlotte's arm compressed the rounded belly while fingers held her sparse bush wide, exposing her clit. Under the fluorescent light, he noted that Charlotte was one of those rare women whose clits resembled a mini-penis. It was at least two inches long and three-quarters of an inch at its base, narrowing to half an inch at the tip. Multiple folds surrounded the stiff, protruding head, darkened to a cranberry-pink blush of arousal. The clit raised and lowered rhythmically, most likely in concert with her pulse.

As his eyes traveled downward, John took in the glistening rim of the outer labia. Charlotte's fingers lifted, and a viscous string of moisture tethered her fingers to her lips. John sighed as the string was drawn taut and finally snapped before her hand cleared her waist.

"So *this* is where you went last night. And you said she wasn't your type." Cal chuckled, startling John as he watched the realtor pleasuring herself.

John felt a flare of annoyance at this interruption. Yes, he and Cal had shared many a woman, yet he couldn't put a name to the cause of his flash irritation. He covered his displeasure with a snort. "Laugh if you want, but there is much to be said about a woman who hasn't had a stiff cock in years." John winked.

"Really?" Cal asked, unconvinced.

"Really. It didn't take much to get the engine running; then that old girl worked my cock like she was thirty years old," John bragged.

Cal's eyes widened in surprise. He'd thought the older women got, the less they wanted sex.

"Yessiree. And man, she's got these long nipples—and you know I know nipples—that you can practically wrap around your fingers." John nodded. "Look at her sweater. See how her nips are pushing the bra out?"

There was no repudiating the hefty points stabbing the front of the cowl-necked sweater. Cal licked his lips when, as he watched, the hard erasers pushed out even farther. He floated down, hovered in front of the closed-eyed realtor. Her breasts were abundant beneath the thin yarn and jiggled with every movement of her arm.

From the anguished whimper and sudden grimace, John knew Charlotte was losing her bid to re-create the ecstasy she'd felt last night. No problem.

"Cal, how about you grab that tit, I'll grab this one, and we help her out," John suggested, knowing what road it would lead them to.

Cal didn't need additional encouragement. His fingers covered the left breast as John's covered the right. They pulled in sync. Charlotte moaned; a slight smile slid onto her face as they tugged outward. She shifted on the desk, spread her legs wider, and sped up her fingers.

"See what I mean? With the right know-how, you can turn any woman on," John preached. Only one test drive and now he was the conductor. Hot damn!

Cal heard but paid no attention. He wanted to up his sexual ante, be inside her mind while he pleasured her. As John prattled on about his prowess, Cal let his head slide between the dyed strands of hair and seat within her cranium. In milliseconds, her mind rebelled—slapped him, hacked at him, backed him to the periphery. Knowing he was hanging on by a thread, Cal pressed forward and was ambushed with a mental mule-kick that totally ejected him from her brain.

"Damn." Cal shook his head. His mind felt tender, raw. What did he do wrong? With Mina, he'd been pushed and shoved, but he'd managed to get inside.

"Man, what are you doing? Why is she frowning like that?" John barked.

Determined not to be denied, Cal pushed back into her mind . . . and pulled up short. There seemed to be a physical wall present that wasn't there before. He pushed, pried, but he couldn't seem to penetrate this mental barrier no matter how much he tried.

"Quit playing around in her head," John huffed as he watched Charlotte wince, then rub her temples slowly. "If I'd known you were going to mess things up for me, I would have thrown you out when you showed up." He glared at Cal, his ire rising as Charlotte's arousal fell. "Just stay over there and watch. I'll show you how it's done."

John covered both of her breasts and massaged the globes slowly. At first, there was no reaction from Charlotte, but after a few minutes, her hands drifted from her temples, returned to her chest, squeezed.

"See. Watch and learn."

Cal harrumphed but his cock rose to attention as Charlotte uncovered a breast, gathered the heavy mound in her hands, pushed a long nipple between her lips.

John stuck out his tongue, twirled it into the recesses of her belly button. He licked around and inside the hidden corners. Charlotte gurgled, her hand returning to her clit. John smiled as he let his tongue drift lower, following the path of her hand. He tickled her pubic hair as he parted it. Charlotte's fingers seemed to read his mind as she splayed herself wide, clit saluting. John gave the mini-penis two swipes, then sucked deeply.

Cal watched silently as juice puddled between her legs, then dripped to the floor. His hands now stroked and choked his rigid cock.

Charlotte's hands blindly felt behind her, across the desk, searching. She stopped as they rested on a slim bottle of lotion. She dragged the plastic bottle to her, her intentions obvious.

John saw and was unwilling to allow the bottle to have his orgasm. He quickly closed his eyes, telepathing his thoughts to Charlotte's mind.

Fuck me, not the bottle.

Charlotte heard the plea and just like that, *he* was there. Suddenly seeing him, kneeling before her naked pube, startled her a bit . . . but only a bit.

Two days ago, Old Charlotte would have screamed, run off, thought she was losing her mind.

But that was two days ago.

Instead, New Charlotte shed her clothes, got comfortable, and spread wider.

I'm yours, baby.

John knew the moment Charlotte truly saw him—her eyes widened, the hand on the lotion stilled, her breath hesitated. Lust finally won. She lifted the sweater over her head, unsnapped her bra, and stepped out of her pants. She quickly shed her panties, then sat in her chair and opened her legs in invitation.

How'd you do that? Cal thought, miffed that John seemed to be able to get inside her head and he couldn't.

John didn't pause as he positioned himself between her legs. *Don't do the body-transference thing. Just think the thought and share space with her brain cells,* was his silent reply.

Oh.

John drove his cock slowly between the thick lips, sighing as Charlotte's warmth surrounded him. His hands twirled the long nipples as he stroked lightly inside the wet cavern. Charlotte panted, writhed beneath him, eyes glazing. With a growl, she pulled his hips forcefully, slammed his body into hers.

"Fuck me, dammit!" she yelled.

John needed no further persuasion. He pistoned long and deep. The chair rocked as he swirled his hips and swished in her juice.

Cal couldn't take it any longer. He was about to erupt. He closed his eyes and made a request.

Double your pleasure?

The question came from a new source. Charlotte's mind was fogged with lust, but she clearly saw the man, the fair man, standing beside her chair. Only one word came to mind—delectable.

New Charlotte urged him onward.

Cal knew he'd been successful as Charlotte's eyes sprang open, stared directly at him. She then did something that took him by surprise—she crooked her index finger.

He stood beside the bouncing chair, began to lean toward a long nipple when she stopped him. Instead, her finger closed around his concrete pole, pulled him toward her coral-stained lips.

Cal's cock turned to steel as her tongue flicked the crown. She let her lips nibble down the shaft, then back up. Everything in him wanted to plunge his cock deep down her throat, but he held back, let her set the pace.

John stopped and watched the sex play.

Charlotte covered the head, sucked it into her mouth. Her saliva collected and rolled from the corners as more cock slid into her mouth.

Her mouth felt good, but it was obvious she was a novice.

Cal wanted the entire cock-sucking experience, not a half-assed performance.

No time like the present to teach an old gal a new trick.

He grabbed her head between his hands and methodically fed his dick into her mouth. Whenever she gagged, he'd retreat a bit but push right back. After the thirtieth stroke, the gags were less and the depth was right. Cal began pumping like he was in her pussy.

John, no longer able to hold back, resumed his stroking. The chair reeled and tottered beneath the vigorous sex play.

Charlotte cupped and squeezed Cal's balls. Cal wanted to scream. He was close! After a few more delicious sucks, he knew Mount Cockhorse was about to erupt. He grasped a handful of thin hair as the hot cum surged upward, shot outward, and dissipated into the air.

Charlotte turned her attention back to John. Her actions belied her age as she rotated her pelvis and pussy-gripped John's pole. Invigorated, John pounded into her wet hole. Charlotte eagerly matched him stroke for stroke.

John felt a frisson of ecstasy ripple up his back. It wouldn't be long now. He wrapped a long nipple around his finger, pulled it to his waiting lips. Then he massaged her dick-clit.

"Goddamnitgoddamnitgod*damn*it!" Charlotte yelled, hips slinging and jerking. She galloped on John, soaked him in liquid. His ass staccatoed in response. It took only a few seconds before she squirted juice and clenched.

It was John's turn to blubber as pussy walls vised him, made his cum boil as it bubbled up and out his slit . . . and rendered him an eager captive of ecstasy.

13

———————

Joseph and his crew left shortly after dinnertime. Honestly, Mina was famished, but she was too excited to stop and eat. She visited room after room, making notes and tweaking her original design ideas.

Seeing a forgotten hammer lying in the back bedroom, Mina couldn't resist picking it up and slamming it into the wall. She ignored her caked fingernails and blistered palms as she banged, pulled, banged at the drywall. When she was halfway down, she banged and the hammer flew out of her hand, into the recesses of the wall.

"Damn."

Mina peered into the hole and saw only darkness. She was leery of just sticking her hand inside. There might be a rat waiting to scramble up her arm, and she'd have a coronary if that happened. She grasped the drywall and gave it a hefty yank. It broke easily.

She gazed back inside the hole, and her eyes widened. Inside, she saw a book and an old satchel perched on a thin piece of plywood. Her heart sped up. Rats now forgotten, she reached in and pulled the book out first, then wedged the satchel through the narrow hole. The satchel plopped to the floor from its weight. She hadn't expected it to be heavy, but it was.

She looked the bag over. It was constructed of thick leather, and from the amount of mold patchworking the surface, it had been in the wall for years. Curious now, she tried the metal clasp. Locked. Mina searched for something to pry the catch open. She found a bent nail and jimmied it inside the keyhole. She poked, prodded, wiggled, and finally dug at the metal fittings.

Nothing.

Frustrated, she flung the nail against the wall and turned her attention to the book. Mina flipped it open and stopped. Inside were photos. Her eyebrows quirked higher as she studied the first page. The photo was yellowed with brown age spots dotted across the front. She looked closer at the photo and was brought up short. Joseph stood beside a man, their arms loosely around each other's shoulders as both smiled into the lens. He wore a plaid shirt and jeans, goatee framing his white teeth as he gave a thumbs-up. The other man—Mina had a feeling she'd seen him before but couldn't place him just then—wore similar clothes but stood with one hand on his waist, an abundance of teeth visible on him also.

Why would Joseph have a photo album in the theater?

Unable to answer her own question, she shook her head and studied the photo some more. It appeared that Joseph and the man stood in sand or light-colored dirt. An old convertible— really old, as in it was brand-new when she was a little girl—sat in the background.

Curious now, Mina lifted the yellowed picture from the page and turned it over. Her breath stuttered in her chest as she read the heavy scrawl on the back of the photo—JOHN AND CAL, 1969, LAS VEGAS. CASH, GRASS OR ASS!

Goose bumps zipped across her body, the lightbulb flashed in her head, the puzzle pieces aligned themselves.

Daylight and Dusk.

Cal Toledo and John Whitmore.

The missing owners of the theater . . . and one of them was Joseph's father.

"Well, the cat's out of the sack now," Cal commented as he watched Mina stare at the photo.

"Definitely." John didn't want to admit it, but he was past worried. Watching her sitting there hugging herself, he knew her mind was zipping all over the place faster than a freeway at rush hour.

"Guess when we visit her again, we should introduce ourselves properly." Cal chuckled.

"And say what? Hi, I'm John, your dream lover and, oh yeah, I've been dead for thirtysomething years? Man, laugh if you want, but she could jump up, slap a For Sale sign on the building, and then we'd be right back where we started."

Cal twisted his mouth and shook his head. "John, she's not going to do anything of that sort. Yes, she might be surprised"— he held up his hand, stopping whatever comment was about to exit John's mouth—"but I've got my money on her. Hell, it's obvious she loves a challenge. She bought this building, didn't she? And you think she'll run off because the men in her dreams happen to be dead? As good as we shagged her? Shoot, she ought to bottle us up and sell us on the street. She'd make a mint."

It was John's turn to laugh. "You think so?"

"I can't speak for you, but I know I laid the pipe down like I had a certified plumber's degree." Cal winked. "She might be out of sorts right now, but believe me, that little lady's not going anywhere."

John watched as Mina turned the pages of the book. True, she looked calm, but he knew better. There was no way a person got this big of a shock and not be stressed. And a stressed mind could throw a curveball into any situation. But he hoped, fervently hoped Cal—for once in his dead life—was correct.

She had been sexing dead men.

Mina was stumped. How in the world had she managed to conjure up these two men? All the live ones out there and she managed to imagine—and then screw—not one, but *two* ghosts. Friendly ones, yes, but still, they were D-E-A-D yesterday, today, and no change on tomorrow.

Who says they will stay *friendly?*

Thunder boomed, shaking the building, seemingly punctuating this thought. Gory scenes from *Nightmare on Elm Street* and *Jeepers Creepers*—watched in its entirety solely because of a dare—flashed in her head. Apprehension crawled up Mina's spine just like the dead kid climbing the stairs in *The Grudge*. What if they *weren't* as friendly as they seemed? What if they were using her as a portal or something between the living and the dead? What if she was just an innocent headliner in a prelude to *The Exorcist*?

Mina jumped from the dirty floor, tense, jumpy. Thunder boomed again, giving weight to her flash anxiety. Then, the overhead light flickered.

"No! No! No! Please don't let the electricity fail!"

Fear spurred Mina into action. She tucked the album under one arm and dragged the satchel with her free hand, eyes darting and bouncing all around. She knew that if so much as a spiderweb touched her crawling flesh, she'd become hysterical. At the top of the staircase, she flung the satchel to the lower floor, skipping and jumping treads as she hurried behind it.

The lights flickered again.

Mina's heartbeat galloped, adrenaline surged, pupils dilated. She gave Wonder Woman a run for her money, snatching the bag's handles and lugging it toward the door, arms crying under the weight. She ignored the pain. All she knew was she had to get out of this haunted house and into her car before she was trapped in inky darkness. She focused her eyes on the glass door five feet in front of her and shuffled faster.

The building went completely dark.

Mina dropped everything and ran toward where her eyes had last visualized the door. She almost wet her pants when she felt the handle, and she eagerly pushed it open.

That's when hands grabbed her from the side.

Mina screamed and slapped and punched and kicked. She heard the pained "Oomph" but kept hitting and kicking since her harried imagination—aided by one too many *X Files* episodes—had fabricated an attacker of demonic proportions. Just as she pulled her leg back for another bruising kick, she heard, "Mina! It's me! Joseph!" Mina was unable to stop her trajectory and felt her booted foot connect with a leg, the thud solid and loud.

"Ow!" Joseph howled before stringing together a line of cuss words that would have made even the lowliest of sailors proud.

A flashlight was suddenly switched on, blinding her. The beacon was then turned to the man's face. It was definitely Joseph . . . and he wasn't too happy.

"What are you doing here? You scared me half to death! I thought you were a mugger!" The words poured from Mina's relieved mind and out her mouth.

Joseph took a couple of deep breaths before he replied, "I was worried about you. I figured you'd hang around here, and the weather was turning nasty, so I sent the guys on home and I backtracked over here. I don't know . . . I just wanted to spend more time with you and I also thought you shouldn't be in an empty building half the night. Looks like you're more than capable of taking care of yourself, though." He rubbed his shin.

Mina's face flamed. "I'm so sorry. I . . ." *The album!* "I got spooked and then you grabbed me . . ." The words hung in the air.

"Did you see something?" His eyebrows quirked, hand on the door handle.

"No! It was nothing. Really."

"You sure? I've been known to go a round or two and come out on top." He flexed his free arm.

"No, really. I'm fine."

A smile teased at the corners of his mouth. "So . . . How about dinner?"

"Of course!" *Anything to get away from this building right now.*

Joseph shined his flashlight inside the building. "Looks like you dropped something. Let's grab it and go."

"No!"

"Come on. It won't take us but a sec to load that stuff in your car," he assured her.

Mina dreaded going back in the building, but Joseph already had the door propped open, waving her inside. She was horrified to see that the album's spine had snapped open and pages lay strewn about. Mina began grabbing the pages, trying not to let him see, but Joseph managed to pluck a few of the ones farthest away from her anyway.

"This is interesting," Joseph remarked as he shined a light on the photos. "Who are . . . ?"

Mina knew from his pause he'd seen *that* photo. All the ones in the album and he gets THE photo. She was afraid to look at him and afraid not to.

"Mina. Why does this . . . this man look like *me*?" There was accusation in his voice.

"Well . . ." She rotated her head slowly toward him, wanting to delay the inevitable conversation that was coming.

"And what are you doing with these photos?"

Mina decided the truth was the best tact. "Joseph, I found the album in the wall of the back bedroom."

"Okay. But why am I in here? I've never seen these folks. I mean, what is this? Some kind of joke?"

"No, no joke." *Tell him!* Mina took another deep breath and said, "Joseph, I think the photos are of the men who owned this theater."

"The missing men?"

"Yes."

"But . . . but he looks just like *me*." His face was a mass of total confusion. Mina could see the cogs turning in his head, trying to make up a plausible explanation besides the obvious.

"I know."

Their eyes met—unasked questions in his, answers in hers.

"I think one of them is your father," Mina said quietly.

"F-father?"

Mina covered the hand holding the photo, but Joseph pulled away. "Joseph, I know this is a shock, but—"

"Shock!" He waved the photo in the air. "We are past the shock phase, lady. This is . . . is . . ." Joseph fell silent, face contorting as he searched for the proper word.

"Amazing?" Mina supplied, hoping to stymie the negative vibes emanating from him.

Joseph gave her a look that said she'd either sprouted wings or had horns growing out of her head. Then he turned and stomped to the door.

"Joseph? Joseph?" Mina quickly trotted behind as the darkness returned.

He continued out the door, not answering. Mina grabbed his arm, slowing him. He stopped but refused to look at her.

"Joseph, let's go eat and talk this out. It might be your father; it may not be. But at least let's talk and think this through."

Joseph's voice was defeated. "Mina, I've got to take a rain check on our date. I've . . . I've got too much stuff to process right now. I'll see you Monday."

"You sure?" She hated for him to find out this way, hated for the night to end on a down note.

"Yes. Have a great night." With that, he lifted himself into the cab of his truck, threw it into reverse, and zoomed down the street, out of sight.

Mina stood there staring at his wake, then she remembered where she was. She fumbled about, glad when the car's interior light broke the darkness around her, and fell inside the vehicle, relieved. That relief was short-lived as she remembered the building was unlocked—and her keys were inside.

14

_____

"She shouldn't be out there by herself," John commented, watching as Mina stared back and forth in the darkness.

"What do you suggest? Float the keys down to her, drop them on the hood, and scare the bejesus out of her more?" Cal joked.

"I'm just saying, it's not safe. Anything could happen to a woman sitting alone on this dark street."

Cal had to agree with him as he watched Mina shiver and then lift to look in her backseat. "Why don't we just stay here and watch over her. If anyone comes along that's suspicious, we could always do the chain rattling and scare them off."

"We hope. If it's somebody wired on drugs, it might not work."

The conclusion of that type of situation was one neither of them wanted to contemplate for long.

"I'm going to talk to her," John said after a few moments.

"How?" Cal asked, eyes wide, eyebrows hitched to the sky. "Since when are we able to just sit down and hold a conversation like living folks?"

"Of course I can't just plop in and start talking. But I think I know a way."

Cal remained unconvinced but held his words. "Go ahead. I don't think we can muck things up any worse than they already are."

"Hopefully, I can make things right as rain."

"Do your thing. Do *your* thing," Cal urged, wondering what John had up his transparent sleeve.

Mina's eyes darted back and forth, halfway wishing some wayward soul was walking this time of night, but as thunder boomed again and rain splattered her windshield, she knew her wishes were hopeless.

She hugged her arms around her belly, berating herself again for leaving the keys behind and for being too afraid to enter the building to search for them. It didn't help that flashes of every scary movie she'd seen since childhood popped into her head, reversing and replaying clear as the best quality high-definition system on the market. She found herself glancing up and down the sidewalk constantly, interspersed with cautious peeping into the darkness of her rear seat. Visions of blood-red eyes popping open in the darkness, a bloody hand smearing her window, a thump on the hood made her slump deep into her seat. Her mind was under siege! Honestly, if a lightning bug lit up, she'd pee where she sat.

She didn't know how long she stayed awake, but eventually sleep claimed her tired body and harassed mind.

John hovered over the car, watching as Mina slept fitfully. She lay sideways, legs pulled onto the seat, arms wrapped around them. Every few minutes, her body would jump, tense up, but she stayed asleep. His eyes roved over the bare skin cresting from her shirtfront, her petite ankles inadvertently exposed to the night. He sniffed the air in the car. She smelled of oil, plaster, and sweat mixed with a hint of flowers. He groaned.

He'd fed Cal a bullshit line about wanting to talk to her, lay everything out so she'd understand, but honestly, part of him wanted to talk and the other—he rubbed his now throbbing cock—wanted to fuck her senseless. No matter what Cal said, the truth was he wanted to sink his cock deep in her pussy and pump like this was his last fuck.

Yes, Joseph *might* be his son and he *might* even be interested in her, but he hadn't gotten a taste of her *yet* . . . and that made Ms. Mina fair game in his mind.

A light tapping on her window woke her.

Mina jumped a foot, banging her head on the roof of the car. Through suddenly awake eyes she saw the light. She peered through the window and could clearly see Joseph standing on the other side, a flashlight shining onto his face. She threw the door open in relief, grabbing him in a bear hug and wrapping her legs around his waist for good measure.

"Joseph!" How glad she was to see a familiar face!

He said nothing, just placed his arms around her, hugging her close. His hands rubbed up and down her back, comforting her as they rocked in place. His arms felt just as Mina knew they would—strong and safe.

After a few minutes, Joseph pulled back. But what he did next took her by surprise. He slammed his mouth onto hers, twirling and swirling, stoking her fires. Mina hesitated, wanted to ask necessary questions, but fingers threaded into her hair, held her captive as his tongue plundered deep and long.

Mina's surprise quickly morphed into desire as a hand slid down, covering her butt. She left the questions unasked as she sighed around the tongue when a hand squeezed her cheek. His tongue licked at her earlobe and her legs jellified. She held tightly to his muscular shoulders as his tongue stabbed inside her canal. The tongue moved lower, down her neck.

She knew she needed a bath, but he licked her like she'd just stepped out of a rose-scented shower. Her pussy clenched, focusing her attention back on Joseph's actions.

He leaned her back against the car. Knees held her in place as hands ripped her shirt open, baring her flesh to the cool night. Other than her pebbled nipples, the cold barely registered as pulled her tits from the bra and latched on. Her blood boiled, her pussy-juice factory revved into overdrive as he deeply tugged the berries.

Mina whimpered when hands gripped her ass, thumbs pressed into the seat of her crotch. Her hips bucked as her clit was located and mashed. His pelvis ground into her, his cock brick hard. This double assault had her grasping at his skull, his back, his ass.

He began pumping her through her clothes. Her pungent fragrance wafted between them as his covered cock made her clit sing with every contact. Mina wiggled, pulled his hips to her, felt herself melting. But she needed more.

"I need you in me!" The anguished cry wrenched from her lips.

He lifted, allowed her legs to slide to the ground. Nimble fingers unbuttoned her jeans, unzipped her fly, slid the panties down her legs with the pants. Mina was turned, hands now on the hood. A cock quickly nestled at her opening, then surged inside.

Mina's nails raked the hood as his cock filled her over and over again. She lifted her hips, allowed more shaft inside her sopping love hole. He pistoned, rammed, and stroked her gloriously. Hands captured her nipples and pulled as he humped her. She felt his leg lift, sit on the fender; his intensity increased.

He yielded no quarter as he pounded against her hips. Mina

mewled low, held on to the hood, meeting each thrust, matching each stroke. Suddenly, her body tensed, her clit swelled, and firecrackers exploded behind her eyes. Mina shrieked in the black night as darkness clouded her mind.

"I thought you said you were only going to talk to her?" Cal accused.

"I did talk to her. You just couldn't hear it."

"Oh, I heard her moaning all right, just no talking."

"Believe me, we were talking. We just used sign language." John's teeth shone brightly in the darkness.

"That's what you are calling it now?"

"I am."

"You know she thought you were Joseph, don't you?" Cal had overheard her call out Joseph's name.

"Yep." John turned to look at Cal. "But the important thing is, I never said I *was*."

The sharp yellow glow beneath her eyelids forced her awake. Mina squinted into the bright sun aiming its beacon directly into her windshield. She stretched, stopping when her hands plunked into the ceiling of the car.

Then she remembered. Joseph had returned, they'd had hot passionate sex, and . . . the events went blank after that. But why would he leave her here? In this car on the street?

Her mouth tasted like old dishwater, and she wiped away sleep boogers as her eyes scanned the theater. The door remained closed, but the interior showed light. Mina flipped the mirror toward her. Just as she'd thought. She looked like she had slept in her car.

Mina glanced up and down the sidewalk, not wanting to alarm anyone walking at—she winced as she looked at the car clock—six-seventeen in the morning. Not seeing anything other than a stray dog, she quietly opened her door.

She took more than one deep breath as her hand closed around the door to the building.

Here goes just about everything.

The air was cool and smelled of plaster dust and mildew. The photos were still strewn about, the satchel sitting front and center amongst the chaos. Nothing seemed to have been disturbed.

She took a tentative step inside. "Hello?" Not that she thought anyone—living, that is—was actually inside. She did it by rote, anything to appease her anxious mind and delay the inevitable.

No answer, as expected.

She was being a ninny, a big old baby. Mina squared her shoulders and bolstered up her fragile mind, determined to find her car keys. She held her head high as she strode to the pile of articles. Her eyes searched but saw no keys among the mess.

Shoot!

That meant her keys were most likely . . . upstairs.

She groaned, fear lapping at her heart like the family dog. *Why hadn't Joseph hung around?* She eyed the staircase suspiciously. Inviting light shone at the top. But she didn't feel invited at all. She was afraid.

Either deal with the situation or cut bait and run, her mind chided.

Cut bait and run. Those words reverberated around in her head, stiffened her spine. Cut bait and run. She'd run away from her home, her job, her friends, spent half of her the-reason-why-she-was-running money on this dilapidated building just to run off again? Uh-uh. She was sick and tired of running. Sick of wondering if she'd run far enough, fast enough, or if her "visitor" and his cronies would hunt her down and finish her off.

Mina lifted her chin, determination shining in her eyes. Dammit! She wasn't going to run another step. If she had unfriendly ghosts, she'd find a ghost buster. Everything she had was riding on turning this building into a business and a home, and she'd be damned if ghosts—real or imagined—were going to run her off.

She snatched a heavy wrench from the floor, waded through the dust, and stomped up the stairs. That way, everyone—living or dead—could hear her coming. Because she *was* coming.

The library stood as she'd left it. Mina had to smile as she spied her keys in the center of the bed. She didn't hesitate, didn't show any apprehension as she walked calmly over to the bed and retrieved the ring of keys. She then retraced her footsteps back down the stairs, stopping only when she reached the satchel and photos. She gathered the album contents up, grabbed the satchel by the handle, and dragged everything to the car. When she reached the motel, she'd look everything over thoroughly.

15

"Holyschmollymamamia!"

Mina's eyes were glued to the satchel, disbelieving what she saw. Inside were bundles of hundred-dollar bills. Lots of bundles. Eyes big as marbles, she pulled thousand-dollar packet after thousand-dollar packet from the satchel, mentally counting as the pile grew. When she reached the bottom, those marbles grew into saucers as she stared at the two gold bars—as in, Fort Knox-only-seen-on-television gold bars—sitting there.

GodalmightyhelpmeJesus! There was more than one hundred and fifty thousand dollars in this room!

Mina stared at the ceiling, trying to understand the events of her life. "Let me get this straight," she said to the empty room. "First off, I see a shooting in a parking lot; then some mobster-type guy shows up with a case full of money and suggests I get out of town. Scared, I run off, leaving everything familiar behind, end up in this sleepy little town where I buy a dilapidated building, where I now have mind-blowing sex with two ghosts who left a secret treasure buried in a bedroom wall?" She bopped her head. "Unbelievable! My life is a made-for-television movie!"

She pulled the album onto her lap, stared at each picture, looking for clues. Most of them were of either Cal or John alone or with others. But the remainder shocked Mina. They showed naked people engaging in various sex acts—conventional and perverted. All looked happy. She flipped the photos over, not surprised to see names and dates. These were obviously blackmail photos.

The last photo in the album piqued her interest. It showed an airplane and Cal standing with his hand on the cockpit door. On the side was the name *The Goose.*

Hmmm. Okay, maybe they flew away, leaving everything behind. But why leave all this money in the wall? It's obvious they didn't run off and tell their families. Otherwise, the building would have been gutted years ago as people searched for the hidden treasure. But if they were dead—and you didn't have live men who disappeared thirty-odd years ago appearing in dreams unless they had some hellova psychic energy—then how and better yet, why?

More than curious now, Mina decided to call Charlotte Charles to see if she could shed any light on the photos. Charlotte answered after the third ring. She quickly agreed to see Mina and gave her detailed directions to her house.

Mina showered, dressed, and strode out the door within fifteen minutes.

Mina thought Charlotte looked refreshing when she answered the door. The realtor was sporting a peach wind suit, her hair was styled differently, and she wore full facial makeup.

"Wow. You look different, younger," Mina complimented the older woman. And she did. The make-up was artfully applied and gave her skin a pleasant glow.

"Why, thank you!" Charlotte gave her hair a girlish bounce. "Just got a mini-makeover. I thought it was time for a new look."

"It suits you."

"Thank you again." Charlotte grabbed Mina's forearm, propelled her forward. "Come on in, show me what you have."

Mina pulled the album from her armpit. "You know we've started renovating the building." Charlotte nodded rapidly. "And last night, I found this album in the wall. I wondered if you knew any of the people in the photos. If so, I want to contact them, see if they know what happened to the two men who owned the theater."

"Well, it's worth a try." Charlotte eagerly pulled the album onto her lap, and then gave Mina a lopsided smile. "I find it admirable that you are still trying to find out what happened to those men." She flipped open the book. "The town gave up . . ." She suddenly stopped, hands fluttering up to cover her mouth. Mina leaned forward, saw she held the photo of John and Cal with the convertible.

"What? You recognize someone?"

Charlotte's eyes vacillated between Mina and the photo. The hand holding the photo trembled. Her color whitened to paste.

"What's wrong? Charlotte?" Mina didn't know if the woman was in shock, having a heart attack, or something worse. She quickly grabbed her hand. It was cold and sweaty. Mina, alarmed now, shook her fiercely, slapping her face lightly to get some sort of reaction from the mute woman.

Charlotte's eyes finally focused, stared directly at Mina. "Where—who are these men?" Charlotte's voice was a shell-shocked whisper.

"If you turn it over, you'll see the inscription says it's Cal Toledo and John Whitmore."

Charlotte turned the photo over and read, then lifted confused eyes back to Mina. "But it can't be . . . they can't be . . . aren't they *dead*?"

Mina played a hunch. She gathered Charlotte's cold hands inside her own, forced her head into the woman's personal space, and stared into her eyes. "Charlotte, have you *seen* these men? Recently?"

Charlotte visibly swallowed; the muscles worked in her jaw, but no words exited her mouth. After long seconds, during which time her facial muscles ticked and warred with each other, then relaxed back to normal, she finally spoke. "I'm not sure how to answer your question. If you are asking if I've done business with these men or if I know them personally, then the answer is no . . . but—" She fell silent, eyes closing and squeezing together, leaving the remainder of the answer unspoken.

It was obvious Charlotte knew more than she was telling. But Mina was an old poker hand and knew when to call and when to hold. She skipped over the sexual stuff and lifted out the photo of Cal standing beside the plane. "How about this plane? Ever hear of either of them owning a plane named *The Goose*?"

Charlotte perused the photo for long moments. "No, I never did, but that doesn't mean they didn't own one. The only airport around here is the St. Paulus County Airport. Why don't you stop over there and see what they can tell you?" Charlotte stood suddenly, walked to the door, and held it open before turning back to Mina. "I don't think I can help you further"—she slid a candied smile onto her face—"but I will stop by and see how the renovations are coming along."

The conversation was obviously finished. Mina gathered up the photos, more than puzzled by Charlotte's behavior.

Mina spied Joseph's truck as she turned into the motel parking lot. His reverse lights lit up, and she tooted her horn before pulling up behind him, blocking the truck in. She hopped from her car just as he exited through his door.

"Hey, why did you leave me on the street last night?" She hadn't planned to ask the question, but it flew out of her mouth on its own. "I mean, we have brain-stunning sex and you couldn't stick around to help me get back to the motel?"

"Good morning, Mina." His voice was stoic, stern.

"Do you treat all your women friends like this?" Yes, he was sexy as hell and screwed her like nobody's business, but leaving her in her car during a power outage, on a deserted street, shifted him into the "cad" zone.

Joseph's face had turned blister-red. As he opened his mouth to respond, someone in the truck cleared their voice. He glanced in the cab, then back at Mina. "Mina, I'd like you to meet my mother, Lauren."

Mina wanted to sink through the asphalt and disappear. Her face blossomed a beautiful spring pink as a petite woman coughed, spat on the ground, then walked around the truck. Lauren's face was a road map of life lines caused by too much sun, fun, cigarettes, and beer. Her movements were smooth, graceful, belying her aged face. Her crimson-painted lips separated, forming a smile and unveiling perfect, white dentures. The hair was Lucille Ball red.

"Good morning, young lady." The voice was as rough as brand-new sixty-grade sandpaper. "Don't worry about me and what I heard. I've had to upbraid a man or two who'd left his manners in the gutter as well." Lauren's eyes shifted to include Joseph. "I just never thought it would be my son who would need the upbraiding." Censure was all over her face.

Mina turned discreetly and stuck out her tongue; Joseph bit his lips.

"Now, my Joseph tells me you may have figured out what happened to his daddy."

"So you know who his father is?" Mina wished she could take the words back the moment they wiggled out.

Lauren stood taller, eyes sphinctered. "*Every* woman knows who the father of her child is."

Mina had the good sense to remain silent.

"I'd like to see the photos, see if we can find out, for sure, what happened to John." Lauren's eyes grew sad; her shoulders dropped. "It's been past hell not knowing."

Mina retrieved the album from the car and held it out to Lauren. Brown-spotted hands took the book while her head nodded at Joseph. He put the tailgate down, and Lauren laid the book on the plastic-coated lip.

Mina studied the emotions playing across Lauren's face as she looked at each photo. Sometimes she smiled, other times she frowned, but most of the time she had a wistful look of remembrance.

"I'd forgotten about *The Goose*," Lauren said quietly, her finger running over the outline of the plane photo. Mina's heart thumped in her chest. "Well, actually, I didn't know much about it." She gave a half-laugh. "John talked about it one time when we were . . . together. He didn't go on about it, just mentioned it in passing, you know, after lovemaking. Said Cal had lost his Mississippi mind, gone pink-elephant-wearing-clown-shoes dumb and bought a plane. A week later, he disappeared."

"What happened to the plane?" Mina's gut clenched. The conclusion to this puzzle was definitely near.

Lauren cocked her head in thought. "You know, I don't know. I never even thought about it again. I was too caught up in finding myself pregnant and unmarried; then news reached me that John and Cal had disappeared." The voice got low again. "I never even had a chance to tell him, and then he . . . never came back."

The look on Lauren's face fueled the fire in Mina. "I've got a hunch." Two pairs of eyes studied her. "I'm not sure, but let's load up and drive over to the airfield. It may be a long shot, but something tells me *everything* leads to there."

"Think she'll put it all together today?" Cal asked, drifting above the small crowd below.

"Sounds like she plans to." John spoke quietly, his eyes fixed on Joseph and the woman.

"John . . . do you remember her?" Cal studied him.

John squeezed his eyes shut; he remembered Lauren as the thin girl who'd given herself to him freely. They'd not shared many beds, but apparently the few times they had had been enough. "Yeah. I remember her."

"Which one was she? She come to the parties a lot?" Cal's mind claimed only the standouts, the ones whose sexual prowess was memorable. Nothing about the name or face sparked any recollection in him.

John shook his head. "No. She wasn't one of the party women. She was the one hanging around the theater that we kept telling to go home."

Cal's eyes flared, chin diving into his neck as he looked back at Lauren. "*That's* her?" He cleared his throat. "I guess there are some advantages to dying young after all, eh?"

As John looked at the young girl turned into an aged woman, he couldn't dispute the truth.

16

After riding around for an hour on one wrong rutted road after another, they finally spied a large tin building in the distance. Lauren saw it first and wiggled her hand toward it. "Look! I think I see a hangar!"

There was expectancy in the air of the truck as they finally found the correct road and drove into the airport parking lot. It was a small affair. Three small planes—two two-seaters and one crop duster—stood angled toward the corrugated-metal building. A thirty-foot-wide tarmac strip led away from the huge structure, its end disappearing in the haze of heat monkeys. A lone Jeep was parked catty-corner to the open bay.

They tapped the horn as they stopped in front of the building. An older woman stepped outside, flannel shirt unbuttoned over a T-shirt and jeans. The forehead crinkled mildly under windblown brown hair as she watched the trio exit the truck. "Howdy. I'm Sarah Burns. What can I do for you folks?" The speech was clipped and precise but friendly.

Mina strode over, shook the outstretched hand. "I'm Mina

Sinclair and this is Joseph and Lauren Turnbull." She waved at the others.

"Glad to meet you all. What can I do for you?"

"Well, we've got some questions about a plane."

Her eyebrows hooked. "Which one?"

"It was named *The Goose*." Mina held her breath hopefully.

Sarah let her eyes shift toward the planes, thinking. She shook her head after a minute or so. "I don't recall any plane named *The Goose*. When was it supposed to have come through here?"

"Thirty-odd years ago."

"Thirty years?" Sarah's head vigorously shook now. "I've only owned this outfit for fifteen. Heck, our logs don't go back beyond five." She looked at the group askance, hands now planted firmly on her hips. "Why in the world would you care about a plane coming through here thirty years ago?"

Mina let the air out of her lungs, disappointed but knowing an explanation was expected. "The men who owned it disappeared, and we were searching for any lead, any thing at all that could tell us what happened."

Sarah tilted her head, stared. "What are these men to you?"

"It was my father and his friend," Joseph inserted quietly.

Sarah nodded, eyes vacillating between Mina, Joseph, and Lauren. "I'll tell you somebody who might know, and this is just a might, but he worked here for forty years, so he'd be your best bet. His name is Arnold Hunt."

Mina wanted to jump for joy. "Is he around?" Her eyes darted and flitted about the area, searching for this Arnold Hunt.

"No. He retired last year, but he doesn't live too far away. If you'll hold up a minute, I'll write down the directions." She turned to enter the hangar.

"I told you all things led to the airport, didn't I?" Mina whispered, excited.

"Yeah, but we still don't know any more than we did when we got here."

"Not yet. But hopefully, Arnold can pull this scattered puzzle together." Mina refused to let her spirits be dampened.

Sarah returned, directions written on a torn, coffee-stained envelope. "He's got an old mutt that barks like he's the devil's number-one guard dog, but don't pay him any mind. That mongrel doesn't have a tooth in his head. At most, he'll gum you to death." She chuckled at her own joke.

They thanked her quickly—Mina with a tight hug that caught Sarah off guard and almost pitched them both to the ground—and piled back into the truck.

"You sure this is the right road, son?" Lauren asked, grasping the ceiling handle to steady herself as they jiggled, bumped, and skittered down the gravel road.

"That's what the sign said." Joseph squinted ahead, dust churning behind the truck.

"Whoa!" Duplicate screams as Joseph lurched to a sudden fishtailing, rock-spitting halt. When the dust had drifted past, both women gasped. In front of them lay a wide crater, big enough to swallow the truck whole—and right now, they couldn't see the edge because the bumper was over the lip.

Joseph flipped into reverse and gunned it. The four-wheel-drive vehicle shot backward. Once in the safety zone, he turned the steering wheel hard, directing them around the road cavern.

"That was close," Mina squeaked, images of them flipped upside down, pinned inside the truck making her shiver.

A few hundred yards later, the road stopped in front of a small, seen-better-days house. The brown paint was peeling off in sheets, the low-hanging porch roof sagged, and the top step was missing. A thin dog bounded off the porch, setting up an eardrum-splicing racket while running back and forth around the truck.

"Guess that's the dog Sarah mentioned, so this must be the right place," Lauren surmised.

"Shut up that fuss! Hector! Hush up!" A small man followed behind the voice. His back was slightly bent, the clothes two sizes too big. In his hand was a long shotgun, which he propped across his forearms and aimed toward the truck.

No one moved.

"Hector, come here and hush!" the man yelled again. The dog squelched his noise midbark and slowly retreated until he stood beside his master. "Yes?"

Joseph opened his door, careful to keep the metal between him and the man as he answered. "You Arnold Hunt?"

"Yep. You?"

"Joseph Turnbull. We'd"—he indicated the women in the truck—"just like to ask you some questions about a plane."

The shotgun's nose dropped to the ground; a smile spread across Arnold's face. "Why didn't you say so? Come on in! One thing I love to talk about, it's airplanes."

They emptied from the truck and made introductions. Arnold pointed at some rickety chairs on the porch, and they all sat down.

"Now, what plane are y'all interested in?"

Mina spoke up first. "Well, we were hoping you'd remember a plane called *The Goose*. Two men from St. Paulus owned it." Mina hoped her description sparked a memory.

Arnold's face froze. "Two men, huh?"

"Yes."

"One white and the other black?"

"Yes."

Arnold sighed, tilted his chair back, and rocked. "Yeah, I remember those two . . . and the plane."

"I guess you know they disappeared thirty years ago, and nobody has seen head nor hair of them. We were wondering if you could shed any light on the situation."

Arnold's lips pulled in and out, sucking his teeth in the silence. He finally spoke. "That was a long time ago. I had a sick wife and four younguns running around here, and we all had to eat. Wasn't no reliable jobs at the mill for a man like me. I was lucky to have gotten on the cleaning crew at the 'port as it was."

Mina knew something profound was happening.

"They came in there one night, arguing and joking like friends do, but they were happy. Real happy. Nobody was around but me. We didn't let folks fly off at night, so nobody else was needed. My job that night was just to clean one side of the hangar and keep an eye on things."

Lauren scooted her chair closer and leaned in.

"They begged me something fierce. I told them there wasn't nobody there to put out the landing lights when they came back." He twisted his lips, shook his head. "They didn't care. They just wanted to fly off somewhere right then, right there."

Mina left her chair and sat on the edge of the porch in front of him. Hector snuffled her hand, apparently found her worthy, and draped his belly across her feet.

"It wasn't until they bribed me with the thousand dollars that I gave in." He eyed the group, held up his hands. "I know I was going against the rules, but I . . . I needed the money." The head rocked as the mind moved backward. "I was barely scratching by, and my Matilda was sick; she needed medicine I couldn't get for her regularly. That money was a whole lot of food and medicine."

Mina knew well the power of money. "So you helped them."

Arnold nodded slowly. "Yeah, I helped 'em. It was supposed to be a 'just between them and me trip,' one I couldn't write down on the books if I wanted to keep my job. They flew out of there happy as June bugs on moonshine, told me they'd be back in two hours."

"Were they?" Hope infused Lauren's voice.

Arnold's eyes dropped to the ground; he shook his head. "I set the landing lights out after an hour or so; just got ready for whenever they moseyed on back. I started getting worried after three hours had come and gone and no sign of them. By the time six hours had passed, I was scared out my head. But it was close to five o'clock—the time the boss came in—so I picked up the lights, put everything back like it was, and drove on home, praying I didn't pass him coming as I was going."

"What about later? Did they show up later?" Lauren's pitch rose. "Maybe they came back later. Had the plane pulled away while you were gone?"

Arnold turned sad eyes to her. "Ma'am, ain't no way a plane that size flies around five or six hours on the fuel it holds. It just ain't possible."

"But I didn't read anything about a plane crash. Surely someone would have heard or seen if the plane crashed, right?" Mina needed to *finish* it, make the pieces fit, connect the dots.

A bird chirped in the stillness. Knees popped as Arnold rose from his chair. "Y'all follow me. I want to show you something."

The dust puffed around their ankles as they trailed Arnold to a leaning shed behind the house. The tin door screeched as he pulled it open. A stick was plucked from the ground, banged about the outer walls, and poked into the mass of stuff ready to spill out. Arnold turned, said, "For the snakes," then banged some more. Lauren and Mina took a few steps backward . . . and then a few more.

He finally stopped after five minutes. He then listened. Satisfied, he stuck his hand between what looked like a chair leg and a box spring. Arnold leaned and pushed, rocked and grunted, his face showing the strain. He motioned at Joseph. "Hold up this stuff so I can reach a bit farther."

Joseph pushed against an old bicycle tire and the mass shifted. Arnold's head disappeared into the widened hole. They heard mumbling, and then he popped back into view. Cobwebs coated his salt-and-pepper hair. He glanced at Joseph. "Now grab this here and yank it out." He shoulder-pointed to something out of the women's view.

Joseph reached in, grabbed whatever it was with two hands, planted his feet against the base of the building, and yanked. He grunted as he pulled again. His foot slipped, and a white object sailed out, thudded into the back of the house. Hector barked and howled. Mina and Lauren moved closer for a better look.

A surfboard?

It was a wide, oblong, white fiberglass board, edges ragged on one side. Barnacles formed an intricate network across the top and, as Mina flipped it over with her shoe, the bottom surfaces. The underside had dark markings. Mina tried to figure out what the markings were when Arnold shuffled over, turned the board clockwise, one hundred eighty degrees. It was obvious that the lines and circles were the top parts of an *F* or *E* and a *C* or . . . *G*?

Mina turned questioning eyes to Arnold. He nodded. "You figuring right. I believe that's part of the wing of the plane, the *E* and the *G* from *THE GOOSE*."

"You sure?" Lauren asked, letting her hands travel over the weathered fiberglass.

"I'll grab the photo, see if it matches," Joseph said, trotting to the truck.

"But where did you find it? Why didn't you say anything?" Mina had to ask. Someone should have been told.

Arnold crossed his arms, let his chin rest on the back of his hand. "I pulled it out of Meadow Lake when I went fishing one day. When I snagged this here, I thought I had caught the granddaddy of all bass." His eyes lit up as he recounted the story. "The durn thang was so heavy, I thought my line would snap. It didn't, so I kept feeding line and reeling it in, all the time formulating the speech I'd say for the newspaper, that is, until I finally saw what my prize catch was—a piece of what us old folks call *flotsam*. But the closer it got, the more I knew it wasn't just *any* old piece of flotsam. I saw planes day in and day out, and nobody had to tell me what it was—part of a wing."

Joseph returned, held the photo beside the board. There was a shared sigh as the *E* and *G* from the photo undeniably matched the wing board in front of them. Tears streamed down Lauren's face; she slumped to her knees, hands flat on the board. Joseph kneeled behind his mother, gathered her into his arms, and tucked his chin into her neck. They rocked in silence, staring at the board, both wishing and wondering.

Arnold continued his story in a low voice. "I know I probably should have told somebody, but I couldn't risk it. If I went to the sheriff, then it'd come out that I let somebody fly at night; the airport would get fined, and worse, I'd lose my job. And I couldn't lose my job." The tone was granite. "I was all my family had, and I'd do whatever I had to to keep them safe and healthy. I ain't saying what I did was right. But those men were already dead, and me and my family had to survive, so I did what I had to do." Shoulders lowered. "Y'all can take the wing if you want, tell somebody. I'm too old for them to do anything to me about it now." Glum eyes peered at the trio one more time before he shuffled around the side of the building, leaving them in their private pain.

Officially dead.

Mina had played a hunch, badgered strangers until they squealed, and pieced together the puzzle. Heck, she'd even figured out where their bodies were located. So it was official.

"Guess this makes it official. We are now D-E-A-D," Cal stated, nodding at John.

"Newsflash: We've been dead for thirtysomething years." John's eyes did a slow roll.

"No, we were missing persons. We are now bon a fide deceased, sans bodies." Cal suddenly glanced over his shoulder and then heavenward.

"What's up with you?" John asked, watching the jerky movements.

"Ah . . . isn't this the part where we should see a bright light leading the way? Harp-holding angels strumming us to Glory? A sign with 'Pearly Gate' and an arrow on it?"

"I . . . I don't know. Maybe."

Four eyes darted about in silence, bodies tensed, waiting.

After a few minutes of nothingness, John said, "Guess they forgot about us, huh?"

Cal let out a deep breath. "Yeah. Sure looks that way."

John's smile broadened to a wolf's grin. "In that case, all I can say is, let the games begin!"

17

A few months later . . .

The building gleamed—fresh paint, varnished floors, and flowers on the tables. WARM SPIRITS was emblazoned on the sign and stenciled on the door. Women—many past their prime—milled around, reading, chatting, and taking turns visiting the "Member's Only" area. The smiles were as broad as their matronly hips.

Mina watched as Tracey counted out the customers' change and tore off the receipt. What a find she'd been. Tracey was the first to respond to her ad for a clerk. She'd said the home-supply company job was a dead-ender, and she needed a change. It didn't hurt that Mina had doubled her salary. She'd been here from day one.

Tracey slammed the cash register drawer shut and turned to her employer. "Looks like you've got a gold mine here."

Mina giggled as she scanned the room. "That was the plan."

"It sure worked."

They both turned as a door banged closed, and then loud

humming drew their attention. Gertie skipped down the stairs, stopping at the bottom and curtseying low. She'd become their best customer . . . and the most frequent visitor to the upstairs room.

"My word! Lass, that was pure bliss." Her eyes rolled in her head. When they righted, she reached into her purse, pulled out her checkbook. "I must insist on a year's membership." Her forehead wrinkled. "Wait. Do you have a lifetime membership?"

Mina chuckled at the question. "Not yet, but I may add it. What did you watch today?"

"*Cowboy X.*" She fanned at her face. "You should have seen the protuberance he possessed! Reminded me of my Robert. Just magnificent!"

Gertie, like many of the "members," had no set limits on her erotica. Action, adventure, mystery, or downright porn, she was an eager, willing sponge for all of it.

"Glad you enjoyed," Tracey piped in as she slid Gertie's check into the cash register.

"I did. Well, let me get back to work. My lunch hour is up. See you tomorrow." Gertie waggled her fingers at the others she knew before leaving.

Joseph walked into view as Gertie exited. Mina tensed. Things had been strained between them since *that* night. She had a hard time forgiving him, and he'd not made reference to it, so she let the situation lie. But she wanted, so wanted, to clear the air, understand why he'd done what he did.

Joseph stopped in front of Mina, hands shoved into his pockets. "I see business is going like gangbusters in here." He waved at a petite blonde furiously waving at him.

"They are." Her voice was tight. His attention and too-quick smile at the blonde made her strain her TMS joint.

His eyes met hers. "Got a minute? I think we need to talk." Her heart sped up. Was today the day? "Sure. Let me grab my purse." She turned to look at Tracey. "Can you handle it alone for a bit?"

"No problem."

Mina walked into the office, grasping the side of the desk as the door closed behind her. Her nerves were frayed; her mind reeled. What would she say? More importantly, what would *he* say?

She quickly swiped lipstick across her lips and ran a comb through her hair. As she grabbed her purse, she heard a loud thud, then excited voices. Mina quickly headed back into the main area to see what the commotion was about.

Charlotte Charles stood by the door; dirt, a large plant, and a broken pot lay around her feet. Her mouth was open, her hands stopped halfway to the open mouth, and her eyes were glued on Joseph.

Mina walked over to the still woman. "Charlotte, what happened?"

No response.

Mina patted her arm. "Charlotte?"

Blank eyes focused on Mina. "Nothing. It was nothing. I was just . . ." Joseph had walked over by this time. Her eyes fixated on him. "Who are you?"

Joseph held out his hand. "Joseph Turnbull. I was the contractor on this remodel."

Charlotte let the hand hang. "But . . . you . . . you're . . ."

The way Charlotte stared and stuttered, Mina had a good idea of the reason behind her reaction and her previous actions as well. She took her arm, guided her around the mess, and said, "Charlotte, why don't you go upstairs, rest your feet, and pop a DVD in? You work hard, and this will relax you a bit." Mina handed her off to Tracey. "I'll be back to check on you."

Tracey took Charlotte's arm. "Don't worry about the mess. I'll take care of it once I get Ms. Charlotte comfortable." She guided Charlotte slowly up the stairs. This was no small undertaking, since Charlotte couldn't seem to take her eyes off Joseph. Those blue eyes held his until she was pulled into the library and the door closed.

"That's a strange woman," Joseph commented quietly.

"Nope. My guess is, you remind her of someone."

"You reckon?" He cocked an eyebrow.

They both laughed aloud at that.

They rode in silence, cresting hills and passing fields Mina had never seen before. Finally, Joseph stopped at the edge of a huge lake. Egrets lifted into the air, fish flipped from the water, frogs croaked, and crickets sang in the fresh air.

"Where are we?" Mina stared at the ripples radiating across the water.

"Meadow's Lake."

Mina nodded and waited.

Joseph leaned back in his seat, stretched his legs out, and began. "Mina, I need you to explain what you said to my mother. That stuff about me sexing you and leaving you on the street."

Mina expected the question but still had no ready answer. "Well . . . I . . . I just think that it was . . . callous." And cheesy and flaky and lowlife and disrespectful.

"*What* was callous?" Forehead wrinkled, eyes pitched skyward.

Now he's got amnesia. She couldn't believe his nerve. Her anger simmered. "We had hot sex in the middle of a pitch-black street, and when we finished, you just up and ran off, not making sure I'd gotten back to my motel safe or that I could even get back to the motel, which I couldn't, but you didn't know because you didn't care enough to stick around. What kind of crap is that? Hell, for all intents and purposes, you just used me and left me there!" The hesitant voice had become a cauldron of pisstivity by the time she finished.

Palms flipped into the air. "Whoa! I have never, *ever*, had sex—in *any* form or fashion—with you. Where that idea came from, I sure would like to know. I don't know how you usually do things, but I have to get to know a person, really know them first, *then* we'll move it up a notch. One night stander? Not me." He shook his head. "I'm a slow lover. So, I don't know who you had hot, sweaty, obviously fulfilling sex with on the street that night, but it wasn't me." His face was pure earnestness.

Mina's mind spun. She'd felt his hard arms circling her body, felt his tongue nibbling her ear, felt his fat cock pumping into her pussy. He was imprinted on her brain. Had his name stamped all over her pussy, was . . .

My God! No!

It couldn't . . . but it could. Just like that, she knew the truth.

She slumped back on the seat, her ire totally dissipated. Had there ever been a bigger fool than she felt like right now? If she were Joseph, she'd definitely be slapping labels all over her body—and none of them would be remotely positive. Face flaming like the evening sun, she mustered up all her courage and faced Joseph. "I . . . I think I owe you an apology."

"No shit, Sherlock," he spat, eyes locked on her face.

She winced at the coarse words. Time to lay it all on the line. Yeah, she'd sound like a fool, but damn, he was worth it. With a deep sigh, she said, "Joseph, I . . . I've been having these dreams . . ."

The sun slid into the water, and the moon rose in its place as two separate lives began traveling the sweet path to becoming one.

Cal drifted above the semicomatose woman lying on the chaise lounge. John floated over, a wide grin on his face. "That makes how many?"

"Eight today. You?"

John nodded. "Six. We beat our personal best of five from yesterday." He shook his head. "We sure couldn't have this much fun when we were alive."

"Uh-huh. There are definite advantages to being dead." And Cal planned to take advantage of each one of them.

A small flaxen-haired woman entered the library. Her dress was short, tight, and barely kept her voluptuous curves confined.

"My, my, my, a new recruit." Cal rubbed his hands together.

The woman quickly skimmed through the DVDs, then pulled one from the pile. Both men smiled as they saw the title—*The Chain Gangers.* She popped the movie into the DVD player and settled on the couch; her legs slid beneath her hips, her dress riding up, baring her thighs.

John licked his lips. "Seems she likes 'group' activity."

"It definitely appears that way."

John drifted down, let his hand cover a spilling breast. The woman absently stroked the area, her breath quickened, her legs shifted a bit. "So, you up to the challenge?"

Cal scoffed at the question. "Of course. You know our motto."

If the woman had listened hard, really, incredibly, straining-to-hear-the-slightest-peep hard, she would have heard duplicate voices shout, "Never let a wet pussy go to waste!"

Going Wild

Fiona Zedde

1

The first woman Derrick ever loved left him for his sister. Well, that wasn't quite the way it went, but that was how he liked to think of it. He turned over Tori and Dez's wedding invitation in his hands, smiling despite the ache of sadness at the delicate scent of ginger that still clung to it.

Victoria Jackson had been perfect for him in every way—professional, intelligent, beautifully put together, not to mention sexy as hell. They met at the University of Miami during his last year of college and her fourth year as a PhD candidate. Because of her, he stayed at UM to get his law degree. He even did his clerkship in Miami and took a job in his hometown despite the better offers in New York and Boston.

"What are you thinking about so hard over there, baby?"

Derrick looked toward the sound of his girlfriend's voice but felt Trish slide her arms around him before he could see her, teasing his nose with her light citrus perfume. He put the invitation facedown on the window seat. Beyond the upstairs window of his study, the artificial lake glimmered under the late Saturday morning sun.

"A case," he said. "Nothing serious."

The window's glass mocked him with a glimpse of his lying face—eyes deliberately bland, his mouth, framed by his neatly trimmed goatee, smiling.

"It doesn't look like it from where I'm standing."

"I guess you better come closer, then."

He reached around for her, tugging her forward and down until she sat in his lap, straddling him in the oversized leather chair. With a quick motion, he pushed the armrests down to seat level so she could get even closer and be more comfortable.

Glimmering black in the light, her straightened hair swung forward along her jaw, framing her almond eyes set against teak skin, the smiling mouth.

"You're right," she murmured. "This *is* better."

She'd been drinking hot chocolate, and the scent of it wafted from her parted lips, brushing over his mouth in a warm stream.

"Did you leave me any of that hot chocolate?" His hands fell to her hips.

"In the kitchen."

"What if I want what you've already had?"

"Then you'd have to come and get it." Her mouth hovered near his.

He chuckled, taking her up on her invitation. The taste of chocolate was still rich on her tongue, vibrant and dark but not as interesting as her own flavor. Her tongue danced with his, licked his teeth, daintily tasted until his dick rose hard between them and she moaned very softly, moving her hips against him.

"I thought you had to go to a meeting?" he asked, his hands already lifting her dress out of the way.

"You thought wrong. Right now"—she pulled down the top of her dress, baring her small breasts to his gaze, his mouth— "the only get-together that I'm interested in is this one."

She reached down to grasp him, to peel the thin cotton pajama bottoms from the thickness of him rising between them. Derrick fumbled in the top drawer of his desk for a condom, ripped the package open, and slid the latex over his dick. They both gasped as he slid inside her.

"Ah . . ."

Her breasts waved before his mouth, an invitation he couldn't resist, and he licked the tip of one, then the other. She gasped and squirmed on his lap. Derrick licked her breasts again, then chose one, pulling its velvet tip into his mouth, sucking the hard nub until she was riding him in a gentle rhythm, her mouth open, the other breast gently bobbing. He released her hips and grasped the other breast, kneading its softness, flicking the hardened peak with his thumb.

"Yes, baby."

Her soft cries urged Derrick on, but he didn't need them. His body was already hard and eager, throbbing like a pulse inside her and ready to fuck them both to oblivion. She was hot and wet around him. Pussy grasping him so tightly that he dropped the responsive breast and grasped her hips again with both hands, and she rolled her ass on top of him, moving her hips beyond the slow pace to something faster. And she was gasping again. His dick was close to exploding, but it was too soon. He felt her grasp the back of the chair, moving faster, her breasts jumping in front of his face. Derrick moved back, the air whistling between his teeth as he watched her damp face, her eyes dreamy as she rode his dick.

"Yes, baby!" Her voice rose, and his fingers sank deeper into the flesh of her ass.

The liquid sounds of their fucking and her cries and the squeaking leather chair and their breaths boiling in the room made him even harder, flooded fire in his spine.

"Make love to me." She rode his dick hard, slamming into

him, choking on her words. He was close. *Fuck*. Close. He reached down between them, fumbled for her clit, and found it wet. Juicy. "Yes!"

Her mouth fell open. Her movements sped. His balls tingled. *Fuck. Fuck. Fuck!* His head arched back, and he was jackknifing up, his hips uncontrollably fucking. Fucking her. Trish's soft scream rang out. "Don't stop." Through her cries, he heard the phone ring. Derrick pushed inside of her. It rang again. Again. Its cool continental ring sounded from the top of his desk just a few feet away. But he stayed where he was. Inside of Trish. God! She was so hot inside!

"Hey, Derrick. It's me." Victoria's voice stopped the seeking motion of his hips. "Just checking in—" He grabbed the phone.

"Tori." He swallowed, grasping for control of his breathing. "What's going on?"

On top of him, Trish became still. He felt her eyes like daggers. When she would have left him, swept her legs up and taken her hot pussy away, Derrick grasped her hips. *Stay*, he mouthed. He continued to move inside of her, gently. Trish's hand clenched into his shoulder, and her nails dug into his skin.

"Am I interrupting something?"

"No," he said. "Nothing."

He heard the doubt in her voice, but she didn't say anything else. "I'll make this quick. Dez wants you to do her a small favor. Drop off a package for her. Can you?"

"Yes." His hips began to move a little faster, the low smoke of her voice impelling him wordlessly to move. He imagined her mouth close to the phone. Its moist O.

"Great. It's going to arrive at your house in a few days. For her friend Nuria. Can you make sure that she gets it by the eighth?"

"Definitely." Derrick swallowed again. "No problem." Nuria. Another image blossomed in his fevered mind. His sister's hot little friend with the sinful gaze. The two of them—Nuria and Tori—together. His hips twitched.

"Good. Thanks, you're a doll."

"For you, anything."

Victoria laughed. "I doubt that."

He didn't. "Are you doing okay on that boat?"

"Yeah." Her voice dropped even lower and she sighed. "Everything is perfect."

His sister was back in the room. Derrick could tell by Tori's melting tone. "Good. Well, have fun and don't fall off unless you mean it."

"No worries on that. Dez won't let me out of her sight." His friend's voice was warm with love.

Derrick's mouth twisted. "Good. Well go back to the party for two. I'll deliver the package as soon as I get it."

"Great. I'll see you soon."

"Later." Derrick hung up the phone and blinked, bringing Trish's face back into focus. He gently squeezed her ass. "Now, where were we?"

Her face was cool, the passion bled away and gone. "Couldn't you have waited to answer the phone?"

"It might have been important."

She made a noise. "Well, obviously this isn't important." She gestured to their joined bodies.

"Of course it—"

She abruptly pulled her body away from his, struggled off his lap and out of the chair. "I have to go prepare for my meeting."

His dick cooled quickly in the air, bobbing and still hard, abandoned in the mouth of his cotton pajamas with the striped blue cotton rucked up under his balls. "Trish."

But she was gone. *Fuck.* He stripped off the rubber, tossed it, and tucked himself away before turning to face the window and pick up the wedding invitation again. The wedding was finished, brought to a graceful close in Montreal while most of the brides' family and friends watched. The trip up to Canada, the wedding itself, and the reception had passed by in a mad blur. But he remembered the bachelor party, an event that he insisted on planning as part of a scheme to show that Dez was still the same thoughtless fuck machine she always was. But things hadn't quite taken shape as he planned.

He paid strippers to come to the hotel, a suite on the other side far from where his mother lay snug in her bed. They were the kind of girls he always assumed his sister liked—sexually aggressive with big asses and small tits, slim waists, and the willingness to do anything given the right financial incentive. With Dez's friend Rémi and a half-dozen others there, the girls arrived with music and tricks, costumes, and whips meant to excite.

"You don't have to do this for me," Dez kept saying well up until the women swarmed the chair where Derrick stationed her in the center of the room.

His sister's particular preference had inspired Derrick, and he paid the girls extra for half of them to come in drag. As they trooped out, all four of them, he heard several in-drawn breaths in the room, including his own. The feminine ones, two of them, wore corsets that tightly cinched their waists but left their breasts bare except for sequined pasties. Their long legs were made even longer with fishnet stockings, garters, and stilettos. Two women in their red and gold satin corsets, with breasts curving high and smooth and their magazine cover-girl faces. Deep red lipstick, bare throats, sloe eyes.

The ones in drag were no less appealing in black slacks, suspenders, and white undershirts worn tight over their breasts and their hair swept back from their smooth, sparsely made-up faces. The women staged a burlesque fantasy for Dez, dancing around her to Monifah's "Touch it," pressing their breasts against her face, dipping between her legs to sniff and nuzzle her crotch, biting her ear. His sister indulged them. But with her cigar clamped between her teeth and a gentle but firm shake of her head when one of the women tried to unzip her pants or take off her shirt, she didn't touch any of them.

In fact, it was Derrick who ended up with one of the girls on her knees in front of him, her wet mouth pulling at his dick as he leaned against the wall, gasping for air. The party broke up sometime after four in the morning with a sardonic Rémi escorting Dez from the suite to get her ready for the big event only a few hours away. Overall, the night hadn't turned out quite as he would have liked, but it wasn't a complete disappointment either.

Derrick stood up from the chair and walked to the window. It was difficult to tell sometimes where his happiness for his best friend and his sister ended and where his jealousy began. Tori was his first, he wanted to say. But that wasn't quite the truth. She had always been gay, and he knew that. Still, it didn't stop him from thinking that he could get her to change her mind about men. About him. But she hadn't changed her mind. She chose his sister instead.

The moment Tori met Dez—who was nearly as tall as Derrick, was in shape, and had the manners of a prince when she wasn't being a pig—his best friend was gone. The knowledge was there the first time they met as he sat watching them. But the idea of it was so galling that he hadn't admitted it to himself until months later when he was sure that Tori was well on her way to heartbreak and Dez was just fucking around like she always did. But for once Dez was serious, and the two women hooked up, then ran off to Canada to get married.

Derrick sighed and dropped the card back on the window seat. In the street below, he thought he heard Trish's car pulling out of his garage and speeding off.

2

Derrick called Trish's office a few hours later and left a half-apologetic message, inviting her out to dinner with him that evening if she had the time. He grimaced at his tone on the machine, but better too much regret than none. His mother had raised him right, after all. Trish didn't call him back until Sunday afternoon.

"You're an asshole, Derrick," she said.

He winced but said nothing because she was right. It had been wrong of him to answer the phone when he did. But the truth was, if he got the chance to do it again, he would've done the same thing. Victoria would always come first.

As always with Trish, and with so many other women, there was something missing. No matter how beautiful they were, how skilled in the art of fucking, or "making love" as Trish preferred to call it, his mind always tumbled back to Victoria. No one was as sexy or as important as the woman who married his sister.

"But," Trish continued, "I'm going to go against my better

judgment and have dinner with you." She paused. "How about our usual place at six tonight?"

Derrick nodded, almost disappointed that she'd given in so easily. "That's perfect. I'll be there."

Heavy silence lingered between them. "I'm sorry," he finally said, sensing that she was waiting for something.

"Don't say things you don't mean." On the other end of the phone, Trish rustled papers. A sign of her irritation, Derrick thought. "See you tonight," she said.

Derrick already sat waiting at their table when Trish walked in. She wove through the restaurant, deliberately sexy in a high-waisted skirt that clung from ribs to calves. The wide leather belt that sat just below her breasts and a long-sleeved shirt, unbuttoned to show a teasing hint of cleavage, invited more than a few stares. Her stilettos made cruel music as she made her way toward him.

"I haven't seen this outfit before," he said, rising as she approached the table. "You look wonderful."

Knowing that she probably wouldn't allow it, Derrick didn't make any sort of move to kiss her. But as Trish sat down, a "thank you" fell from her lips, and her face softened. The dominatrix became a kitten.

"You fucker," she said with a reluctant smile. "Why do you have to look so damn fine?"

And he hadn't even apologized yet. What he had done was wear the aftershave she liked and the close-fitting dark jeans that Trish once confessed made her wet whenever she saw them on him.

"You bring out the best in me?" His tone was lightly joking, and she reached across the table to squeeze his hand. Just then, the waiter approached their table in his somber white and asked for their drink orders.

Trish briefly scanned the menu. "Iced tea, please."

Keeping in mind that he had work in the morning, Derrick ordered the same.

After the waiter drifted away, Trish leaned closer. Her heavy swing of hair released a tangerine scent that invited Derrick to come closer, too.

"Derrick," she murmured, as if afraid others nearby might hear her say his name. "Your incredible looks aside, you're the most sexual man I've ever been with." Derrick shifted his hand under hers, uncertain where this was going. "Even though it didn't seem that way when I was getting to know you, I soon realized that you're the kind of man who expresses himself a lot through sex. And I don't mind it." Trish squeezed his hand again. "Far from it. I love that you want to experience all this with me, especially after almost two years of being together. But what happened yesterday . . ."

She broke off as if imagining the feel of him inside her, the two of them moving in the leather chair, how she held herself naked over him, only to have him look away to answer the phone, then keep talking as they fucked. Trish glanced down at the table, then met Derrick's eyes again. "I felt like you completely disregarded me."

Before he could say anything, she continued. "Now, I know that Victoria is a big part of your life, Derrick. Not only is she your best friend, but now she's basically your sister-in-law." His eyes briefly flickered down as she leaned even closer. Trish, seeing this, drew her hand from under his to pluck closed the V of cloth over her breasts. "I want boundaries. Answering a call when we're in the middle of making love doesn't show me any respect at all. And I really want that from you, Derrick."

He nodded. And kept his eyes from her breasts. It was only fair. He closed his mouth over the easy excuses that came to his mind. How to explain that he had some vague hope that Tori would change her mind on the honeymoon and discover that it was Derrick she wanted after all and not his substitute sister? His hopes were unrealistic, even a little bit foolish, but that didn't stop him from holding on to them.

"You've always had that, Trish. But I will make sure to *show* you that more in the future."

She smiled in relief, her fingers still toying with her blouse. "You know, I had all sorts of ideas that this dinner wasn't going to go well. I don't know why."

"I don't know why either." He sat back in his chair. "Let's just enjoy tonight and carry on with our lives. Okay?"

"Okay."

Although he thought briefly about it, Derrick didn't invite Trish to spend the night with him. His excuse of work in the morning was technically valid, but he didn't need that much sleep in order to function at work.

That night, he worked out in the weight room until well after two, doing sit-ups and lifting weights, pushing himself through rep after rep until sweat ran down his tight and twitching body in a swift river. His muscles burned and trembled. The mirrored walls reflected his body back at him—shoulders and back rippling with tight muscle and sweat, ass solid under the loose gray shorts, thighs and legs thick and contoured. Derrick rubbed his palms over his solid pecs, his abs standing out in sharp relief under his skin, his damp belly. He didn't want to think about Trish. Didn't want to think about Tori with Dez. Didn't want to think at all. But no matter how hard he pushed his body, no matter how he ached, the thoughts crashed down on him in the mirrored room until he was just as weak as before.

3

The package Dez sent was actually an envelope with two smaller ones tucked inside. One addressed to him and the other to her friend. Derrick called Nuria the next day. The phone rang twice before a slightly accented female voice answered.

"Yes?"

He leaned back in his chair, watching his computer boot up in preparation for the day. "Nuria. This is Derrick. Dez's brother." Silence. "Hello? Are you still there?"

"*Si.* Um. Yes. Sorry." Nuria's breathless laugh made him stop his pen's slow tap against the desk. "I'm just a little surprised."

"I know. Sorry to catch you off guard like this, but Dez gave me your number. She also gave me a package for you."

"Really? That's interesting."

"If that's the word you want to use. Listen, where can I drop the package for you?"

"You don't have to drop it anywhere. I can meet you and get it."

"How about"—he filed through the calendar on his Black-

Berry—"Thursday night at Yamagata's? I have a meeting there at eight."

She made another breathless sound. "Ah, that sounds good. I'll see you then."

"All right." He waited a beat to see if she wanted to say anything else; then he hung up the phone.

Nuria's hair lay across her back like a whip. The lights from the overhead lamps plucked out the colors in the separate strands of her dreadlocks—red, mahogany, deep amber. Even from behind, she was a beautiful woman. Focused and animated, she spoke quietly with her friends at their table in the Japanese restaurant. Her hands gestured. Her head turned to look at each woman in turn. The brown skin of her back looked like velvet framed in the white halter dress. Derrick crossed the restaurant, passing with murmured apologies between the full tables of laughing patrons. Wondering if her skin was as soft as it looked, he walked up to Nuria and touched her shoulder, said her name. She didn't stiffen, only turned around with a wet smile. Her platinum labret stud glinted in the light.

"I smelled you before you got here," she said.

The others at the table, Sage, Rémi, and Phillida, looked briefly at Derrick, greeting him with nods before turning back to their private conversation.

"I didn't think you remembered what I smell like. It's been a long time since I've seen you." *Too long*, his body said.

The times before when they'd run into each other, usually when she was a part of his sister's entourage, an electric attraction flared between them. He always ignored it. She was beautiful poison, but poison nonetheless.

"Has it?" Her eyes flickered over him, taking in the Joseph Abboud navy suit and blue paisley tie, and smiled just a bit more.

Derrick produced an envelope from his pocket, the package

from Dez, and handed it to her. "Here it is. The message was to make sure that I put it in your hands."

"That Dez." Nuria laughed softly. "Always one for the personal touch."

She didn't open the envelope. "Want to stay for a drink with us?"

"Thanks, but no. I have clients." He gestured vaguely behind him.

"That's too bad." She managed to pout and smile at the same time. "Maybe next time?"

"Maybe." He answered her smile with one of his own, then nodded at the other women at the table. "See you around."

He turned and walked away from her, his hand tingling from where he touched her skin. Derrick swore that he could still smell her hot perfume, something dark and sweet.

"That's a . . . lovely young lady," one of his firm's clients, Rafael Costa, said with a subtle leer as Derrick sat down at their table. The dark-haired man with the sprinkling of white at the temples looked old enough to be Nuria's father.

"Yes. Very." Alex Meyer turned slightly in his seat to get a better look at Nuria. His wedding ring winked under the light. "Is she yours?"

"No."

"Not yet, you mean." Costa chuckled. "I saw that look. It's only a matter of time."

Derrick gave them his most sincere fake smile. At the corner table, she shimmered brightest of all among her friends. He didn't find anything appealing about any of the others. They were too hard for him. Even the feminine one named Phil. Despite her soft clothes and flirtatious pouts, there was something about her that didn't appeal.

"She's not quite my style," Derrick said. "But either of you are welcome to try."

"You better watch what you say in front of Rafael here," Meyer said. "A wedding ring never stopped him before."

Costa shrugged. "My wife and I have an understanding. Just as we as men of business have an understanding." He lifted a hand that gleamed with a diamond pinky ring, signaling the waiter. "Send a drink to the young lady over there with the bare shoulders and the white dress," Costa said to the tuxedoed man when he came to their table. "Whatever she is drinking. With our compliments."

The waiter nodded and went to do the millionaire's bidding. When Nuria got the drink, she glanced over at the table, lifted her glass in salute, and smiled at the men. Derrick didn't know if he was disappointed or relieved when she didn't approach their table.

She and her friends left the restaurant before his table did, creating a small scene as they walked out, laughing softly together. Derrick was very aware of eyes watching the women, covetously snatching glimpses of their tight and toned bodies as they wove carelessly through the restaurant. The scent of a long night's party trailed behind them.

Derrick's attention and eyes returned to the table only to encounter Costa's amused smile. "Only a matter of time," the other man said, cutting into his steak.

At home later that evening, Derrick sat on his patio with a glass of tomato juice and his thoughts. He rubbed his eyes tiredly. The firm had been working him long hours over the last month. Rafael Costa, one of their biggest clients, found himself in very real danger of going to jail if Silverman, Johnson, and Meyer didn't build up a credible defense and pull a rabbit out of their ass at the last minute. Derrick was on that team of weary magicians. He sighed and took a deep drink of his juice. The next few weeks were going to be even more intense, more crucial. That meant this was going to be his last night of rest.

"That's why they pay you the big dollars." Derrick smiled wryly to himself as he gazed up at the stars.

Without looking, he reached over to the patio table and picked up the envelope that Dez sent him in the mail. It smelled slightly like the sea.

Take a night off from the usual, Dez wrote. *There's something at this place I think you'll like.*

The thick slip of paper under her note was a ticket. Black with silver lettering, it detailed an address, date, and time. Saturday. In two days. In a part of town he'd always thought of being too full of itself. Though a night off did sound good, he wasn't sure if he was ready for Dez's idea of not-his-usual. Derrick picked up the cell phone at his elbow.

"Hey, Jake," he said when his friend answered. "Have you ever heard of a place called Flaunt?"

Jake laughed. "Seriously? Flaunt is really hot right now. I'm surprised you haven't heard about it." Jake paused. "Then again, maybe not." He laughed again.

Derrick had known the other man since their undergrad years at the University of Miami. Jake enrolled in school not knowing what he wanted to do. When Derrick mentioned that he wanted to become a lawyer like his father, Jake shrugged his shoulders, saying, "I could do that, too." But barely a year into the program at UM, his friend shrugged his shoulders again and said it just wasn't for him. Now Jake was a jazz musician earning a decent living in the city. "I'm not rich," Jake often said when Derrick chided him about getting a real job. "But I'm not sleeping in the streets either."

"Tickets to get into that place can be hard to come by, especially if they're having a good show."

"Is that right?" Derrick turned over the ticket in his hand. "I have one for the show this Saturday. How hard do you think it would be to get one for you?"

Jake laughed. "No worries. I know someone there."

"Cool. If you can't get the ticket, let me know. I'm sure we can work something out."

"Whatever, man. See you Saturday. I'll drop by your place to pick you up."

Derrick almost offered to drive. Jake owned a silver 1998 two-door Honda Accord. He kept the car in good shape, but it wasn't exactly a pussy wagon. But he let it go.

"That's cool," Derrick said. "See you then."

On Saturday night, Jake showed up looking fresh and ready. His dreadlocked hair was pulled back and bound with a plain leather thong in a style that went well with his simple black shirt and black slacks.

"The ladies there are hot, man," Jake said at Derrick's smiling look. "Even standing next to your ass, I'm sure I'll get some play tonight. Not every girl is taken in by the green."

Derrick's own look was all money. Gucci sunglasses covered his tired eyes, while designer jeans and a thin moss-colored long-sleeved shirt draped nicely over his body. The platinum Rolex flashed briefly against his wrist as he closed the car door.

"So Trish knows you're going to this place, Rick?" Jake put the car in gear and pulled smoothly out of the driveway.

"We're not together like that."

"You sure? Because I think that girl wants to lock you down for good. She might even have the wedding dress picked out already."

"Stop talking shit. She and I never had that conversation. As far as I know, that's not standard procedure after dating somebody for not even a year."

Jake laughed. "I hope you haven't said that to her face. Even *I* know that it's been about two years since you started kickin' it with her."

Really? It seemed like just a few months ago that he'd met Trish at the fund-raiser in Key West. Derrick made a dismissive noise. "People don't even have that conversation until year five or so."

"Shit. By then, some guys are ready to trade up for a new model."

"Only if you're a dick."

"You are what you are."

Derrick hummed in response but said nothing else. He'd known for a while now that he didn't want to marry Trish. She was a nice woman and a decent bed mate, but there was nothing about her that made him want to make her a permanent part of his life. They were having a good time with each other, and, for now, she fit well into his life. Trish knew a lot of the same people he did. Their tastes were similar. And they could always carry on a conversation on nearly anything under the sun. But that was it. Just because his twin had found a partner didn't mean that he was next in line.

"Trish is a nice woman," Derrick said. "She'd make someone a great wife."

"But not you?"

"Twenty-seven is too young for a man to get himself stuck with one woman."

"And which rule book are you going by?" Jake tossed an amused glance his way.

Derrick smiled slightly. "Mine."

From the outside, Flaunt looked like any other nightclub. The clientele was well dressed in silks, leathers, the latest hip-hop, and men's magazine fashions. Men, women, and people in between sauntered, sashayed, and glided by as Jake pulled the car slowly to the club's off-street parking lot. The trickling crowd making its way from the well-lit back parking lot watched the steady stream of cars just as the drivers and passengers watched them. One woman, wearing dangerously high

heels and a tiny mandarin-collared red dress that barely covered her ass cheeks, walked in the road, forcing cars to drive
slowly behind her, taking note of each shift of her bottom under
the red silk. Someone far back honked their horn, but Jake
seemed content to watch her parade of one until that dangerous
body of hers disappeared around the corner and into a large
SUV with its stereo blasting the latest Justin Timberlake song.

"I hope she's performing tonight." Jake flashed him a grin.
"That would be something to see."

"There's only one kind of show somebody like that would
put on," Derrick said.

"And there ain't nothin' wrong with that."

Both men laughed. Jake parked the car, and they walked the
gauntlet of stares, seeming to meet the approval of the critical
eyes passing over them. They gave their tickets at the door and
went quickly into the dimly lit club. Despite the relentless
stream of people making its way through the tall double doors,
the inside of Flaunt was surprisingly comfortable. The cavernous, two-level space easily fit the crowd, allowing most people to move about without having to squeeze chest to chest or
even shoulder to shoulder with everyone else there. Cool air
washed through the club while strobe lights flashed, conversation buzzed, and laughter fizzed fresh and intoxicating, like
bubbles from the first sip of champagne. It was early yet.

The people at Flaunt were sharper than the ones Derrick
was used to. Their smiles rested on the edge of razor blades,
and their sexual energy burned electric along his skin. A woman
brushed against his shoulder, not because she had to but because she could. And Derrick felt her heat, smelled the pungency
of her sex, through the poured-on black slacks and barely-there
lace blouse. Her look was wet and inviting. When he didn't respond to her less-than-subtle command, her entire body seemed
to shrug and move on, cutting through the throng like a scythe.

"Trust my sister to know about someplace like this." Derrick raised his voice to be heard above the loud thudding music.

"Dez was the one who gave you the ticket?" Jake asked as the two men made their way to the bar.

"Who else?"

"I didn't think you two were that tight anymore."

"We reconnected over the Tori thing." Derrick shot Jake a look. "And don't say it." Jake knew how pissed and jealous he was that Dez hooked up with Tori.

His friend chuckled. "I wasn't going to say a word." He leaned against the bar and signaled the bartender. "But that's nice. She'd definitely have the lowdown about tonight."

Jake had met Dez a few times over the years, and Derrick's friend was inexplicably attracted to her. For reasons of her own, Dez entertained Jake, going out with him on a few "dates" that she'd later dismissed as "boys' night out." During one of these get-togethers, she told Jake the deal with her liking women, and he showed his disappointment but remained respectful. He still asked Derrick about her every now and then.

When the bartender finally came their way, Derrick ordered a Red Stripe while Jake had his usual Miller Light. Flaunt was shaped like a coliseum, with a bar level where they stood, and above, a higher, wider level with a railing that people leaned against, watching the action below. There was a railing on their level, too. Derrick nodded toward it and Jake followed, barely paying attention to him. Everyone in the place was appealing, and he couldn't seem to keep his eyes from bouncing from stimuli to stimuli while Derrick chuckled softly. And *he* thought he'd be the one looking like a bumpkin tonight.

At the railing, the room sank, opening up to a view of a stage and another room below. The stage was empty, but it was still early. Barely eleven o'clock.

"We'll get a better view if we go downstairs." Jake gestured to a staircase near a wall leading down. The room below was nearly an exact replica of the one they came in through except that the stage was at the very center of the room and there was no railing to separate it from the crowd. By sheer luck, they found a small table with two stools and sat down.

"Can you even see with those things on?" Jake indicated Derrick's shades.

"Not really."

"Then what's the deal?"

"If I see something worth looking at, I'll take them off."

"Poser."

"Somebody's got to do it."

Derrick smiled at his friend, knowing that Jake saw him as flawed and fucked up but still liked him anyway. They'd been through too much for the affection not to be there between them. He'd seen Derrick through the worst of his infatuation with Victoria, warned him to back off and not hold hopes about her turning straight just for him. But Derrick never listened, and here he was. Nursing a six-year-old wound that would probably ache for a lifetime.

"Remember when I first met Tori?" he asked suddenly, taking a sip of his beer and watching the beautiful throng ebb and flow around them.

"Yeah. Your mind was gone the second you saw those tits of hers."

True enough. Then what kept his interest was her willingness to accept him for who he was. Between his recklessness that led to an AIDS scare, his general moodiness, and obsessive need to succeed, Derrick was surprised that Tori stuck with him. She hadn't taken any of his shit, but she never gave up on him either. Derrick really loved that woman.

"They are definitely nice tits," he said.

Jake watched him quietly. "Why don't you drink something a little stronger? It's been a long week."

Derrick's gaze swept the room. Anticipation throbbed in the

air around him, bouncing off his skin in waves that made the small hairs prickle. "I just might do that."

A few minutes later, Jake left the table, then came back with a glass of scotch. Neat, just the way he liked it. Derrick nodded his thanks and tossed his drink back, mentally saying good-bye to a sober night. By the time the music stopped, signaling that the show onstage was about to start, the edges of his mental exhaustion had been rubbed smooth by the scotch. After a second glass, then a third, he was floating.

Strobe lights flickered around the otherwise dark room, directing the attention of the thickening crowd to the raised stage. With a sound of boot heels in the suddenly quiet club, a tall woman strode onto the stage. She held a microphone loosely in one hand and wore a cool but strangely inviting smile. Derrick put his nearly empty glass down. The riding boots, jodhpurs, and white long-sleeved shirt fit her slender body well, pressing tightly to breasts, flat belly, and curved hips. Her hair, pulled back from her face to show off its severe lines, trailed down her back in a long ponytail. The crowd hushed.

"Welcome to Flaunt," the woman said, her voice a cigarette-roughened caress. "This evening, we have something very special for you."

She paused and the crowd applauded loudly on cue as if they knew exactly what that special thing was. As the applause died away, she smiled, flashing white teeth that burned against her brown skin.

"A birthday girl will have one of her dearest wishes fulfilled for her tonight." The woman's eyes gleamed. "If you want to help make this night a memorable one, there's a line for spanks backstage after the show." Delighted laughter erupted with the applause this time. "Now, without further delay—Lady Leo!"

The woman sauntered off the stage to more applause that quickly tapered off as the crimson curtain lifted. A bed lay in the middle of the stage, slowly turning. Derrick's skin jumped as a thick, rhythmic drumbeat, like a heart at rest, began to bleed from the speakers.

A woman lay on her back in a pool of light against white sheets. On the bed, her body was soft and seductive, the face relaxed. Derrick knew that face. Nuria. She sighed against the sheets, her mouth the perfect picture of innocence corrupted.

"Nice," Jake breathed at his side.

Derrick blindly reached up and tore the sunglasses off his face. Nuria's body lay sprawled on the bed in sumptuous abandon. And in case anyone in the club wasn't lucky enough to see every sigh from her wet mouth up close, the image of her flared to life on every monitor scattered throughout the club. The pulsing music grew louder.

As the bed stopped its slow revolution, men in bright color began to appear. Red. Blue. Green. Purple. Liquid latex covered their gym-hardened bodies. The glistening material clearly outlined each part of them, showing that they wore nothing other than a cup and string that were supposed to be underwear. In other circumstances, this scenario would be laughable. Nearly naked grown men prancing around in public with only their faces uncovered by latex but still hidden with simple Zorrolike masks. Right. But under the bright lights with the heavy music and Nuria resting in the white bed, an air of palpable menace settled in the room. The music rose higher. Thicker.

Light glinted off the men's flesh as they came closer to Nuria. And closer. They neared the bed, and she finally seemed to become aware of them. She sat up in the sheets, and Derrick lost his breath. Her dreds tumbled around her shoulders in disordered curls. Her breasts heaved under the loose lace nightgown. The wet red of her mouth parted in a terrified gasp.

Nuria shivered and the music made choreography of her fear, her curls shaking as she stared at the creatures surrounding the bed. Her long thighs spread wide under the short dress. The creatures crawled onto the bed, and she scrambled up on her knees in fear, breasts heaving under the white lace, nipples hard. She licked her lips. Derrick swore her eyes flashed on him. The alcohol rushed potently through his blood, but it felt like her gaze, flaring like heat over his skin. The animalistic men crawled toward her, hands grasping, pulling at the barely-there fabric, at her skin. They squeezed her thighs. Her nightgown ripped, exposing a shoulder, the tops of her breasts.

I want to fuck you like an animal.

Derrick shuddered as the words of the song settled into his spine and spilled into his hips. He swallowed past his dry throat. With Purple and Green at her back, the bed began to turn again, and she leaned into their caresses. Red dipped between her thighs with his thick hands, and her neck arched. Her face was gorgeous in its pleasure. But Green spun her roughly to him, completely ripping off her nightgown. Her look changed. She pushed him and the others back and leapt gracefully from the bed. Standing up and closer to the crowd. Derrick could see that she wore latex, too. The material glowed a deep chocolate brown, matching her skin perfectly. Brown stilettos made her taller than usual under the lights.

Before the latex men could follow her, Nuria grabbed a bullwhip from the shadows. The first crack shook the crowd. It snapped through the heavy industrial music, bringing everyone's attention to the sleek muscles in her arms. Derrick swallowed again. She was truly Lady Leo, a lion with her thick mane long and curling around her face, eyes fierce as they surveyed her territory. The latex men stiffened, then subsided in the bed, their eyes fastened onto Nuria. When she turned away from the audience to face them, Derrick's dick jumped. Her ass was a miracle of symmetry, a curving apple that made his teeth ache to bite into it. The muscles of her back shifted just beneath skin and latex as she moved in a lightning motion, cracking the whip toward the captive men. Green flinched. The latex over his belly split open. The whip sounded again, and Purple, with his back to her, arched forward in agony as his latex split from the whip's expert slap.

Nuria stalked toward Purple and ripped back the ruptured latex skin covering his back, baring his pale flesh, the swell of muscle and sinew, peeling more of the purple skin away to bare a muscular buttock, a solid thigh. With a sneer, Nuria shoved him down to his belly in the bed. Green flinched again when she turned to him, the whip in one hand, the fingers of the other hand curled to talons that ripped away his green skin, cleared the fake color from his thickly muscled chest, his belly, showing the black string of his underwear, the sharp line of muscle, the swell of his dick under the cloth. Her finger hooked in the string, and Nuria arched a naughty eyebrow at the audience. A chorus of whistles rose in the crowd, both masculine and feminine encouragement to strip the man naked. But Nuria only snapped the string against his supple flesh and moved away.

She modeled for the crowd again, showing off the flex and release of the muscles in her thighs and legs. The delectable bounce of her ass and breasts. With an abrupt turn, she cracked the whip in the air, snarling, and the men slid meekly from the bed. They crawled on the floor toward her feet, grasping at her long legs.

Another crack of the whip and the men flinched. They jumped back from her. She lashed the floor in front of her. Once. Twice. Three times. The music pulsed. And they all lined up on their bellies in front of her, their bodies writhing to the music. Doubling the whip and grasping it tightly in her two hands, she backed up toward the now-stationary bed until she was sitting on it, her thighs splayed wide. The liquid latex made it obvious that her pubes were completely shaved. Her clit stood up hard and thick under the glistening material. The platform holding the bed began to slowly turn again.

Nuria summoned to her animals on the floor with an imperious finger. The green man settled between her thighs, hands resting lightly on her knees and his head held low so the audience could see her. He began to lap at her pussy through the latex.

The music throbbed, thick and sex-drenched, reaching for a high crescendo. But Nuria seemed to hold it off, gesturing again to the men. And they all came, one after the other, worshipfully, pushing her back gently on the bed and tending to her. Blue knelt upside down over her to settle his mouth over her breasts, licking and sucking her latex-covered nipples. Red and Purple abased themselves at Nuria's feet. They licked her shoes and worshipfully stroked her slender calves. The camera zoomed in on Red's tongue moving wetly over the brown leather of her stilettos. Glistening with effort and latex, the men's muscled backs, thighs, and asses rose and fell to the music. The sound of drums dropped away, leaving only tinny piano music and the low moans coming from Nuria in the bed. Darkness abruptly descended on the stage. Applause erupted. Wolf whistles and catcalls sounded from all corners of the club.

"I think I just came in my shorts."

"Maybe you should have kept that one to yourself," Derrick said, but he wasn't far from that himself. He knew that Dez and her friends were into some kinky shit, but he'd never seen any of it until now. He felt like someone abruptly flung a door open on something that he wasn't ready to see. Something that made his balls ache and his mouth go dry.

"I wouldn't mind giving her a birthday spank," Jake said.

Derrick shook himself out of his stupor. "There *is* an open invitation to go backstage and help her out with that."

Jake looked at Derrick like he'd lost his mind. "Seriously?"

"Why not?"

After asking the bartender how to get backstage, Derrick went to find Nuria with Jake a nearly panting presence behind him. They found her in the darkened dressing room surrounded by adorants. Still wearing her latex, she lay over Green's knee squirming under his light slaps. His hand connected with her shapely bottom with a delicate sound.

Nuria laughed and stood up when he was finished. "Somebody has to do better than that."

Derrick was surprised that no one rushed to take her up on the offer. Then again, maybe not. She looked delectable just standing there in the flesh-colored material, shimmering and gorgeous for the eye and the cock to appreciate.

"Happy birthday," he said, raising his voice to be heard.

Her eyes immediately found him along with everybody else's. "Thanks. I wondered if you would show up." She slid through the crowd of two dozen or so and came closer. Her smell—of rubber, sweat, and spiced perfume—made him want to slide into her skin. "Dez said you might." In her high heels, she was nearly at his height. Her breath teased his face.

"Can I take you out for a drink to celebrate your birthday?" Derrick found himself asking. He didn't know where the words came from, but he certainly didn't want to take them back.

Her lashes flickered in surprise. "Sure. Why not?"

At his side, Jake cleared his throat and straightened the collar of his shirt.

"Oh, this is my friend Jake." He gestured between them. "Jake, this is Nuria. A friend of Dez."

"A pleasure," he said, kissing the back of her hand. Nuria chuckled and watched him through slumberous eyes. Her hair slid over her shoulders.

She reluctantly took her hand back and turned back to her crowd. "*Gracias*, all. Thanks for coming. As usual, much love. After-party at my house."

The people quickly dispersed, leaving Nuria, Jake, and Derrick alone in the suddenly large dressing room. Nuria kicked off her shoes and turned her back to Derrick.

"Help me get out of this thing, will you?" At his puzzled look, she smiled. "Just peel it off."

Jake cleared his throat and backed out of the way. Between Derrick's hands, the latex felt slick and warm from Nuria's body. He ripped it away, gradually revealing the cocoa brown skin, its tiny hairs, and the richer smell of her sweat. And her arousal. The latex parted over her back, her bottom, the lean length of her thighs. On his knees, Derrick could smell her, could almost taste the salt sea of her. Up close, he noticed that she had a tattoo of a black sun sitting in the shallow cup of her lower back.

He vaguely heard Jake mumble something about having to make a call before his friend stumbled from the room. At the front of her body, he peeled up, slowly, over her pubes, her belly, and her breasts until it was just her. He crushed the latex in his hand and threw it in the trash bin under the make-up table.

"You're very thorough," Nuria murmured. Her dark-tipped breasts moved with each breath. A fine layer of sweat rested above her upper lip.

"I like to think so," Derrick said, equally softly. Then he was leaning closer, his breath brushing against her lips.

She kissed him. Lips gently brushed his, almost to see if he would turn away. Derrick took what she offered, opening his mouth over hers, licking her lips open before diving into her sweetness. Nuria tasted like hot spices. Even through his alcohol haze, he savored her uniqueness. Suddenly, he had to have more of her. He pushed her against the wall, devouring her mouth like a man starved of nourishment. And she opened up for him. Groaned for him. Nuria sank her fingers into his back. Her skin burned hot through his shirt, and her scent nearly overwhelmed him. Derrick lifted her, grabbed her ass, and pulled her against him. Her legs slipped up and around his waist.

His dick rose hot and hard between them, pressing against her heat. He fumbled with his zipper.

"No," she gasped. "Not here."

Why not here? He pushed against her, imprinting her wet-ness on his jeans.

"Where?" He gasped the question, beyond thinking. Then, "Come home with me." He kissed her full mouth, biting her lip. "Come home with me."

She nodded. "Okay."

With fists clenched in his pockets, Derrick watched her with hawklike attention as she dressed, shielding her body from his gaze, in a gray tube dress and black high-heeled boots that came up to her knees. His body ached with need for her. He felt feverish, hand trembling, his belly whirling with butterflies.

"Ready." Nuria grabbed her purse and kissed him roughly, igniting the taste of blood between them. "I'll drive."

In her car, a surprising white BMW Z4 convertible, he forced himself to keep his hands off her as he gave gruff direc-tions to his house in Fort Lauderdale. The miles crawled by as they sat in the silence saturated by their desire. She drove com-petently, quickly, her full lower lip caught between her teeth. Her thighs, shifting beneath the short dress as she changed gears, hypnotized him. Derrick's heart beat a fierce tattoo in his chest, thumping in what he was sure was an audible rhythm. It had to be the alcohol. There was no other reason for him to want her like this. None.

Before the car even pulled into his driveway, he was reaching for his keys. She turned the car off and came to him in a click of high heels and the scent of good things to come. Their mouths met, and they crab-walked backward to the door, stuck to each other. Wrestling the key into the hole, the door open, and the alarm off, Derrick had never felt so hungry for another human being in his life. They fell back against the door, still joined at the lips, panting into each other's mouths.

He reached for her dress, pulled it over her head, then impa-tient with his own clothes, tugged off his shirt, exploding but-tons all over his hardwood floor.

"Wait," Nuria said, her mouth wet and bruised. "I want to see you." she stepped back, naked except for her boots and the diamond studs winking in her ears.

Her eyes moved over him, devouring his body, his taut belly, curved shoulders and rigid biceps from his daily work-out, the tent his dick made under his pants. Derrick unbuckled his belt, unzipped his jeans. She turned and walked away from him. *Ah. That ass.* He followed.

"I thought you were getting me a birthday drink."

His brain froze. *A drink? Was she joking?* A shake of her head told him no. As he poured her a scotch with shaky hands, Nuria posed against the railing, spreading her arms along the burnished metal, resting her body against five rungs of rounded railing. Away from the stage, away from the club, she was even more incredible—gym-hardened muscles shifting under soft skin, small breasts that would nicely overflow his mouth, her shaved pussy. Beyond the railing and upstairs lay his bedroom, but he doubted they'd make it that far.

"Your place is nice," she murmured as he approached her with the drink in his hand.

"I'm glad you like it."

Right now he didn't care if she thought this was a hole she never wanted to set foot in again. As long as she let him touch her.

Nuria watched him, tongue darting out to lick her lips. It was as if she'd licked his dick. His hips jerked. Derrick handed her the drink. But she didn't take it.

"That's for you," she said.

What the fuck?

She shook her hair back off her shoulders, pushing out her breasts even more, drawing his eyes to their dark peaks, the flat belly, and the clit swelling between her spread legs. Nuria was performing for him, only now his living room was the stage.

"Pour it on me. Drink it off."

She didn't have to tell him twice. He poured the scotch on her, soaking her shoulders, breasts, belly, thighs, legs. The golden liquid splashed down on his dark cherry hardwood floors. But he didn't give a damn. He caught his breath at the glistening temptation of her. Derrick moved in quickly, mouth open, dick hard. The whiskey was hot and burned his throat going down, but she burned hotter, the slick curve of her shoulders, the weight of her breasts, her nipples under his tongue.

Derrick dropped to his knees, worshipful, licking her belly, drinking every drop from her skin as he went. Whiskey dampened his pants. Above him, she moaned softly, encouraging him with a light hand on his hair. He spread her legs even wider as he came to the juncture of her thighs. There was no whiskey there, but he parted her cunt lips with his tongue, dipping in to taste her salty heat, then out again to suck on her clit, to tease it, to hum against it. She gasped. Nuria was wet, and he was hard, aching. He needed to bury himself inside her. He would die right here without it.

Derrick shoved down his pants and stood up. He looked at her, with her skin wet from his mouth, from the whiskey, her dark eyes watching him with insistent desire. Groaning, he moved toward her again.

"Where's your rubber?"

Stupid. Stupid that he should have forgotten. Derrick stumbled back, pants around his ankles, as he rummaged in the side table and came up with a packet; he ripped it open and came back for her.

"Go ahead," she said. "I want to see you put it on. I want to watch you."

He rolled the rubber over the thick length of his dick. It throbbed for her. It ached to be inside her. Nuria took him in her hands, feeding him the warmth of her through the latex.

"I'm really enjoying my birthday," she murmured, lightly stroking the upward curve of him. His pulse thundered in her fingers. Derrick's cock surged forward in her hand, hungry for friction. He would burst if she didn't give him what they both wanted. But he knew if he made a wrong move, if he did something she didn't want, this night would be over before it began. "Fuck me," she hissed.

And he almost cried in relief. Derrick parted her pussy lips, skated his fingers over her wet clit as he guided his heavy dick inside her. She was liquid heaven. Her pussy swallowed him, clenched him so tightly within its walls that he nearly sobbed with pleasure. Her booted legs immediately wrapped around his waist, pulling him even deeper into her.

"Fuck me."

He shoved into her, desire hot and hard in his belly, his need for her making him incoherent. She sizzled. Her flesh burned against him. Her gasping breath scorched his throat. Derrick grabbed her hips, holding her steady for his relentless thrusts, for his own driving heat that was driving him out of his mind. She clasped him, met him thrust for thrust, lust for lust. The slapping wetness of their bodies moving together loosened a groan in him. Her fingers curled around the railing, her anchor while she dueled with him. Their hips moved faster.

Her fingers flew from the railing. She grasped his head, twisted her fingers in his hair, and forced his mouth down to hers. Their teeth clashed, their tongues twined, their hips fucked. Sensation tumbled in his belly. His skin was aflame. Around him, her pussy grasped hot and certain. Nuria gasped in his mouth. Her fingers tightened even more in his hair, the nails digging into his scalp.

She came hard around him, her pussy walls undulating with her pleasure. And pushed him over the edge. The world exploded in a kaleidoscope of color behind his tightly closed eyes. *Oh fuck. Fuck. Fuck.* The railing shuddered as he spasmed inside her, his hips jerking before finally resting still. Her breath puffed against his chest. Slowly he pulled back so he could look at her, but her legs twisted around his waist and the leather boots pressed into his ass, not allowing him to withdraw from her pussy completely.

Nuria twitched around him, and they both groaned.

"I like this." She grasped his face in her hands, rubbing her fingers through the thin oval of hair surrounding his mouth. "One day soon I'd like to feel it rubbing against my pussy again." Smiling, she drew her thumb over his lips. "I want to see my juices caught up in it."

Derrick smiled back at her. "That can be arranged."

"Good." She let him go, unwinding her legs and pulling away so his softening dick slid wetly from her. "I have to go."

What? He'd caught himself imagining her in his bed all night, fucking her until they were both sore and satisfied.

"You can stay the night if you want." Then his mind flickered to Trish. Before he could correct himself, Nuria shook her head.

"Nice of you to say, but I have a birthday party to go to." She bent to retrieve her dress from the floor, then drew it on in one quick motion. "Thanks for the drink."

Nuria blew him a kiss as she walked quickly to the front door and disappeared through it.

4

"Did you fuck her?"

Jake's voice on the other end of his cell phone woke Derrick from a very deep sleep. He didn't even know why he answered the phone. Yes, he did. On the off chance that it was Nuria calling.

He sat up in bed and scrubbed a hand over his face. "What do you think?" A groan leaked out of him as his feet pressed into the Berber rug on the hardwoods.

"I think that Trish is looking in the wrong place for an engagement ring." Jake's tone was glib.

"This doesn't have anything to do with Trish."

Jake was silent for a moment. "Is that how you're going to play it?"

"For now, yes. I might not even see Nuria again." But he wanted to. Badly.

"All right, man. Just don't be surprised when this shit blows up in your face."

Derrick stopped in midstep across his bedroom floor. "Are you going to tell her?"

"Why the hell would I do that?" Jake didn't wait for an answer. "You know that this town is very small. Not to mention karma's a bitch."

"Karma is not my problem." Derrick chuckled, throwing open the window. The sun sparkled on everything below, burning the landscape in brilliant shades of red, green, and terra-cotta. "But I will make sure to keep my private business on the low-low."

"Good luck with that."

Derrick laughed again. "I don't need luck."

After he hung up with Jake, Derrick showered and changed, then grabbed his briefcase and headed to the office. It was a Sunday, but he still needed to do some research and prepare briefs for the Costa case before work on Monday morning. But sitting in front of his computer with his eighty-page document open on the screen, Derrick's mind kept wandering to Nuria. His fingers stubbornly clung to the memory of sliding over Nuria's skin, touching her nipples, peeling the latex from her body, gripping her hips to fuck her deeper. In the brightness of day, he thought that his drunken obsession with her would go away. But if anything, it was the opposite. Now he knew what she tasted like. How she sounded when she came. And he wanted more.

His dick hardened, begging for the chance to slide into her again. Derrick adjusted himself and refocused on the computer screen. *I don't have time for this bullshit.* With the mouse gripped beneath his palm, he neatly excised a paragraph from his growing document. *Better.* Derrick nodded to himself, about to replace the deleted text with another when the phone rang.

"Hey, Derrick. I thought you were going to call me yesterday." Trish's voice bit him lightly on the ear.

He straightened in his chair. "Shit, I'm sorry. I didn't realize." A quick glance at his watch told him it was nearly two. *Shit.* "Do you have time to have lunch with me today? I'm at the office right now."

"Of course I have time for a quick bite with you." Her voice was softly apologetic, as if he'd accused her of neglect. "I didn't know you were working this weekend."

"There's nothing to be sorry for." Guilt grabbed him neatly in the throat. He coughed.

"Here I am about to complain when you've had to slave away for your firm all weekend."

"What they pay me is hardly slave wages, so I'll survive." He didn't correct her assumption that he had worked Saturday as well. "So can you meet me here in a half hour?"

She paused as if double-checking her calendar. "How about an hour?"

"That's good. It'll give me time to wrap some of this up."

A little over an hour later, she breezed into his office, smelling of the ocean and sun. Trish's hair lay pinned back against her head, revealing the curves of her heart-shaped face while the belted yellow T-shirt dress and sandals made her look like a college girl on spring break.

"Hey, handsome." Trish leaned down to kiss him briefly on the mouth.

Did she like the facial hair? The thought crept unbidden to his mind, along with the image of eating Nuria's pussy, smearing her cunt juices all over his face and into the hair around his mouth, then kissing her deeply afterward. What the fuck was wrong with him?

"We can walk to Thai food down the block," he said to Trish, dropping his BlackBerry into his pocket.

Outside, Derrick squinted at the sky, irritated at himself for forgetting his sunglasses.

"So"—he pushed his extra thoughts aside and forced himself to focus completely on Trish, who slid her arm through his and grinned up at him—"how was your beach meeting?"

5

_____

Derrick waited four days to call Nuria. When it became obvious that she wasn't going to take advantage of caller ID and seek him out, he used the number that Dez gave him.

"When can I see you again?" he asked as soon as she answered the phone.

Her husky laughter made him immediately hard. "Would it bother you if I said never?"

"I wouldn't believe you." His briefcase made a dull sound as he dropped it on the couch. With a few quick tugs, he loosened and pulled off his tie.

"You'd be a cocky fucker, then. You and your sister have that in common."

Here comes Dez again. "People are too quick to interpret self-confidence as cockiness," he said.

"I just call it like I see it."

"So, when can I see you?"

Her laughter stroked him again. "How about Friday night?"

"Okay."

He had to work late that night but would meet her wherever

she wanted. Hopefully here at his house. Derrick poured himself a glass of scotch, watching the golden liquid braid into the glass. Remembering how it had tasted fresh from Nuria's skin.

"There's a party in the Grove. I'll text you the address."

"What's the dress code?"

She paused. "Whatever you're wearing now is fine."

Derrick looked down at his dress shirt and slacks. "You sure about that?"

"Positive." She hung up the phone.

Derrick would have liked to say that he waited patiently for Friday to come. But that would be an outright lie. He almost took Jake up on his laughing offer of two Ritalin tabs to help him focus on work instead of the way it would feel the next time he slid into Nuria. Or the way her mouth was lush and red and pink inside and how it would enfold his cock and suck him into heaven.

On Friday, he showed up at the address she sent him dressed in slacks and a long-sleeved shirt rolled up at the elbows. The house, surrounded by tall palm trees and with a circular drive and front yard hidden from the streets by a gate, was not far from his mother's. As he stepped out of his car, he took out his phone and called Nuria.

"Are you here?" she asked.

"Why don't you come out here and find out?"

"Uh-uh, baby. I'm not playing that game." Laughter exploded somewhere near her, and Derrick missed whatever she said next.

"Sorry, I didn't catch that. Say it one more time."

"Come into the house. Walk up the stairs and go to the back of the house. I'm on the terrace."

Derrick's mouth twisted. They were going to be playing her games, then. "Yes, mistress," he said. "Whatever you say."

"Don't say that to me unless you mean it," she purred. "I could use an obedient boy in my life."

He found her easily, leaning against a garden terrace sharing space with a bunch of what his sister would laughingly called "urban professionals." Nuria's curled hair moved like eels around her face as she spoke with a graying bright-skinned man, hands gesturing gracefully through the air with each word. The man looked relaxed with his hand in his pants pocket, not at all intimidated to be facing a sex goddess. As Derrick drew closer, begging pardon as he passed through the light crowd, he realized they were speaking in Spanish.

"Derrick," Nuria exclaimed softly when she saw him. She gave him a light peck on the cheek, sliding her hand under his jacket to rest against his back. "I'm glad you could make it." She glanced back at her friend. "Tony, this is Derrick."

Derrick gripped Tony's hand and smiled politely. Somehow he'd expected a raucous party with half-naked women and men, not this polite gathering of accountant- and lawyer-looking types that made Derrick immediately feel at ease. Yet not. A woman beside him laughed, brushing his back with her elbow as she leaned into her male friend.

"Good to meet you," Tony said. His mouth twitched as he looked at Nuria. "If you'll both excuse me, I think I've ignored my wife for far too long."

"*Bien,*" Nuria said with a look that made Derrick think he was missing out on some joke. "I'll make sure to find you both before I leave."

"Please do. Maya would like that." Tony nodded once again at Derrick before leaving the terrace.

"You look nice."

"Of course I do," Nuria countered. She twirled, showing off the periwinkle cocktail dress draped modestly over her voluptuous body. "I hope you didn't think I'd show up here wearing thongs and a leash." Whatever she saw in his face made her laugh.

"Not exactly."

She hummed. "But something like, huh?"

Derrick pursed his lips. She must know that what he knew of her—her lifestyle of drugs and sex with her other friends, the performance the other night in the club, and the way she had let him fuck her in his house—could only lead him to expect certain things from her. And none of these things was modesty.

A waiter walked onto the terrace with a tray of martinis. Nuria reached past him for one, stretching her lithe body to show off the naked weight of her breasts through the blue cotton, the hard button of nipple. The flare of his lust.

"Don't let your assumption about me stop you from seeing what's really going on," she murmured, taking a sip of her drink. She closed her eyes in pleasure. "Hmm. This stuff is *fabuloso*. I have to get Maya to tell me how she makes them just so. Seeing his look, she leaned closer. "Do you want a taste?"

His mouth was open and moving closer before his mind could properly formulate an answer. The mango-flavored mix and vodka caught him by surprise. *Not bad.*

"Did you just call me to get laid?" she asked.

He swallowed the drink. It was only by a minor miracle that he didn't cough it up or spew it over the balcony's edge. "Would you slap me if I said yes?"

"I don't know. Why don't you try the honest answer and see."

Without turning his head, Derrick glanced self-consciously around him. But everyone was too busy with their own conversations to pay them any mind.

"I want to fuck you again," he said. "I haven't been able to get you out of my mind."

Nuria sipped her martini, lips pressed delicately over the

glass's edge. As she moved the glass away, leaving a burgundy lipstick stain on its rim, she licked her lips.

"Are you desperate to have me, or only a little blue-balled?" The twining hair shifted around her head as she dipped her head back to look at him. "How much do you want me?"

He stepped closer and pressed his body against hers. On command it seemed, his cock grew harder, nuzzling her clothed flesh. "Very much."

"Hmm." She sipped her drink again. Then deliberately stepped away from him. He could only blink after her as she walked off the terrace and into the thick of the party. Derrick swallowed against his desire, then turned to press his aching cock against the concrete railing, willing its hardness to subside. After a deep breath, he turned to walk into the house. His phone rang.

"What's up, Jake?"

"Hey, what was the name of Dez's friend who owns Gillespie's?"

"Rémi. Rémi Bouchard, I think."

"Cool. I thought so, but I wasn't sure. She's at this party I'm at, and I wanted to talk with her about playing a gig at the club. I don't want to look too stupid by not knowing her name."

"You definitely don't want to do that. From what Dez says, the chick is approachable, so I wouldn't worry too much about it if I were you."

"I'm not worried about approaching her. I just want her to let me play at her club. A lot of people got good exposure by being there."

"You know more than I do about that, but good luck."

"Thanks, though I don't think I'll need it." Jake chuckled. "Where are you anyway?"

"A party in the Grove."

"With Trish?"

"Nope."

Jake made a noise like he'd just discovered something. "All right. Carry on, playa."

It was Derrick's turn to laugh. "Nothing that serious."

"May be soon if you don't watch it."

Derrick made a dismissive noise. "You tend to your business and I'll deal with mine, all right?"

"I always handle mine." *Unlike some*, was the unspoken comment. "Later."

Derrick ended the call. Inside the house, he ran into Nuria's friend Tony. The older man stood in a semicircle with a half dozen or so women. The one next to him was pretty, a thick size twelve at least, with a dimpled smile. Thankfully, they were all speaking English.

"Hello again." Derrick approached the group with his most charming smile.

The women turned their heads. At least two of them did a double take.

"Hey, Derrick," Tony greeted. "Nuria run off and leave you already?"

"You know it. My boring conversation frightened her off. I'll be surprised if she ever talks to me again."

The dimpled woman laughed as she took him in with appreciative eyes. "I doubt that Ria's with you for the conversation." She leaned into Tony's shoulder as she spoke. This one must be his wife.

"That's very generous of you," Derrick said. "I think."

"Maya is more than likely just telling you how it is." A tall woman, easily Derrick's height with a diamond stud in her nose and a closely shaved head, gave his body a far-from-casual glance. "Ria wouldn't be so stupid as to leave a specimen like you alone around here for long."

The other women laughed while Tony chuckled and shook his head.

"Hands off, Mari. Nuria's, remember?"

"Oh, please." The bald-headed woman pursed her lips. "We all know that Nuria usually doesn't mind sharing."

"Usually." This was from a plump plum of a woman with nearly purple skin and large round earrings that danced just above her shoulders. "That's the key word."

"It sounds like you all know her very well," Derrick said, slipping his hands into the pockets of his slacks. He wasn't sure he liked the idea of being discussed like property. This was one of the times he wanted to protest that he had a girlfriend. The women's predatory looks made him uneasy.

"How long have you known Nuria?" Tony asked Derrick.

"A few years."

The other man's eyes widened in surprise. "And she hasn't gotten you where she wanted yet?"

A sweetly spiced scent captured Derrick's nose, and moments later Nuria slid into the group, latching onto Tony's arm on the side opposite his wife. "And where is that, Antonio?" she asked with a teasing smile.

"Underneath your very sharp high heels, of course, darling." He leaned down to kiss her cheek. His wife laughed, completely unconcerned.

"It's your fault that he knows you so well, Ria." Maya leaned over to lightly run her fingers along Nuria's bare arm. "You're much too honest."

"I'll work on my lying skills." Nuria's labret piercing winked in the light.

"We like to call it *subterfuge*." Maya laughed.

"Speak for yourself, my love. I'd rather Ria tell us instead of being caught by surprise."

Maya chuckled. "Good point."

The other women in the loose circle watched the byplay with tolerant amusement, though Derrick still felt at least two pairs of eyes on him during the exchange. He gave his most benign look.

"Sorry to spoil your fun, *mis amigas*. And Tony." Nuria lightly pinched her friend's arm. "But I have a prior engagement."

"I'm sure you do," the round woman murmured with an arch look.

"No comment." Nuria turned to Derrick. "Walk me to my car?"

He only nodded at Nuria when she took his arm. She turned away from her friends, wiggling her fingers over her shoulder. "See you all later on."

"Good to meet you," Derrick said out of politeness, but his pulse was already galloping in anticipation of their "prior engagement."

"My friends seemed to like you," Nuria said as they walked away.

"Your friends wanted to eat me alive," he said with a laugh. "Except for Tony, that is. Although I get the feeling that he would gladly watch that feeding frenzy."

In a swirl of blue cotton, Nuria turned gracefully to face him as they moved through the party. Their arms were still linked. Her lips twitched, as if fighting back a laugh. "You're very perceptive. Our Tony enjoys all sorts of amusements."

"Like most straight men, I'm sure."

Nuria did laugh then. "Most."

They walked down the twisting staircase, occasionally pressing together to avoid bumping into the people walking in the opposite direction. The spice of her perfume brought his nose closer with every step. He found himself trying to decipher where exactly on her body Nuria dotted her perfume. Was it behind her ears, her throat, the backs of her knees, or the dip below her belly button?

Near the bottom of the stairs, she pressed against him again, and his hand lightly gripped the small of her back, crushing her against him. Her breath brushed his throat, smelling of mangoes. This time, no one blocked the other side of the stairs pushing for entrance higher up into the house.

"If you don't ask for what you want, you'll never get it," she murmured, breasts pressed against his chest, slender hand around his biceps. "When you want me, say it. I can only say no."

His skin flushed hot at her words. "You can only say no, huh?"

"No isn't always a bad thing, Nichols."

"Not in my experience."

"You must have a very limited field of experience, then." She drew back, taking in a deep breath, and they continued on their way through the house, past the occasional person wishing Nuria a good night. Their shoes made a loud tattoo against the tile paving the circular drive, then were silent as they stepped into the grass.

"I'm parked not too far from here," Nuria said, digging into her tiny black purse for keys.

Anticipation sat low in Derrick's belly as they approached the sleek white lines of her convertible. The car chirped when she opened it with the remote. At the driver's side, she slid into the car, one leg in, the other stretched out in a high heel damp with moisture from the grass. The sprawl of her thighs drew his eyes.

"Get in."

The beach she took him to was secluded, quiet with only the whisper of the waves, haunting and melodic, that tumbled up on the sand. With a soft hum, the cloth roof of the car retracted until the sky was spread open above their heads, stars glittering against the inky dark. Nuria turned off the car but left the radio on. The swelling notes of a jazz saxophone flowed from the speakers.

Her fingers crept across the gearshift to settle lightly on Derrick's thigh. With a movement of scent and flesh, Nuria swept over the gearshift and settled on Derrick's lap. She sighed and shook her hair out of her face. Her labret stud winked below her red mouth.

"Derrick."

She whispered his name against his lips, teasing him with the possibility of her mouth. The scent of her was hot and thick. He smelled her pussy, too. Her breasts shifted under the thin blue dress.

"You are one sexy man."

The words touched him just before her lips did. Her hips, bare with the dress shoved up around them, called his hands. She moved lightly against him, grinding on his lap as their tongues tangled, their lips slid. *Ah.* Nuria tasted of mangoes and desire as she rode him, rubbed her softness against his hardness.

"I bet you say that to all the men you fuck in your car."

"No. Just the hot ones."

His laugh turned into a heavy groan when she put her hands on him, sliding between them to find his hard dick under the clothes, to unearth it, stroke it, and cup his balls. Derrick groaned again and pushed deeper into her hands.

"You're too good at this," he gasped, unable to hold breath in his lungs.

His balls were heavy with arousal, precum already weeping from the head of his dick. Derrick almost wept, too. Everything he wanted in that moment was pooled in his lap and about to spill into her hands. Still kissing him, Nuria reached blindly for her purse and upturned it in the driver's seat. Her hand came back with a condom, and she ripped the packet open and slipped the cool latex over his dick, inch by aching inch, until a fire built in the pit of him. She soothed him.

"Easy, baby." She pulled back, and her teeth flashed in the moonlight. "We're just getting to the good part."

With a movement of her hand, she pushed the seat all the

way back. Nuria was in control. And he watched her, breasts moving under the blue dress, nipples pressed hard against the cotton. Derrick brushed his thumbs over them, and she made a small noise, a pussy-deep groan, that made his dick dance in her hands. He pulled down the straps of her dress. Under the silver light, her breasts were dangerous. They swayed in front of his face like a tempting last meal. Derrick dipped forward, licked a nipple, and sucked the hard point into his mouth, teasing it with his tongue until she groaned, releasing the sound of her rapture into the air.

"Hmm."

She seemed to love it so much that he had to do it again and again, soothing one nipple with his tongue, licking and sucking the other until she swayed, snakelike, on his lap. Nuria slid against his dick, teased him with her hot pussy. He devoured her breasts until they both shone wet under the light. Her fingers curled into his shoulders.

Derrick reached for her. He needed to feel her around him now. But she pulled away. Turning her back to him, she lifted her dress out of the way and sat on his lap. Derrick gasped as her pussy took him in. Tight. Wet. Perfect. He trembled, feeling her heat around him. Finally. The wind brushed over his face; her warmth pressed back against him. She sighed. And began to move.

The dress fell completely off her shoulders to pool at the base of her spine, a pale slash against her dark skin. Her hair snaked against her shoulders, twisting against her dampening skin as she moved faster on him, breath whistling through her teeth. The wet glove of her pussy was hot and eager around him. Derrick held on to her waist as she rode him, intent on getting hers. His body burned.

She grabbed his hands and put them on her breasts. "Play with my tits, baby," Nuria hissed. "Yeah. That's how I like it."

He cupped her slight breasts in his hands, squeezed her hard nipples, rolled them between his fingers until the noises built in her throat and overflowed. "Uh-huh. Yes. Yes!"

Her praise moved him faster, as the tight fit of her pussy around his dick focused his world to one explosive point. The wet slide of their bodies, her cunt and his cock, her gasp and his groan, filled the car. "Fuck me, baby. Fuck me."

He squeezed her nipples harder, jackhammered his hips until her words became sounds, incomprehensible and guttural. A fireball of sensation rolled down Derrick's body, plunging into his spine, into his balls, his dick. He threw his head back and saw stars. Nuria's pussy pulsated around him as she came, gasping, squeezing his hands over her breasts.

His heart thumped in his chest like a fist shaking out of control, almost frightening in its intensity. Derrick swallowed. Chill sweat stirred over his body, sticking the shirt to his back. Limp with satisfaction, he could only groan when Nuria lifted herself off him and scooped her things back into her purse before getting back over to the driver's seat. She shook her hair away from her face and pulled her dress back up to shield her breasts from sight. With a purring smile, she glanced at him once before she started the car and put it in gear.

The smell of their sex lay thick in the small convertible even with the top down and the breeze rushing over their heads as Nuria sped through Coconut Grove. The coastline flew past them, moonlight glinting on foamed waves, palm trees, and pavement.

Derrick's mind flew, too. When was he going to see her again? Did she have any idea how addicted he was becoming to their sex? Even though his body was slack with completion, he wanted her again.

The car stopped. "We're here," she said.

But "here" wasn't the house where Derrick left his car. It looked like they were in a parking garage in the middle of downtown. In his absentmindedness, he hadn't been paying attention to the passing landscape, only to the feelings throbbing through his body, the echo of her in his pulse. Nuria got out of the car. A flash of smooth legs and thighs. Her hungry smile.

"I want to keep you for a little while longer," she said. "This is my place."

This was her place. They walked together to the elevator, and as soon as the double doors closed, they came smoothly together, tongues tasting, hands searching warm flesh. Derrick shuddered in anticipation of what was to come. The elevator stopped, and Nuria tugged him from the confines of the steel cage and directly into a cool hallway. Her hands pulled his shirt up and out of his slacks, skimmed his hard chest, lingering at his flat nipples. Derrick groaned. Right now he didn't care if everyone in the building came out of their condos and saw him with his dick hard and throbbing in Nuria's hand. As long as she let him cum. *God!*

At her door, they stopped. Him pressing her against the sturdy wood. Her gasping and urging him on as his hands squeezed her breasts, pressed her ass, and caressed her hips.

"I have to—" A wet moan stopped whatever it was she had to say. But she fumbled with her purse, digging into it for something. More condoms? Derrick's hips jerked at the thought. Yes. They would fuck right here against her door. It was more than perfect. And right now, it even seemed necessary. He *needed* to feel her around him. And when he was inside her, they would knock on the door with their hips, break through the wood with their relentless fucking, end up with splinters in their asses, gasping their pleasure and pain into each other's mouths. Derrick groaned again. Then her keys jingled.

She slid her arms from around his neck to open the door. His arms lashed her waist from behind, and her hips settled in the cradle of his. He was going to explode any minute. Her door opened, and they stumbled inside, her keys and purse

falling to the floor as he spun her to push her back to the wall
and fling the door closed behind them. Derrick barely took in
the shock of copper walls, cushions, music already playing, and
the smell of old incense. A table lurched near their rocking hips,
and Derrick reached out to steady it. His hands tumbled into
what felt like a phone. But his other hand tangled in the hem of
her dress, lifting it out of the way.

"Ria, darling . . ."

The voice came from a speaker, the answering machine accidentally pressed, but Nuria stiffened under him anyway. Dis-
embodied, the voice continued on:

". . . It's Mama and Papa." The female voice laughed very
softly, then said something indecipherable to someone in the
background. "Sorry we missed your birthday on the weekend,
but your papa swore me up and down that it was today. Don't
worry, though; we sent you a something extra that you should
get very soon. Look out for it—" Nuria twisted away from
Derrick to cut off the machine with the decisive press of her
finger. A flicker of something crossed her face, but when she
turned to face him, she was smiling.

"Sorry about that," she said.

"Nothing to be sorry for." Derrick leaned back against the
wall, watching her. His breath was rough in his chest, balls
heavy and hot beneath his stiff dick. "You can call her back if
you want. I can wait."

He licked his lips, and the rough beard below his mouth
gently abraded his tongue. It would be hard. He was hard. The
hardest he'd ever been for a woman, it felt like. But he would
wait. He knew how important family was, how tenuous con-
nections could become, how important it was to grasp at them
before they disappeared altogether.

"You may be able to wait, but I can't." She unzipped the
dress from the side and slipped out of it, discarding the blue
cloth at her feet before she came naked toward him. Nuria ran

her hands over his chest and purred. "I have a very nice bed in there." She nodded toward a darkened hallway. "We need to get in it. Right now."

The bed was more than nice; it was firm but fitted with soft sheets, a frilly feminine nonsense of canopy draped with thin copper-colored silk that stirred in the breeze from the open window. It took their weight without a sigh, and Nuria pushed him onto his back, lips parted in a teasing smile as she crouched over him, animal and female. She licked his mouth. Her scent, bergamot and patchouli with a hint of sandalwood, he realized now, tickled his nose.

"This is more like it," she said. "I need room to fuck."

Her hair lashed his mouth as she moved lower, and he fought the urge to throw her onto her belly, to be on top and fuck like he was used to, but her mouth closed on his nipple, and Derrick jerked in the bed. *Ah.* He never knew it could feel that good—his other nipple hardened between her fingers and he groaned.

"Fuck!"

Her teeth grazed the sensitive flesh, and his hand tightened in her hair. The molten scent of her pussy flared again, making him dizzy. A hot breath against his belly, then he felt her going lower. Derrick looked down in time to see her put his dick in her mouth. *Fuck fuck fuck!* His eyes fell shut again. Hot sensation ricocheted through his body. How did she know? How? It felt so good. He couldn't remember the last time a woman put him in her mouth. Nuria cupped his balls, rolling them in her feverish palm, and he groaned, loud and long. What was she doing to him?

Derrick opened his eyes to the sight of his own face. A long mirror leaned against the wall near the foot of the bed. In the mirror, his face was tense with lust, while Nuria's head bobbed over his dick. Her lower back's sweaty curve, her ass, the wide-open pussy, and fingers disappearing into her slippery cunt in a leisurely rhythm. All in the mirror. The heat inside him flared higher.

Her mouth was wet and warm as she held him, sucked him, licked him until the energy built in his body and he was cumming hard, spurting in her mouth. She groaned with pleasure, swallowing him with an enthusiasm that jerked his hips even harder. The sheets felt damp under his back, and her hands were hot on his thighs. As he came back to his senses, she began crawling back up his body.

"That was a nice dessert." Nuria licked her lips and smiled.

The taste of his cum on her mouth shocked a groan from him. It made his knees weak. It made him want to share more of himself with her. Derrick flipped her over, switched their positions in the bed.

"Now that you've had your fun," he said, looking down at her. "It's my turn."

"We don't have to take turns." Her thigh lifted, gently prodded his softened dick. He shuddered from the contact with its sensitive tip. "I'll share mine with you," she said.

Derrick chuckled deep in his throat. "I know you're more used to women, but you have to know that it'll take me a few minutes to . . . um . . . take my turn again."

"I've been known to work miracles."

Her breasts lifted under him, and he gasped at the feel of her. Oh yeah, she was definitely a miracle worker. Their bodies slid together, exchanging kisses and languorous touches. Her pussy spiced the air with its scent, and her groans were like music. Derrick moved his fingers inside her wet heat and caressed her hard clit.

"For a man"—she trembled and her fingers raced over his back—"you're really . . . uh! . . . really good with your hands."

Any real man knows how to work his woman, he wanted to say, but his mouth was full. Her nipples slid like milk chocolate under his tongue, and she twisted under him, her feet sliding against the sheets as he fucked her. Nuria panted above his head, hissing his name between breaths. In the mirror, she was his very own wet dream, head hanging off the bed, dreds flailing, lips parted, breasts shuddering. She spilled wetness in his hand as she came.

"I like your mirror," he said, and she laughed breathlessly.

Her arms snaked around his neck, and she nibbled lightly on his ear. "Show me how much."

Nuria didn't need to repeat her request. They grabbed another condom, turned in the bed to face the mirror, and after sheathing his dick in latex, she sat on him. Breath leaked from his mouth on a shuddering groan, and her back slid wetly against his chest. The heat of her around him made Derrick shiver. In the mirror, their eyes met.

"Fuck me like you mean it," Nuria growled.

She arched back in his lap, breasts small and firm, their nipples hard and begging for his touch. Their slight weight shifted, jiggled, as she began to ride him. This time it was even better than the car. He could see her. Could see her licking her lips, could see his hands on her breasts. The sweat begin to wash over her body, her spread legs wider, showing off her hairless pussy, his dick curving up wet and hard inside her. Nuria moved hard on him like she wanted to be first at the finish line, no matter what. Her fingers flickered over her clit. Nuria's hair hopped around her shoulders as the pace quickened.

She was liquid around him. Derrick groaned and fell back into the sheets. He didn't need to see her. Just feel. The need in him grabbed her hips, thrust hard into her, up inside her devouring heat. He grunted. Groaned. The smell of their fucking throbbed in the air. The cum caught him by surprise, and he found himself shouting her name, groaning it as the last of his juices spurted into her. Nuria laughed as she came. She climbed off Derrick and dropped down beside him in the bed.

"That was"—she laughed again breathlessly, rubbing her

hand over her sweaty face and into her hair—"really, really good."

An understatement, if there ever was one. Shudders of another sort still raced through Derrick's body, radiating from his softening dick and balls down to his feet and up through his torso and chest. Shit. Even his eyelashes were trembling.

"You're like the gift that just keeps on giving and giving," Nuria said.

She propped herself up on her elbow to look down on him. Her hair fell forward, brushing against her jaw and mouth. It would be so easy to love her. Startled at the thought, Derrick jerked up in the bed. *Where did that come from?*

"What's wrong?" Nuria asked.

Derrick shook his head. "I just remembered something."

To give his words credence, he bent over the edge of the bed, feeling for his discarded pants and the phone attached to its belt. Four missed calls. Trish. Trish. Jake. And Trish again. *Why was she—?*

"Motherfucker!"

He was supposed to meet her at his house at eleven. Now it was nearly half past four, and he *really* had to go. Derrick jumped out of the bed.

Shit. "I have to go." *Stupid. Stupid.*

"You really shouldn't schedule anything else the same night you go looking for pussy, Nichols." She rolled over in the bed to watch him.

Derrick barely looked at her as he quickly pulled on his pants, socks, and shoes. His shirt was in the living room somewhere.

"I'm really sorry about this. This appointment—I completely forgot about it." *Trish might not so easily forgive this one.*

"At this time of night, that's not an appointment, my friend. That's a booty call." Nuria chuckled, but her eyes were cool and watchful underneath the spill of hair.

"Believe me, that's not what this is."

"Whatever you say." She sat up in the bed, letting the sheet fall away from her breasts. Derrick paused.

She laughed again. "Go, Nichols. I doubt this 'appointment' is as relaxed as I am."

"I'll call you later," he said, backing out the bedroom door.

"Whatever. Just lock the door behind you, stud."

In the living room, he pulled on his shirt and jacket, fumbling with his phone to call Trish back. But as he started to dial, his fingers paused. Maybe it was best that he wait for a moment and let her think that his phone was out of commission. Derrick dropped his phone back in its holster and left the condo. He leaned back against the rear wall of the elevator, his mind flitting through possible excuses why he didn't answer his phone. But instead of lies for Trish, his thoughts bumped into Nuria. It settled into the sweet pull of her pussy, the wet heat of her mouth around his dick, her tongue licking at the head of his cock before pulling it into jungle-hot mouth. He swallowed.

Now wasn't the time. But his unruly libido wasn't paying attention. That part of him very much wanted to be back in Nuria's bed. Her sex amazed him. The way she used her mouth, her hands, her pussy . . . shit! He'd never had a lover as passionate or uninhibited. Just the thought of the way she moved under him, clasping his cock in her sticky heat, made him hard again. Derrick swallowed. The elevator jerked to a halt, and he jumped out as soon as the doors opened. Then—*Damn!*

He cursed, remembering that his car was somewhere else. Should he—? No, there was no way he would ask Nuria to get out of her bed and drop him off so he could go see another woman. Not even he was that fucked up. Derrick reached for his phone to call a cab.

There wasn't another car in his driveway when he got home nearly an hour later. Not that he expected Trish to be waiting for him when he was—Derrick glanced at his watch—six hours late. He half expected the place to be trashed when he got inside, but everything was just as he left it. With a sigh of irritation, he called her from his landline. He fell wearily into the leather armchair, dropping his head back as the phone rang once, twice, then three times before going to voice mail.

"Trish, sorry about tonight. I'm having some cell phone problems." Not to mention he was getting all his senses sucked out of him in the best blow job he'd ever had in his life. "Call me when you get this."

A complete and total asshole. That's what he felt like. And it wasn't because he was sleeping with both women at once but because he'd proven that he couldn't handle it. He couldn't keep both women happy. Not that Nuria cared. Her happiness came in the form of orgasms, and he'd definitely left her happy tonight. *A perfect birthday gift*, he thought.

Derrick smiled briefly. Then before he could rethink it, he used his Blackberry to log onto the Web site he usually ordered his flowers from. A few keystrokes later, he had ordered Nuria two dozen roses—danger red, like her—to be delivered the next day. Then he checked his voice mail. The messages from Trish didn't start off too badly.

"Hey, Derrick. It's eleven-fifteen, and I'm here at the house waiting for you. If you get this message before you get here, could you pick up some ice cream for me? You know the one I like." Her soft voice sounded relaxed yet distracted as if she was taking off her shoes or slipping out of her jacket while she waited for him to come.

On the second message, she gave all her attention to the phone call. "It's after midnight, Derrick. I hope you're all right and not lying in a ditch somewhere. Even if you're just running late, call me. I'm worried."

The third message made him sit up in the chair.

"Rick, your main girl just called me worried about you."

Jake's voice was loud over the background noise of live music and muted conversation. "She sounded like she was about to cry and shit, so I told her you got caught up at work. You better call her."

Trish's third message came in four minutes after Jake's. She didn't sound worried anymore.

"I don't know what's wrong with you lately, Derrick, but I'm sick of it. You're not picking up your cell phone; you're not picking up at your office. And you stood me up. At your own damn house!" She paused, probably fighting the urge to curse him out. "If you think I'm going to wait around until you have time for me, then you're sadly mistaken." Trish was too ladylike to slam down the phone, even in the midst of anger, but Derrick heard the definite click of the receiver as she hung up.

"Shit."

He got to his feet and headed for his bedroom. If he rushed through his workout, he could be at Trish's house by seven.

6

The two women smelled nothing alike. Derrick pressed Trish down into her bed, his mouth nibbling on the soft skin at her throat. Trish's neck held the scent of oranges, fresh from the orchard, an alchemy someone like him could only wonder at. Did she squeeze the fruit all over her skin? There was no way this smell came from a bottle. But it did. On her skin, the faint bitterness from the perfume quickly gave way to her natural sweetness. God! He loved women.

Trish moaned softly, a whisper of sound above his head when he brushed his fingers over her nipples on his way to peeling the blouse from her. She sighed. He warmed her nipple with his mouth through the thin silk of her bra, and she grasped the back of his head. Softer noises leaked from her mouth. The yellow silk grew wet under his tongue, and her legs fell open to his seeking hands. The matching panties were wet, too. Derrick slid his fingers past them to play in the damp pussy hairs and caress her clit, swirl at the entrance to her pussy. Trish's groans grew louder.

An hour before, when Derrick had walked in with grapefruit juice, bagels, and bullshit to soothe Trish's temper, he didn't think that things would end up like this. He hoped but didn't think it was a certainty. After the apologies and smiles and her favorite veggie cream cheese spread folded into scrambled eggs on a multigrain bagel, Trish relented. Her eyes were so hopeful, so trusting, that Derrick had wanted to give her something for believing him. He wanted to give her at least one honest thing that morning. And that was his lust.

In the beginning of their relationship, he'd rushed between her thighs. Being with her was a respite from his fruitless longing for his best friend. But Trish never moved from being a substitute for the woman he couldn't have. No one had. And although he was far from being over Tori, he was finished with needing a stand-in for her. And Derrick realized, walking into Trish's Orient-inspired home with its thick splashes of red and paintings of cherry blossoms and long-limbed women, that he didn't need her as a substitute anymore. At least not for Tori.

Her pussy swallowed his fingers, and she gasped again. So easy. She was so easy to please. Being with her did his ego good. There was nothing he could do wrong with her, nothing that wouldn't make her moan in pleasure and accept his dick, tongue, fingers, nose, his maleness.

She lay back against the sheets, her eyes at half-mast, her lips moist and parted. With a low growl, he pulled off her panties. Her eyes widened, but she didn't push him away. He knew how she liked to fuck—gently. And no matter how turned on he was, Derrick would never do anything that she didn't want. That was one of the big reasons that she trusted him. Maybe she figured a man who did only what she wanted in bed—didn't try to fuck her in the ass, didn't force her to swallow his dick, never asked her to share her body with other people—could also be trusted out of it.

Sun poured over them in the bed. Over her tousled hair, the

white pillows, her sex-slack face. Derrick pulled his fingers from her cunt. Knelt in the bed and pulled her hips up and wide until she was a backward bow, most of her weight on her knees and her shoulders. She watched him. With one hand, he undid his belt and pulled down his zipper. His slacks slid off his ass to pool around his knees, and his dick jut out, thickly veined, pre-cum dripping, and ready. The lust was a slow fire in him, nothing urgent. Nothing that had to rush him through this Sunday-morning fuck. He reached over for a condom in the bedside table, tore it out of the packet, and rolled it onto his dick. Watching him, Trish licked her lips.

"Touch your breasts," he said. She liked that. He knew she was a little embarrassed doing it and only liked to touch herself when she felt like he was telling her to do it. Trish licked her lips and pulled the bra down off her shoulders and away from her breasts. The thick nipples puckered in her desire. Her fingers brushed them.

"Squeeze your nipples." He slid a finger across her dripping slit. "Yeah, like that."

And he slid into her. Their bodies fit, and she rolled her hips as he fucked her, making soft moaning noises that tickled over his skin and urged him on. Her pussy swallowed his latex-covered dick, slurping around him, telling him that he was making her feel good.

"Oh, Derrick!" She squeezed her nipples, eyes glazing, her fingers tightening a bit more each time his dick slid into her. Faster. The bed rocked, tapped against the wall with each solid thrust. Her breasts shook. She bit her lips. Her stomach trembled. Fucking her was like sailing into sunshine. The warmth built inside him. More. And more. He gasped with her. She shuddered and came with a soft scream.

Panting, she fell limply into the bed. Sweat gilded her body, making her glow in the sunlight. Her hand fell to her bare belly with a light slap, and her breasts shuddered with each harsh breath. Derrick smiled as he watched her. She was the only woman he knew who made getting fucked look sweet.

When her breath slowed, Trish lethargically turned her head to look up at Derrick. She licked her lips before she spoke. "Do you still want to go with me to the party tonight?"

Derrick's body tingled in the aftermath of his orgasm. His skin hummed in the sun from his collapse beside Trish, as if waves of heat licked up from his skin. There was something missing. After a cum, he usually felt depleted, unable to move. But his body was still energized. The brush of Trish's arm against his still made him tingle with want. Derrick knew she was satisfied. But he wasn't. He wanted more. With a slight stretch, he sat up in the bed.

"Come take a shower with me."

She was relaxed and pliant under his hands, gliding across the bed to him, her head a limp bud on the long petal of her neck. Trish smelled like sex and satisfaction. Her lips parted as she smiled, inviting him to do whatever he wanted with her. Derrick took his time undressing her completely, unhooking her twisted bra, pulling off the rumpled beige skirt that had been crumpled around her hips as he fucked her. He pulled her off the bed and into his arms.

In the bathroom, he draped her over the toilet seat, and with her head leaning back against the toilet tank, her legs loose and splayed against the floor, she watched him. Derrick quickly shucked off his slacks and briefs.

"You look good like this," she said.

He felt her eyes on him as he turned on the water, first to scalding to get the steam rising up, then to the moderate temperature she liked. Like a physical touch, Trish's eyes caressed the hard globes of his ass, the thick thighs, and the heavy swing of his dick and balls. He turned and she licked her lips, he leaned his head slightly back to look at her. Trish was looking at his dick like she was hungry for a taste of it. Obediently, it rose even higher, thickening, lengthening under her steady gaze.

"Very nice," she murmured.

Tease. She had to know how he wanted her mouth on him. Wanted to be enclosed in her heat, to invade the place that they kissed, where she ate, those delicate lips that she seduced her clients with. Derrick scooped her into his arms.

Her shower was one of those luxurious ones that he liked to fuck in, with three tiled walls enclosing enough space for four. The glass door was far enough away that he didn't need to worry about breaking it at a particularly good moment.

"You ready?" The words felt rough in his throat.

Steam curled up around them in the glass and tile cage of the shower. Trish's straightened hair was already beginning to wilt in the humidity, but she didn't seem too concerned. Instead her eyes devoured him, hungrily watched him pull the door closed. Nuria would have reached for him already. She would have— fuck! All Derrick's thoughts flew beyond him when Trish's hands closed around his dick and gently squeezed.

"Make love to me," she said.

Water rushed down his back in hot jets, warming him. But her hand around him was warmer.

"Yes." He pushed into her hand, and she squeezed him again before lifting her arms to receive him.

She tasted like the Altoid she'd had in her mouth when she first opened the door to let him in. She smelled like sunlight and sex. Derrick backed her against the shower wall, feasting on her mouth. He fumbled up above to the caddy with the condoms. Not too long ago she'd decided on taking the pill so they could have raw sex, no rubbers. But he still insisted they use them. The pill was no guarantee that she wouldn't get pregnant, and, thanks to Tori, he was conscious about germ-sharing even though they'd both been tested and came out clean.

But that night in his living room with Nuria he'd almost forgotten. The sight of her standing against that railing with the whiskey dripping like liquid fire down her body made him lose all his senses. He was ready to fuck, and if she hadn't remembered and insisted, he didn't know where they'd be right now.

Derrick pointed the nozzle away until it arched over them and splashed against the back wall, raining minute droplets on their flesh.

"Turn around, baby," he growled.

And she did, trusting and sweet with her damp skin and flush of anticipation. Her ass turned up, legs spread wide, her pussy open to him. Droplets from the shower dotted her skin, her back, and the round curves of her ass. Derrick watched, mesmerized, as the water slithered between her cheeks and over the dark pucker of her asshole, then the slick folds of her pussy.

"Touch me," she begged softly, arching her ass even more toward him.

He touched her. Teased her opening with his dick, sliding the thick head just inside her where he knew she was most sensitive. Derrick bit back a groan as his heavy dick caressed the attentive nerves there. Her gasps made him move faster until it wasn't just the head of his cock anymore; it was all of him. The breath climbed frantically in her throat. His fingers dug into her hips. Heat sang through his body, the scorching notes climbing higher. And higher. Trish was loud when she came. Surprising. Her arms shuddered from their brace against the wall. Her thighs vibrated against his.

The orgasm he ached for held itself suspended inside him, just out of reach. Derrick groaned, fucking her deeply, twisting his hips, reaching and reaching. Trish moved gamely beneath him, encouraging with her soft moans. But suddenly he didn't want to do this anymore. Derrick withdrew his body from hers. The water was getting cold.

* * *

Despite Trish's protestations, they quickly had a shower without getting Derrick off again; then they emerged scrubbed clean to get ready for Trish's brunch party. The truth was that he'd rather be with his boys than at this mix-and-mingle for Trish's clients and designer friends. Walking around her decorated apartment and discussing the merits of her design style with fawning women or lisping queens wasn't high on his list of things to do, but that's exactly what happened when the house was overrun by the dozen-plus people nearly two hours later. Well dressed, well read, and obviously well heeled as these people were, they held little interest for him. Too many women swooned over him, touched his back, chest, and shoulders with the pretense of friendly concern for Trish and asking when they would be getting married.

Derrick left as soon as he could, slipping out just before the party ended with the excuse of catching up on work at the office. He intended to drive straight home, but as Derrick coasted down I-95 with the top down and the sun burning on his head, the thought of going home began to seem less appealing. He got off one exit earlier and veered off toward the office. Work needed to be done anyway.

At half past six, he still sat at his desk, wading through the Costa files. He should just unfold a sleeping bag and spend the night here since work started again in less than twelve hours. Derrick slouched back in his chair, staring at the computer screen in irritation. This man was guilty as hell of all the charges and more. It would be a minor miracle if the firm managed to get him off. He was still glaring at the gray screen when his cell phone rang.

"Are you just down to one girl now?"

"Very funny, Jake." He picked up a pen. "What's up?"

"Just checking if you're still alive. Trish didn't seem too happy with you last night."

"Well, now she's *very* happy with me." He tapped the pen against his desk.

Jake made a noise of disbelief. "You really must have the magic dick."

Derrick grinned. "The last thing you need to worry about is my dick. Still, thanks for trying to save my ass last night. I got caught up and didn't notice the time."

"No big deal. I know you'd do the same thing for me if I was in the same fucked-up situation."

"It's not fucked up. Just a little complicated. It's just about sex, getting something a little different. Once it's over, Trish and I can go back to usual."

"As long as you know that her usual probably means marriage."

It better not. He wasn't anywhere near that stage with her. Derrick shook his head. "Anyway, what are you up to tonight?"

Jake laughed. "Whatever, man." But he played along. "I'm about to leave for a gig on Miami Beach. A private party."

"Nice. Feel like company?"

"Yeah, why not? You can shake the tambourine or something."

"Cool." He stood up to gather his keys and jacket. "I'm at the office, but I can be at your place in fifteen."

"All right."

Going to the party wasn't a good idea. Derrick went with Jake as the roadie, helping to set up the equipment and getting drinks for them both when it got too hot out on the Spanish-tiled patio with its view of Biscayne Bay and the glittering lights of the city. Derrick's skin prickled under his clothes. He wasn't comfortable. The laughing and brightly dressed people at the party only made him ache for his own quiet space, the peace that he'd denied himself when he left this morning for Trish's without even taking a nap. Now he desperately wanted sleep. Or something. After barely two hours rubbing elbows with the rich and not so famous, Derrick left the large house for his more modest one.

At home, he was equally restless but worked away most of it in the gym, doing reps until every muscle burned with effort and all he wanted to do was collapse in his bed. Later, lying against the sheets, his mind a careful blank, he almost didn't hear his cell phone ring.

"I was starting to get worried about you." His mother's light voice reached him through the receiver.

"No need to worry." He felt himself smiling despite his exhaustion. "I've just been really busy at work. We should have brunch this weekend."

"That would be nice, but I'm heading out of town for a few days."

He rolled over in the bed and sat up. "Where? Is everything okay?" Ever since his mother's cancer scare a few months ago, Derrick had been more aware of her mortality and importance in his life. The doctor gave her a clean bill of health, but that didn't prevent the occasional spurt of worry in his chest.

"Everything is great. I'm actually going up to Maine with a friend and won't be back until next week. I'll take a rain check on that lunch, though."

He breathed a quiet sigh of relief and dropped back against the sheets. "Sounds good."

They talked for another half hour before his mother, teasing him about the fatigue in his voice, wished him a good night and hung up the phone. Moments later, he fell asleep.

7

"Good work, Derrick." Fiametta Johnson intercepted him on his way to the office kitchen for another cup of coffee. "I saw the work you did over the weekend on the Costa case. Very impressive."

The small woman looked impeccable as always in a charcoal skirt suit and a circle of pearls sitting high on her throat. Derrick had always thought she looked like a fairy with her short hair cut close to her elegant head, pointed ears, and wide eyes. But she was coldly ferocious in the courtroom and brought in nearly as much business as Alex Meyer, the firm's founding partner.

"Thanks, Metta. It's going to be tough, but I'm sure we can get him out of this thing."

"You're the only one who's that confident." Her mouth stretched briefly in a smile. "Good luck." She nodded once before continuing down the hall.

He looked after her with a deliberately bland smile, aware that he was being watched. If she thought he was doing a good job, then he must be knocking the socks off the other partners.

In his pockets, his fists tightened with triumph. The late-morning lethargy he'd felt abruptly disappeared. Suddenly, lunchtime didn't seem so far away. He turned around to go back to his office and spent the next two hours buried in work. At one o' clock, instead of walking down to the Thai restaurant on the corner like he planned, Derrick found himself picking up the phone.

"Are you busy?" he asked Nuria when she answered.

She wasn't. And she was home, only three blocks away from the office. Derrick asked if he could come over and didn't waste any time when she said yes.

Nuria came to the door in something ordinary. Jeans. Her mouth was free of lipstick, and her braless breasts lay under a tight white T-shirt with something Spanish scrawled across it. Her feet were bare.

The intensity of her look flashed sparks over his skin. And the need he felt in Trish's bed returned as if it never left. The fuck under the sun hadn't burned the desire out of him. The sex in the shower hadn't quenched him. His skin burned. His balls ached. His dick hardened. And he couldn't separate the need of Sunday afternoon from now. But he was sure that satisfaction, if he got Nuria under his hands and around his dick, would be his. And hers. Absolutely hers.

Derrick opened his mouth to say hi but ended up capturing hers instead, licking the smile from her face and devouring what she intended to say. Pleasure illuminated her face. Yes, she wanted this, too. *Yes.* A shudder ran through him. This was what he'd been wanting. She felt warm against him, and soft. Her jean-clad backside the perfect thing to have under his hands, to squeeze in his frantic fingers. He'd been hungry all day. And this was the food he wanted.

They stumbled into her condo with her clinging to him, his hands pulling apart her clothes. Her fingers plucking at his shirt, baring his chest. Her body was heavy on him, and hot. The door slammed shut as they sank to the floor, half on the hardwood and half on the copper rug. She'd been drinking pineapple juice. Its sting snaked against his tongue, and he thirstily drank her, searching for the essence of her beyond the pineapple.

Nuria's teeth clenched in fierce pleasure as Derrick squeezed her nipples through the thin shirt. He fought to pull off her jeans, and she helped him, kicking them away, chest heaving, mouth wet, nipples hard under the shirt.

"Take off your shirt," he grated. "I want to see your tits."

And she pulled it off. God! So beautiful. Derrick fumbled with his zipper, crawling onto her at the same time. Dick hard and thrusting into the air. Even harder because she wanted him just as badly. He barely remembered the rubber in the wallet in his pants, which sagged around his thighs, to pull it out and on, and he dove into her. Wet heaven. He trembled inside her, his hands tightening on her hips. Nuria cried out. Yes! And they were moving together, slamming together in a ferocious rhythm that called up his own cries, grunts, and gasps as he fucked her, as they fucked each other across the slick hardwood floor. Her legs clasped tightly around him, her heavy, dark-tipped breasts shaking with each thrust, each gasp, each groan.

Sweat dripped down his back, into the sharp valley of spine. Derrick felt it dampen his shirt, felt the smell of sex rise up like steam in the room around them. He was hungry. So hungry. His belly clenched tight with his need for her.

"Harder," she said, heels locked at his back. "Harder."

They slid across the sweat-slick floor, wrinkling up and pushing aside the rug. *Yes.* Her head arched back and her teeth bared. She wanted this cum. He needed it. So. Fucking. Badly. Derrick heard himself grunting like a beast. He clenched his bottom lip between his teeth, pounding, thrusting, fucking, until destruction lurked at the edge of his vision. He gripped her hips tighter. Her breasts jumped to the rhythm of their fucking; her breath came in jagged pants. Then she was coming.

Derrick felt her around him, felt her pussy walls milking him. Nuria's throat stretched as she screamed her release. Fuck! Fuck! Fuck! His world ignited. Hips jerking as her spurted inside her. Sensation licking all over his skin. Nuria gasped, laughing softly when he collapsed on her, sliding over her damp belly.

"You're not light, Nichols. Ease up." She shoved at him, and Derrick rolled off her and let the floor catch him.

His body was still. Finally, the restlessness that had claimed him since Sunday was gone. Derrick forced his breathing to slow down. He lay there as the ticks and twitches from his orgasm tapered off, then disappeared altogether. *Thank you.* He wanted to say the words to her but kept them behind his teeth. When she shifted beside him, he turned his head to look at her. She stood up, walking toward what his mind now processed as a ringing cell phone. Behind her on the kitchen counter sat a vase full of deep red roses. Their petals glistened with moisture and thick color. He hoped she liked them.

Derrick pulled off the condom and tied it, still watching her. Her body was perfect symmetry. Full breasts, narrow waist, thick ass, hips, and thighs. The urge to pull her back to the floor and burrow between those thighs with his mouth made Derrick swallow.

"Hey, what's up?" She answered the phone, smiling. Then her look changed. "What's wrong?" Her eyes flickered to Derrick. "No, I'm not busy." Silence. "Yeah, no problem. I'm leaving right now. All right." She hung up the phone.

Before she could say anything, Derrick stood up and pulled on his pants.

"Sorry," she said. "I have to go."

"Me too. I'm on my lunch hour."

At her surprised look, he laughed. "Yeah . . ." With a quick movement of his wrists, his shirt was buttoned and tucked back into his pants. He could clean up at the office. Derrick turned to go, then said, "Have lunch with me next week?"

Her eyebrow rose. "Seriously?"

"Yes. Can you?" He didn't even know why he was pursuing this, but suddenly he wanted to see her in the light with her clothes and with that particular smile that she seemed to have for everyone but him.

"Ah . . . sure. What time?"

"This time next week Tuesday is fine." He looked at his watch. "One o'clock?"

She nodded and Derrick felt as if that was his permission to go. He turned with a brief smile and grabbed the doorknob.

"By the way"—Derrick turned back at the sound of her voice—"thanks for the flowers."

He smiled briefly. "You're welcome."

A warm spot blossomed under his breastbone, and it stayed with him all the way back to the office. The rest of his day passed by in a blur. It wasn't until he got home and stood in his bedroom about to change for his workout that Derrick realized that he'd forgotten to clean up after his afternoon with Nuria. He walked around the office steeped in the scent of their sex and didn't notice it. He coughed up a sound—half groan, half laugh.

Okay, Nichols. You have to get better than this. What if Trish had come to visit him sometime during the day? That would've been a mess so big that even he couldn't talk himself out of it. Still, the thought didn't hurry him to the shower. Derrick pulled on his sweatpants and headed for the workout room. There was nothing wrong with smelling like her for a little while longer.

* * *

A week was a long time to wait and see her again. Especially since everything conspired to remind him of her—the swinging temptation of girls' backsides as he cruised slowly past; the radio station he accidentally programmed his car to that played music he'd heard in her condo; the pineapple he smelled at the market. So it wasn't completely unexpected that while walking through the mall on his way back from meeting with a client, a certain scent in the department store caught his nose. A woman in a black dress more suited for evening wear than department store customer service said it was a perfume called One Thousand. Derrick bought it before he could think too carefully about it and showed up on Nuria's doorstep the next evening with it as a gift, and an excuse.

Nuria blinked at him from the doorway, her body draped in a thin beige robe and little else. She looked at his present, carefully wrapped in black and gold.

"A girl could get the wrong idea, Nichols," she said, holding the package carefully in her hands.

Derrick wanted to devour her then and there, but he forced a smile. He couldn't force his erection away, though. It tented his pants, a betrayal. They both pretended that it wasn't there.

"No ideas, wrong or right," he murmured. "Just a feeling."

She dropped the box on the table beside the couch without opening it. As she turned back to him, the robe fell off one shoulder, catching on the fullest part of her breast. The nipple teased his eyes through the cloth.

"In that case," she murmured, "why don't you feel your way over here?"

And that was all the invitation he needed. Derrick moved quickly across the small space and pulled the robe off her shoulders, burrowing his nose in the curve of her neck for a trace of the scent that was driving him crazy.

"I think you put something in my drink," he gasped around her nipple. "I can't get enough of you."

She laughed, then sighed as his fingers found her wet and ready. Her legs straddled the ground, parted more for him. Nuria pulled at his hair, tugged him back up for her mouth to devour him. They fell to the couch. Her legs around his waist. The robe on the floor. The rubber fumbled for and found. A hot push inside her pussy. Her moaning laugh.

"Don't blame me because you can't control yourself," she gasped.

And he couldn't control himself. Her pleasure and her pussy were under him, and he could think of nothing that he wanted more. Nowhere else that he'd rather be. Derrick was hot and aching. His hips twisted as he fucked her into the couch. Their breaths wove together. Nuria groaned. His balls tightened. Heat lanced through him. He died inside her.

Still panting and joined, they stumbled to the bedroom. Nuria stuck to him like a vine, her legs twined around his waist. Their laughter surprised him as they tumbled onto the bed, not urgent, pleasure still shuddering over their skin. They kissed and nibbled each other until he became hard again and they couldn't laugh anymore. They fucked until their flesh was raw, and countless orgasms later, she was breathless and cried, "Enough."

He slept.

"There's something I've always wanted to try with you."

The roughly spoken words pulled Derrick out of sleep. He surfaced, blinking into the sheets, smelling Nuria over him. She pressed against his back, her breasts dragging against his skin, the nipples hard and hot. He shuddered as she traced her fingers along the muscles of his back, and the light strokes brought his dick up hard against the sheets. Her breath brushed against his cheek, scented with toothpaste and desire. Feeling at a distinct disadvantage because she'd brushed her teeth, Derrick tried to get up, but she gently pushed him back into the bed. He struggled with himself before the admission: her control felt good.

"I've smelled morning breath before," she whispered against his skin. "I like you like this." Her fingers trailed down his ass, along the fault line between his cheeks. "For someone with facial hair, you don't have too much body hair." The fingers dipped between his thighs, nuzzled his balls. "Do you shave?" She cupped him. "Or wax?"

His body tingled to life, all of him waking up with enthusiasm with each caress of her hand, each kiss of her breath.

"Neither," he choked, losing the battle to steady his voice.

"Hmm," she murmured. "I'm envious."

He felt her body stretch across the bed, heard a drawer open. Her mouth returned to his ear, lightly nipped it.

"What are you doing?"

"Taking advantage of having you in my bed," she said. "What else?"

Her light fingers returned to his ass and, before he could protest, slid between his cheeks. Something cool and wet touched his asshole. Derrick clenched up. But she stroked his ear with her tongue, nibbled on the back of his neck.

"Have you ever been fucked?" she asked, as if inquiring about the weather or the current price of tea.

"No."

She must have drugged him. Otherwise there was no reason for him to lying under her so tamely, almost begging her to put her fingers all the way inside him. Derrick wanted to rise up, push her off him, but his limbs felt leaden. Her breasts dragged across his back again. Two fingers, he could feel them distinctly, settled in at his asshole as if asking his permission to enter.

"Relax." Her words were sweet poison at his ear. "You're

here to feel good, right?" Nuria didn't wait for his response. "This is going to blow your mind."

She teased him. Scraped her nails along his back, whispered things he wanted to hear. Wanted to do.

"You remember how it feels when I massage your dick with my pussy or milk you with my mouth? It's going to be like that." Her breath steamed his neck. "But better."

The words opened him like a key. His thighs fell apart, and she stroked his hole, probed with wet fingers. Derrick's breath shuddered in his chest. Morning light poured into the bedroom, predawn and gray. The windows let in the damp sweet smell of newness. Somewhere in the condo, coffee brewed.

There were some things that he never thought he'd do. One of them, maybe even number one on the list, was let someone fuck him up the ass. But by turns stroking and probing, Nuria's fingers felt more than good inside him, trailing vapors of sensation through his body. A groan burst from him. He lifted his ass higher, and the fingers went deeper, bringing more sensation, more sounds from his mouth. She moved down to tease the flesh of his ass with her breath, then with her teeth. The fingers. Damn, those fingers!

They fucked him smoothly, and her other hand grazed his balls, slid beneath to enfold the head of his dick. *Ah!* He felt Nuria's laughing breath against his skin. Knew she was getting off on her power over him, but he didn't care. She was tearing him apart with pleasure. Sweat ghosted all along his back. The fingers left and Derrick groaned with real loss only to gasp when something else took their place. Something colder.

"What are you—?!" But hot sensation caught him by surprise. Cut off his voice.

Something harder than her fingers. Cool. Wet with lube. Filled him. And he couldn't say no, couldn't say he didn't want it because he was in the grip of an agony of delight. Her fingers stroked his dick, pacified him. Pleasured him. Harder. Faster.

While the thing in his ass turned him into a whimpering, gasping fool. Sounds he'd never heard before bubbled up his throat. She found a place inside him, somewhere amazing, a new source of delight that had him crawling out of his skin. Crawling to her. Fuck!

She worked him harder. Her fingers stroking his dick until he shouted, groaned, and howled his release. And came all over her hands.

"Don't ever do that to me again," he panted, blinking away the stars that exploded behind his tightly closed eyelids.

His ass felt sore. Empty. Derrick rolled over shakily, suddenly aware of the rapidly cooling wet spot under him. Nuria grinned. With her teeth, she tugged a latex glove from over her hand and threw it toward the floor. As Derrick watched, she picked something up. A something that had a lube-smeared condom on it.

"Is that a candle?" he asked, incredulous.

"It felt great, didn't it?" She peeled the condom off the stiff white candle and threw it in the same direction as the dirty glove. "I love these things. Just put them in the freezer for a few hours and they're ready to go."

She stroked it briefly, as if in memory of good times past, then tossed it aside before falling on Derrick. His breath huffed out of him at her unexpected weight, but he caught her easily. She kissed him.

"That was *muy caliente*, no? Very hot. Did you like it?" Her hands skimmed up his sides. "I can tell that you liked it." Nuria grabbed his hand and put it between her legs. She was sopping wet. "I *really* liked it."

Derrick groaned. And it seemed like the most natural thing in the world to work his fingers over her clit, to keep kissing her, to plunge his fingers into her hot pussy, fingering her clit and kissing her hungry mouth until she came noisily above him. Nuria curled up on his chest, panting softly, then not at all.

The smell of their sex wound around him like steam, pressing into his senses until his arms tightened around her. More. He wanted more.

"Are you tired, baby?" Her voice was low but very awake. As she stirred, her hair tickled his chest.

"Not right now," he said. His dick was already beginning to stir again.

"Good." She moved up his body, hard nipples brushing briefly against his mouth. "Because I want you to eat my pussy. I want you to eat me until I scream."

Much later, they had coffee and croissants, then crawled back into bed. Derrick loved that she was insatiable, more ravenous for sex than any woman he'd ever known. Her mouth swallowed him, his mouth devoured her pussy, he fucked her, and she fucked him, again and again until they were both limp against the sheets.

When the sun fell across the bed in patterns of late afternoon, Derrick's ears started paying attention to something besides the rhythm of Nuria's moans.

"I think my phone's ringing."

"It's been ringing all damn day," she said. "Whoever's calling seems very eager to get in touch with you. Is it the same woman from the other night?"

"I don't know." But it was. Derrick sent Trish a text message saying he was busy, then turned the ringer off.

"If only everything was that easy," she said from her sprawl in the bed. Her knee pointed toward the ceiling.

As Derrick crept slowly back to her—all the better to appreciate the fan of her hair against the adobe-colored sheets—her knee stretched out to give him room to maneuver.

He kissed her eyelids, her nose, and the somber curve of her mouth. Nuria shifted abruptly under him.

"You know that I'm in love with your sister, don't you?" she asked.

"Now I do," he said, blinking down at her. Yet, somehow he wasn't surprised.

"Do you mind?"

He laughed, though the sound had a slightly bitter edge to it. "It wouldn't matter if I did. Dez is married and she won't cheat on Tori."

"And Victoria's not bi, so she's never going to fuck you." She looked steadily at Derrick, as if daring him to deny her words.

"And Victoria's not bi," he agreed.

Against him, her flesh burned with heat. Despite the truths that Nuria threw at him like iced water, he was still absolutely focused on her. Tori wasn't here in the bed with them. Neither was Dez. Right now, he wanted Nuria to the exclusion of everything else, and he was more irritated that she forced him to acknowledge other people when all that mattered now and here was their hunger for each other. At the back of his mind, the truth of that jolted him. But he wasn't ready to pay attention to it.

Derrick dropped a hand on Nuria's thigh and leaned closer. "Let's talk about that later," he said. "I have more important things to do with my mouth right now."

8

A few days later, they met as planned for their lunch date at Novlette's Café. When he got there, Nuria already waited at a table on the terrace with her eyes shielded by dark glasses and her hair loose around her shoulders. At a few minutes past one in the afternoon, the crowd was thick with people laughing and eating quickly, trying to make it back to their offices before the hour was up. Red-shirted waiters and waitresses wove in and out of the tables with their trays held in front of them.

Nuria's burgundy lips widened in a smile as he got close, and she turned her cheek for a kiss. Derrick obliged, inhaling her perfume and feeling it work its familiar magic on him. She looked gorgeous in tight jeans and a spaghetti-strapped white blouse that lightly skimmed the curves of her breasts and provided an alluring frame for the slender platinum chain and its dangling key pendant around her neck. The titanium piercing just below her full lips winked in the light. Standing there, with her distinct scent playing in his senses, Derrick became hard as the proverbial rock.

Clearing his throat, he sat down opposite her and adjusted

himself under the table. "Do you always do this to me on purpose?" he asked.

Her eyes burned him through the dark glasses. "You and your sister have a lot in common."

"What do you mean by that?" Although he wasn't in the mood to be compared to Dez, Derrick consciously made his tone playful.

"You both want what you want, when you want it." She took off the glasses and put them in the center of the table. "And you usually want sex."

He stiffened as a thought occurred to him. "Did you ever fuck her?"

The waiter chose that moment to walk up to their table. The sable-skinned boy who looked all of nineteen in his red shirt and black pants paused before asking them if they wanted anything to drink. Derrick asked for water, the same thing that Nuria was already drinking. When he left, Nuria continued as if they'd never been interrupted.

"And what if I did let Dez have me? Would you run home and scrub your skin? Or do you want to scrub mine?" She bared her teeth. "Is that what you want to do? Strip off my clothes and scrub me in hot water until all traces of her are gone?"

He calmed himself, reading her body language. The sneer. The helpless flicker of unfulfilled desire in her eyes when she mentioned his sister's name.

"You didn't fuck her." Derrick relaxed in his chair and stretched his feet out under the table.

Nuria did the same, dismissing her pique with a shrug. "I wanted to, though. She's a hot one."

"If you say so."

"Oh, I do. Heat seems to run in your family."

Derrick allowed himself a small smile. "I'll make sure to let my mother know that."

Nuria wrinkled her nose and glanced down at the menu. "I wouldn't go that far."

The waiter came back with Derrick's glass of water and whipped out his pad to take their food orders. She ordered pancakes, eggs, and vegetarian sausage.

"What do you recommend?" he asked the boy.

Before the waiter could speak, Nuria leaned close and caught the top of the menu with a burgundy-tipped finger, lightly pinning it to the table. "You should try the stewed parrot fish with the brown rice," she murmured as her perfume floated to Derrick again. "Your body would appreciate it. And your tongue, too."

Their eyes met across the table. And Derrick nodded. "I'll have what the lady recommends."

The boy's eyes skittered over Nuria's cleavage before he nodded. "Would you like anything else?"

"No, thank you," Nuria answered.

With another nod, the waiter left. Nuria leaned back in her chair and crossed her legs. Sitting across from Nuria with her cool, undemanding gaze, Derrick abruptly realized that he'd never actually sat down to have a conversation with her before. The wind ruffled her hair, rearranging the dark strands around and in her face. Instead of brushing them back, Nuria glanced at him through the twisting vines, looking like some otherworldly creature with the bay glittering behind her. They didn't know each other at all.

"What is it about women that you like so much?" he asked. It was a question he wanted to ask for a long time but never had the courage to. He might as well have asked her, "Why are you bisexual?"

"Why don't you ask yourself the same question? I'm sure the answers will be similar." She toyed with the fork beside her empty plate. "Unless you don't like women at all."

"I love women. You of all people should know that by now."

Nuria shook her head. "You love to fuck me. And you love it when I fuck you." Her teeth flashed in the light. "That's not the question."

Irritation scuttled like beetles under his skin. "Of course I like women. My mother taught and showed me respect. Because of her, I have respect for her and most women."

"Most, huh?" Her smile appeared again.

"Definitely not all. Like some men, there are women out there who don't deserve it."

"Fair enough."

Just then, the waiter appeared with their lunch. Nuria sat back to allow him to place the dishes on their small table. He seemed to have enough trouble keeping his eyes off her body as it was. Better give him all the help she could, Derrick thought with a wry twist of his mouth.

When the boy left, Nuria wiggled in her chair, smiling, and dug into her mound of butter-topped pancakes. Apparently, the subject was closed.

"Do you respect the other woman you're with?"

Derrick looked up, deliberately blank-faced, and Nuria laughed at him.

"Don't give me that look. Dez does innocent a lot better than you. Which isn't saying much, by the way." She laughed, waving her fork at him. "I know there's someone else. Remember the night you ran out of my bed like your dick was on fire?" She picked up the sausage with her fingers and took a bite. "So just answer my question. Do you respect her?"

"I didn't ask you to lunch for you to interrogate me."

"It's not always about what you want, stud." Nuria licked her fingers, then reclaimed her fork. "Right now I'm curious about you. We've never had a meal together before now, or any sort of conversation. I'm interested in who you are, not just how you fuck."

Derrick felt the weight of her stare, the weight of her question. When Trish had asked him, it was easy to give the obvious response.

"How can you justify cheating on her?"

"Look, Nuria, we're just dating. Nothing serious."

Her eyebrow rose. "Does this woman know that?"

Derrick felt his cheeks grow warm. *Just don't look down. Don't*—But his eyes floated to the table, to the fish that still looked good on the plate but tasted like ashes in his mouth.

"She doesn't, does she?" Nuria put down her fork, her face suddenly even more serious. She finished chewing, then swallowed. "I won't be your side piece, Nichols. It's not fair to her, and it's not fair to me."

"No," Derrick said. "This isn't about fairness." The tightness in his chest caught him by surprise.

"I've wanted you for a long time," she said. "But screwing other women by screwing their boyfriends was never my style." A crooked half-smile took over her mouth. "I usually like to leave out the middle man."

Nuria dabbed at her lips with the paper napkin, then slid it under the edge of her plate. As she stood, Derrick reached out for her, but Nuria stepped back, moving gracefully beyond his grasp.

"Thanks for lunch." She pulled thirty dollars from her little black purse and dropped it on the table. "It was fun."

Derrick's cheeks still burned. He could feel people watching them, watching her replace the glasses on her face and slip the purse's tiny strap around her wrist. He leaned back in his chair instead of grabbing for her again like he desperately wanted to. *This can't end now.* But she turned, ignoring his silent demand, and left him sitting at the table. Alone.

9

"I'd have left you there sitting by yourself, too." Tori sighed at him through the phone. "When did you become such an asshole?"

"Not you, too?" Derrick leaned back in the chair on his balcony and closed his eyes to the stars winking above him.

"You know how I feel about dishonesty, Derrick."

Why did he even tell Tori what was going on? He should have known that she would side with Nuria. Derrick fumbled for the glass of whiskey in its holder on the patio chair. The tumbler was cool in his grasp. Comforting.

"Maybe I thought this thing with Nuria would be finished by now." He took a long gulp of the whiskey, wincing as it burned in his chest. "But I can't get enough of her, and I don't want to let her go." He didn't know where the deeper ache for her came from. But it was there.

"That's a bullshit excuse if there ever was one. Nuria was right to drop you when she found out. Don't crawl back into her bed with a lie."

A voice in the background, his sister's, called out to Tori and said something that made his friend laugh.

"Okay, I'm coming," tumbled amid the laughter from Tori's mouth. Derrick knew she wasn't talking to him. "That's Dez," she said, still laughing. "She wants to go scuba diving."

"What? It's the middle of the night."

Victoria chuckled. "She likes to do things a little differently."

I'm sure she does, Derrick thought. He imagined them on their borrowed boat, towels draped across their shoulders from an earlier swim, their bodies warm with the happy flush of love. In the middle of the Caribbean, their twenty-two-foot sailboat rocking gently under the sharp moonlight. Derrick was surprised by his lack of jealousy. "Go ahead. I wasn't thinking. You're on your honeymoon, after all."

"It's never a problem talking with you." Dez's voice came again. This time, there was a distinctive growl in it. Victoria laughed again. "I have to go. But please." She sobered. "Do the right thing. Treat these women well."

His mouth twisted. "I'll do what I can."

"Oh, Lord." He could imagine Tori rolling her eyes. "Talk with you later," she said, and this time he heard the smile in her voice.

"Okay. Have fun and come back to us safe."

"I will."

Derrick heard a playful scream in the background, then Dez's laughter as he hung up the phone. He smiled.

10

Nuria's door was the gateway to riches. The thought echoed in Derrick's mind as the woman currently hijacking his thoughts appeared in the doorway of her condo. She wasn't smiling, and neither was he.

"I didn't think it was fair for you to leave me like that," Derrick said.

"Fair for who?" But Nuria didn't back away from him at the door. Derrick reached for her.

"You're who I want." He slid his hands over her gently and sighed at the feel of her skin through the cotton dress. White again, of course. "Very badly. Can't this just be about us?"

"No, it can't. All bullshit aside."

But she allowed his hand to rest in the small of her back, let him pull her close until their breaths were the same and her palms lay against his chest. Derrick knew if he moved too quickly she would pull away. If he acted as if he was starved for her and desperate, like last time, she wouldn't let him have her. But he *was* starved.

The door closed them inside the condo. Her eyes were wide

and curious, watching to see what he would do next. He swallowed against the need to take. To fuck her against the wall, hammering her pussy until paintings fell, until she clawed his back, until he came, howling his desire in her hair, then got hard enough to do it all again.

Derrick held her face gently between his palms and kissed her. She tasted of spice. Of Mexican hot chocolate and something peppery from a late breakfast. Derrick tongued every inch of her mouth, the corners, the slack lips, the sharp teeth, her tongue that tasted him back. A groan of victory vibrated in his throat. She almost pulled back. But he held fast. Held her with gentleness. Calmed her with his hands stroking her shoulders with light butterfly touches, until she moved toward him again. Her mouth opened wider for him. Her body moved against his. Wordlessly, he backed her in the direction of the bedroom.

She had tidied up. All the pillows were off the floor, the canopy tied back to allow their bodies tangle-free access to the mattress. Derrick fell backward against the soft bed, pulling Nuria along with him. The weight of her on him was sweet. Precious. His dick throbbed with the need to be inside her.

"I want you," he murmured against her throat.

Scented with eucalyptus and roses, her hair fell into his face. Her low moan vibrated against his lips as he bared her to his gaze, pulled the dress from her shoulders, revealing inch by inch the smooth slope of her breasts, the dark nipples, the cupping arch of her ribs. "So beautiful."

The ache for her sat in his belly, gathered in his balls, echoed in the iron hardness pressing against her. He switched places with her in the bed. She blinked up at him, breathing through parted lips. With reverence, he tugged the dress completely off her, leaving her naked under him. Her skin seemed to vibrate with each pass of his hands over her.

"I want you to know how you make me feel."

He pressed his lips between her breasts, moving down, calling up her desire, ghosting breath over her clit, over the wet slit of her pussy that her open legs revealed. Nuria smelled ready. Salty. Like the ocean he wanted to play in. Derrick touched her with a finger, dipped inside her wetness. She gasped, watching him as he licked the finger, tasted her. Her mouth opened. She licked her lips.

"Do you want to taste this?"

She nodded, still watching his mouth.

He dipped his finger again, sliding deep into her wetness, coating his finger, plumbing a gasp from her throat.

"Here."

Her mouth closed, like fire, around his finger. He fought back his own groan. Her mouth pulled him, sucked the finger deep inside, and her tongue stroked him, lashed the tip, then his whole finger. His dick jumped harder in his pants. Heat flashed over his skin, and he desperately wanted to be rid of his shirt. Derrick grit his teeth. And watched her, watched her cheeks hollow as she sucked at his finger and turned up the heat in the room.

"You're greedy today," he said roughly. "Don't worry. You'll have your mouth full later on."

He pulled his finger back, muscles aching with the need to fuck, to devour, and to claim her as his. Another shudder rippled through him. He took her foot in his hands, kissed it, and grazed his nose along the instep, down her calf, the back of her knee, absorbing her scent, the salty tang of her excited sweat. The flesh between her thighs was soft under his tongue. Derrick licked higher, closer to her dripping pussy, touched her with his nose.

"Fuck me." The sheets whispered under Nuria's body as she writhed against them. She gulped for air.

And that was the plea that gave him strength to continue. "No."

Derrick pulled off his shirt and smiled as she feasted on his bare chest with her eyes, ate up the bulge of his dick beneath black cloth with her stare. He started again. This time turning Nuria to her belly so he could taste her neck, the hot line of her back with its tattoo, and the soft mounds of her ass. He slid a finger between them, and she called out. Her fingers clenched in the sheets. Her muscles trembled. Her ass arched up in the bed.

His eyes licked over her weeping pussy. She was ready for it. He was ready for it. But not yet. Derrick lifted her hips in the bed until she was kneeling with her face buried in the pillows. He nuzzled between her cheeks, smelled her musk, her desire.

Nuria's pussy was summer rain against his tongue. Hot. Wet. Intoxicating. She groaned in the sheets. Called his name. Calling him to go deeper. So he did, sliding his tongue over the wet folds of her, between the plump cunt lips, and inside the dew-soaked oasis of her. Nuria's pussy clenched around his tongue. It was like she pulled on his dick; he slid deeper, fucking her with his tongue, tasting her marshy wetness, sucking her swollen clit into his mouth.

She called his name again. And again. He felt her come close to the edge. And he withdrew.

"No!"

He turned her over in the bed so he could see her face. Her features twisted with desire and want. Lips bitten. Eyes tightly closed. Neck stretched taut in an arch. Her breasts shuddered. Her belly flexed and released as she fought for air. Slow tears escaped between her spiky lashes.

"Fuck you," she gasped. "Fuck you."

"No, baby. You already got your chance; now it's my turn."

The sound of his zipper split the tense silence. Then the crinkle of the condom wrapper. Derrick's pants sagged around his knees. He fell between her thighs. Her fingers sank into his ass. Flesh connected. Heat around his heat. His cock in her pussy. *Shit.*

"Oh!"

Nuria's sharp cry echoed his deeper one. Fuck! And it was like it should always be—the rock-fuck motion in the bed, him stroking slowly in her heat, forcing himself to be gentle, and the sweet liquid sound of their flesh meeting. At last. But her nails cut deeper into his skin; her hips moved frantically beneath his. Her walls clasped tightly around him. Derrick gasped and threw his head back. *Yes.* Then he couldn't stop himself if he wanted to.

They came together, hard, like rain and dry soil. Pleasure, like lightning, flared over his body, flashed through him until he could see it reflected in her eyes, in the wild joy she took in having his body inside hers, in the wet noise of their passion, the grunts and growls they drew from each other. They fucked each other like their lives depended on the cumming, like nothing else mattered. The flame flashed through Derrick, driving hard into his dick, into Nuria's pussy. The bed slammed against the wall to the rhythm to their sex, to the shouts that Nuria sent into the room, urging him to be faster, do it harder, to fuck her like he meant it. His muscles burned. Their damp bellies slid together. Sweat dripped down his back. His balls clutched with his impending release.

"Fuck!"

Nuria shuddered in the bed and clutched around him, her pussy swallowing him as she came, pushing him, too, over the precipice of orgasm. Sensation captured Derrick, and he moaned, his body wracked with tremors. He tumbled back into himself with a harsh groan, gasping down at her, at her wildly blinking eyes, her sweat-soaked face, her bitten red mouth. *Fuck.* A shudder ran through his arms at the effort of holding himself above her. He let go and rolled into the sheets next to Nuria.

They lay together, panting. Sweat drying. Drained. His eyes fluttered closed and languor settled over him. This was how is should be. He forced his breath to calm.

"Were you playing with me the other afternoon at Novlette's?" Derrick asked.

The smell of their sex. Her eyes watching him under heavy lashes. "No. This afternoon was a mistake." Whatever she saw in his face made her laugh. "I don't fuck other women's toys."

He grew still. "I'm nobody's toy."

"But we are yours, right? To do with as you like? To tell or not to tell about each other?" Her body moved languorously in the bed. Full breasts, soft nipples, a sloping belly that called his hands. Lush nakedness and her unexpected morality making him feel like an ass. She turned over, the pillow under her head and hands clasped beneath it. Her eyes turned away from him. "I was wrong before," Nuria said. "You're nothing like Dez."

Derrick felt the words like a blow to his belly. Again a woman telling him that his sister was better. The curve of her back in the sheets was warm but uninviting. Like Trish, she had given in to the sexual sorcery he spun. But she hadn't forgiven him. She didn't forget. Derrick silently drew on his clothes and left.

On the drive home, he called Trish and left a message. She was just stepping out of her car when he pulled into the driveway. The night air was moist with the smell of impending rain, and she looked flower-soft in a caramel dress that waved over her breasts in the fragrant breeze. Trish smiled.

"We have to talk," he said.

11

Derrick smiled back at Metta Johnson across the churning room and raised his glass. They won. Champagne sparkled in crystal flutes. Teeth flashed in triumph and jubilant laughter echoed and reechoed around the open-air restaurant overlooking the Atlantic. Even the fire pits, lit and crackling cheerfully in the twilight, seemed to celebrate, too. Rafael Costa stood in the center of a colorfully dressed group, his words swelling with the story of his victory and of the firm's success in getting him out of one of his stupidest messes. Mrs. Costa, thick and voluptuous in mourning black, nodded at her husband's story with her arms folded across her belly, elbows cupped in her palms.

All evening, Derrick had been getting exuberant claps on the back from other lawyers at the firm. Metta personally guaranteed him a raise, and he got an additional week of paid vacation time if he chose to take it. The firm of Silverman, Johnson, and Meyer was very pleased. If they could get Costa off, then any success was possible. Derrick and the partners anticipated a massive influx of new business. Mostly criminals.

Derrick smiled ironically at Alex, but his boss only grinned. "Don't look so serious, Derrick. This is a party."

Yes, it was a party. Costa had rented out the beachfront restaurant at the Ritz and invited over a hundred of his closest friends and business associates. And although Derrick was relieved that the case turned out in their favor, he wasn't quite in the party mood. He hadn't seen Nuria in days, and all his phone calls and visits to the places he expected her to be had yielded nothing.

Derrick patted Alex on the back. "This *is* my party face," he said.

The other man laughed and shook his head before wandering off to a nearby table. The umbrella fanned out above the five heads celebrating noisily in their chairs splashed a bright red against the darkening sky.

"I'm glad you could come," Costa said as he came up to Derrick. "Did you bring your pretty friend from a few months ago, or did she come with someone else?"

"Trish came with me."

But as soon as Derrick said the words, he knew that Costa wasn't talking about Trish. His eyes floated around the restaurant and quickly found her. He didn't wonder about his lack of surprise at Nuria's presence. It seemed only right that she should be there. She stood at the railing overlooking the ocean, a margarita held high in her hand, nearly surrounded by admirers. The wind blew her loosened hair around her bare shoulders and face. A tuxedo-cut blouse and matching pants skimmed her slight figure in red, making her glow against the railing and outline of the sea.

"Hey, Derrick," a low voice came from behind him. "I wondered where you went off to."

As Trish appeared at his side, Costa grinned, then shrugged at Derrick. "Good luck," he said, gracefully making his exit.

Trish blinked in confusion at the older man. "Who was that?"

"The reason we're celebrating tonight," Derrick said. His eyes darted back to the railing, but Nuria was gone.

"Oh, that's him? He looks taller on TV." She touched his shoulder but quickly drew back.

Feeling guilty, he reached for her. "It's okay to—"

"Derrick. What a pleasant surprise."

His insides jumped to attention at the sound of Nuria's voice, but he took his time turning to face her. Up close, she was even more devastating. The weeks' separation had only sharpened his weakness for her. Her sandalwood and patchouli scent snaked around his senses, drawing him up tight in his clothes. Her teeth flashed, but she wasn't smiling.

Unexpectedly tongue-tied, Derrick greeted her with a nod, but she wasn't looking at him. Her eyes swallowed Trish, who looked at Nuria with interest, eyelashes blinking as she took in the sex-shaped body.

"You're very beautiful," Nuria said. And when Trish didn't back away, she added, "Tasty-looking."

Derrick glanced at Trish. *Was she?* The sleeveless black cocktail dress with the pink satin trim and ruffled hem draped nicely on her slim figure, giving her the look of a sweet sophisticate. Nothing that Derrick would consider "tasty."

Trish gave an uncertain smile, then stepped closer to Nuria. "I'm Trish," she said, extending her hand and the smile.

Nuria shifted her margarita to grasp the other woman's hand, then looked fully into her face. "It's really good to meet you."

Derrick ignored Trish's puzzled yet intrigued look. "I didn't expect to see you here," he said.

"By now, you should learn to expect the unexpected." Her mouth stretched briefly in his direction. "Anyway, I'm not staying long. Congratulations on winning your case." The flash of her labret stud drew his eyes to her red mouth. She smiled again at Trish. Nodded at him. Then turned to disappear into the crowd.

"Who is she?" Trish blinked after Nuria and turned to him, the satin-edged ruffles at her knees fluttering in the breeze.

"Someone I used to know."

Her face grew still. "She's the one?"

Derrick nodded once. "Yes."

Shame prickled his cheeks. Trish turned her head away, but not before he saw the anger. She clutched her purse more tightly under her arm.

"I'm going to pass out some more business cards," she said.

He couldn't watch her walk away.

Barely an hour passed before he abandoned the party, leaving Trish to go home in her own car. Thoughts of calling Nuria followed him home, made him drum his fingers into the steering wheel as he drove. But each time he picked up the phone to call, he remembered the cool look on her face. And behind her bravado, the hurt he didn't know how to fix. When he fell into the cool sheets hours later, she still lay heavy on his mind. But the scotch helped to dull the pain of it.

12

The words on the computer blurred in front of Derrick's eyes. New case. New problems. But this was nothing that would absorb his time or energies like the trial that had eventually gotten Rafael Costa acquitted of fraud and money-laundering charges. As anticipated, the firm had gotten a large influx of clients, and a surprising number of them ended up in Derrick's lap. But he could barely focus enough to read the background information on one of their newest clients, a South Beach madam who got tossed to the cops by one of her ex-hookers. He shook his head, squeezing the bridge of his nose. When his office phone rang, he absently reached for it.

"Derrick Nichols," he answered.

"Good, I've got the right Nichols this time." Nuria's laughing voice jerked his attention from the computer screen. "Are you ready to go all the way with me?"

His hand tightened on the phone. After almost three weeks of not hearing from her, he nearly sagged in his chair with relief, but he was also pissed. "What are you talking about?"

"If you're interested in finding out, you should meet me at

the Bay Diner in ten minutes." She paused. "I know you drive fast, so if you're not here in fifteen minutes, then I'll assume you have better things to do."

Derrick glanced at his watch. It was barely two o'clock. He'd just come back from a solitary lunch an hour before and didn't think it would look good if he left now when he had work to do. "Give me twenty minutes," he said.

When he pulled into the parking lot of the small restaurant across the street from the beach, Derrick immediately saw her car. She wasn't in it. Inside the restaurant, she leaned against the counter, chatting up the lean-faced boy at the register. Snug jeans clung to her backside, and a white tube top hugged her torso, baring her lower back and the tattoo sitting on the base of her spine. The boy, Mando, according to his name tag, gave Derrick a skyward nod as he approached. A New York Yankees diamond stud flung light from his ear.

"What can I get for you, man?" Mando asked.

Nuria turned and smiled at Derrick. She straightened and the tattoo disappeared under her shirt.

"I have what I need right here." He nodded back at the boy, but Nuria claimed all of his attention. "Now what?" Derrick asked her.

"Now we go." She turned back to Mando, and the boy wordlessly handed her an ice cream cone, vanilla dripping with chocolate sprinkles. "See you next time, Mando," she tossed over her shoulder as she walked away with her arm tucked around Derrick's. "Tell your sister I said hey."

The boy nodded again, smiling for her this time.

"After the party, I didn't think I'd hear from you again. Where have you been?" The words left Derrick's mouth without thought or invitation.

Nuria licked her ice cream and, with her shoulder pressed against his arm and her scent snuggled up against him, urged him across to the other side of the street. They walked past the sidewalk, down the incline of sand, and past the naked lawn chairs spread across the beach like sunbathers. The ocean rocked gently under the blistering heat of the sun. Derrick was glad that he left his jacket in the car. Between the sun and Nuria's scorching presence at his side, his skin prickled with heat.

They walked on the beach, parallel to the water, Nuria in her black ballet flats and the jeans folded once above her slender ankles and Derrick in his Italian shoes with specks of wet sand already spoiling the leather. The salt-laced wind brought her scent even closer, and her hair whipped and danced against her shoulder.

"I've been around," she said, finally answering his question.

If "around" meant not answering his calls, then yes, she had been around. Between rounds at the office and sweat-drenched hours in his gym, Derrick had been quietly frantic. His body clawed with desire for her. This couldn't be it. All the things they'd done together, had done to each other, couldn't be over.

"Were you trying to punish me?"

"Do you feel punished?"

She looked at him, her eyes sly between the black lashes and under the thick, curling locks that framed her pretty face with its glinting jewelry. Derrick couldn't answer her question, but he did feel punished.

Nuria's tongue swirled around the creamy head of the ice cream cone that even in the heat hadn't gotten the chance to drip. She ate it neatly, hungrily, as if she didn't want a drop to waste. Against his will, Derrick felt himself begin to swell with arousal. Nuria chuckled, her lips pale with cream. She released his arm and looped hers around his waist. They walked with each other like lovers, Derrick thought. Then didn't allow himself to think anymore.

At three in the afternoon, the beach was mostly empty, with only a few children dashing back and forth in the sand while their mothers kept wary eyes on them. In front of their feet, the glinting sand went on for miles.

Up ahead, a man walked toward them. Derrick moved Nuria lightly to the side to give the stranger enough room to pass. As the man passed, his eyes flickered over Nuria in obvious interest. The corner of his mouth tucked up in a smile.

"Hmm. She's cute," Nuria said as she swallowed the last bite of her ice cream and glanced back at the stranger with a coy turn of her head, her hair flying up in the breeze.

She? Derrick turned and looked again. The stranger looked back, too, and Derrick's eyes adjusted beyond what he expected to see, past the dark slacks and long-sleeved shirt, like a mirror of him only thinner and with skin a few shades lighter than his, to the slight roundness of the face, the soft lips, and the faintest hint of breasts under the white shirt. Yes, *she.* Derrick slowed.

He felt Nuria's hand tighten on the back of his shirt, bunching the cotton in her fist. "Don't you think so?"

The girl stopped, too, turned completely around to watch them from beneath her dark shades, the wind ruffling the white shirt and black pants. Planted as she was in the sand, it seemed then that she could've taken off in flight, lifting above the sand and hurtling toward them. Derrick blinked. She wasn't quite his type, but the idea of breasts and pussy under those masculine clothes made him unexpectedly hard. Harder. It wasn't something that made any sense. He'd seen Dez and her butch friends before, had even dismissed them as not being real women, but this one . . .

"Let's go say hi," Nuria said, already releasing the back of his shirt toward the stranger.

"I'm Eva," the woman said when they drew close, with Derrick bringing up the rear, his mind wreathed in questions. Her voice was light and feminine, a surprise. She offered a hand to shake and grasped his firmly. "A pleasure."

"We hope so." Nuria smiled.

It was that slow revelation of teeth that had first caught Derrick. The wet mouth. Eyes slumberous behind the vines of her hair. Like an unfolding, just for him. Eva tucked her hands in her pants pockets and rocked back on her heels, and it seemed as if Nuria's smile sparked hers until both women shimmered with sensual possibility under the Thursday-afternoon sun. Derrick's cock jumped in his pants.

Despite his generous attitude toward sex and his large sexual appetite, Derrick had never had a one-night stand, tied a woman up, or had a threesome. These things that other people he knew freely partook of—hell, his damn *sister* made a life out of that kind of excess—were only real for him in the porno movies or in the books Trish sometimes read to him when she was feeling adventurous. But now, staring at Nuria on her knees and strapped to twin poles with her ass in the air and her legs spread, he felt like he was born to this.

Eva had taken them to her house not far from the beach and invited them inside.

"I wasn't expecting company," Eva said as they walked past her into her condo.

But the smell of incense and the bottle of wine waiting on the counter between her kitchen and living room revealed the words for a lie. He looked at Nuria, but her face told him nothing. As Derrick passed into the room that Eva indicated with a wave of her hand, he felt her eyes on his ass. In moments, they were in her playroom and Nuria shrugged out of her clothes as if this was where she'd meant to be all along. She crawled across the thickly carpeted floor to the two posts that had padded leg shackles already waiting. Under Derrick's bare feet, the floor was firm yet yielding, like a mattress.

The large room had been designed for comfort. Sound-proofed comfort. The deep burgundy walls were padded and the bed was four-poster, looking both inviting and dangerous with its thick cherrywood, plump pillows, and dark sheets. It didn't have the sensual appeal of Nuria's bed. This one seemed made just for fucking. The thought sent a jolt of electricity straight to Derrick's dick.

"You can do anything to me," Nuria murmured to Eva from the ground. And the look in her eyes said that she meant it.

"I'm sure that goes for you, too, Derrick." Eva smiled, a sexy flash of confidence and teeth.

"That's something that I always wanted a woman"—Eva's eyes found Derrick's—"or a man to tell me." She pulled off her shirt, and Derrick couldn't help but notice that her forearms were strong.

Under the shirt, she wore a white tank top. Her nipples rose hard under the thin material, and the rhythm of her breathing was even as she calmed Nuria, ran her fingers through Nuria's hair and down her face.

"I'm going to fuck you, pretty thing," she said. "But before that, I want you to eat my pussy. I've been thinking about that pretty mouth of yours ever since I saw it."

Derrick unbuttoned his shirt and tugged it from his shoulders. Eva's eyes flickered over him. Their casual hunger as they roamed the hard planes of his chest, his belly, and the bulge at the front of his trousers made his dick even harder. If this woman couldn't resist him, who could?

As if reading his mind, Eva shook her head and laughed softly. She pressed her thumb gently into Nuria's mouth, watching Derrick all the while. They both felt it when Nuria's hot tongue slid out to lick and suck the long finger into her mouth.

Eva groaned, openmouthed and smiling. "Good girl."

Nuria groaned, too. With her eyes closed, legs apart, and ass arched up for fucking, Derrick couldn't resist. He moved behind Nuria and tasted her with his hands. She was already wet. Dripping. She made a low noise as he parted her pussy lips, skimmed his fingers over her swollen clit. Nuria spread her legs wider.

"I have rubbers in the bedside table," Eva said, motioning with her head toward the bed.

"Thanks." Derrick shook his head and reached into his pocket. "But I have my own."

The just-in-case pack of five had been a quick afterthought as he'd left the office. Now he was relieved that he had them. The plastic crinkled in his fist, and he was very aware of Eva's eyes on him as he let his pants fall, tugged down his boxers, and rolled the latex over his bobbing dick. She licked her lips and bared her teeth at him. Between them, Nuria groaned softly, bringing their attention back to where it needed to be.

"Don't worry, baby," Eva said, unzipping her pants. "We haven't forgotten about you."

Nuria groaned at the sight of the other woman's hairless pussy, and even Derrick had to appreciate its slick, simple lusciousness. He grasped Nuria's hips to keep her close. Eva stepped out of her pants and pushed her pussy close to Nuria's mouth.

"This is for you, doll."

Nuria dove in without hesitation. Derrick watched her lick the hairless crease, eyes closed as her tongue burrowed between the slender thighs that opened even more for her. Eva's hand hooked at the back of Nuria's neck, burrowing into thick dreds to pull her harder into her pussy. She braced herself and splayed her legs, her lips parted and wet, eyes half closed as she watched Derrick and his hard dick.

"What are you waiting for?" Her gasped question shot at

Derrick. "Fuck her. I want to see you fuck her and make her cum. I know her pussy must be sweet."

Yeah, her pussy is sweet. And Derrick suddenly felt a surge of possessiveness toward Nuria even as she licked and slurped at the other woman's cunt, sucking on the thick pussy lips and making hungry sounds deep in her throat. Nuria's pussy was hot with juice. It ran wet as if she was about to cum just from eating Eva out. Her ass undulated in the air, pushing back, squeezing as if it wanted something. Something Derrick could provide.

But did he want to do it like this? The smell of her was steeped in the air. It pulled his nose closer, made him want to dine on his own cunt meal. Nuria noisily sucked the pussy under her mouth, making Eva grunt with pleasure. The girl's hand tightened at the back of Nuria's neck, and she fucked Nuria's mouth. And still watched Derrick.

As if when she was finished with Nuria, she would come for him. He shook his head, dipped his fingers in Nuria's dripping cunt again. She was so fucking wet. He slid into her. And gasped. *Ah!* It was good to be inside her again. She fit him perfectly. The firm squeeze of her pussy walls around him, the fit of her hips in the cradle of his pelvis, the smoothness of her skin under his hands. Perfect. Derrick closed his eyes.

For a moment, it could have just been the two of them. The purring glove of her pussy. Her moans. The fire skimming along his body in rising waves. But the sound of her mouth on Eva's cunt drew him back. The animal groans the other woman made. Her low cries of, "Yes. Eat my pussy. Show me you like it," pulled him from his illusion. The other woman's presence was as much of an intrusion as it was a turn-on.

He groaned and sped his movements inside the liquid pussy. Ah. She felt so good. His hands tightened on her hips as the fire flared higher inside him. The liquid slap of Derrick's thighs against Nuria's joined her groans, Eva's growled words of encouragement, and the frantic thud of his heart.

The woman shuddered as she came, her hips jerking against Nuria's still-lapping mouth. Eva jerked the dark head back, and Nuria moaned with the loss of it, but Derrick slid his fingers over her clit and her moan became a sigh. The sweat-slick line of her back slid under his palm and arched even more for him. Nuria panted.

Eva pulled off her tank top, and her breasts tumbled free. Derrick felt his face changing as his orgasm neared, as the pressure inside him built. In the haze of his impending explosion, he saw Eva approach him. Felt her hands on his back. His ass.

"I want to fuck your ass."

He exploded inside Nuria. Gasping and breathless, Derrick tried to hold himself still over her, but his body flinched away from Eva's possessive touch. Even in the midst of its shuddering descent, his body knew what it didn't want.

Derrick shook his head once. "No."

"Really? Not even for this?"

Eva gestured to her own body, its silken skin, the stiff nipples like cherries, and the sloping line of her flat belly that led to her hips and the thick, glistening clit. With the luxury of his recent orgasm, Derrick was able to say no again, to pull out of Nuria's sticky heat with its trailing web of cum stretching between them. She gasped beneath him.

They'd finished together. He felt it. He'd made sure of it. But Derrick also knew that she wanted more. With hunger burning still in her eyes, Nuria curled her body around like a snake to watch him. And Eva. His skin jumped at the thought of the other woman. If he hadn't been here, would she have been able to completely satisfy Nuria? Eva flashed him a smile, sleek body glistening, as if reading his thoughts. Even though his body wasn't ready for it yet, suddenly Derrick wanted to fuck Eva's ass. He reached for her. But she shook her head, dancing away from him, breasts dancing, too.

"Uh-uh," Eva said. "I'm not into that."

She knelt beside Nuria to release the bound girl. "It looks like you'll be the main dish," Eva murmured next to the delicate ear.

Derrick watched her gently undo the buckles that trapped Nuria's legs and arms, kissed each ankle and wrist as she released it. Nuria's body trembled, like a race horse that'd been put through her paces. The muscles leapt under Derrick's hands as he eased her gently to the floor instead of the collapse that she was heading for.

Above Nuria's back, Eva met Derrick's eyes as if to say, "Are you ready for more?"

Derrick had never been shy about sex. When he wanted it, he asked for it, or just reached out to take it. His sexual experience with women was vast—not many women, but many sexual encounters. As many as he could fit into a working and sleeping day. But as much as he'd sampled, he had never experienced anything like *this* before.

Nuria swallowed his dick, squeezing pleasure from him with her talented, endless throat, her eyes fluttering closed as if the most delicious thing she'd ever encountered lay across her tongue. Derrick groaned and clutched her hair. His neck arched back as his mind went up in flames. She seemed wholly focused on him, wrapping her hot mouth around his cock, sucking him deeply into her mouth as if nothing else mattered. As if Eva wasn't behind her, fucking her pussy with a big black dildo strapped to her slender hips. Eva's breasts bounced as she fucked Nuria. Jumping to the jackhammer rhythm of her hips as sweat slid over her body. On her face. Down her belly. Over the muscled arms holding Nuria's hips steady. The hard concentration of her face as she fucked and fucked.

The sounds Nuria made around his cock, sounds fucked into her from behind, only twisted him tighter in the web of desire the three of them created. The dick slammed into Nuria with a wet, ravenous sound, and she met each thrust with a hungry sound of her own. Derrick gripped her hair tighter. Fucked her hot mouth. Her hair tumbled over his fist.

The ropes burned. Derrick was sure of it. Nuria lay across the bed, stretched between the headboard and the foot of the bed, tied with her legs and arms apart. Eva lay stretched over her, lapping lazily at Nuria's breasts, sucking the pebbled nipples into her mouth, drawing sighs from Nuria's open mouth while both their legs swam open, teasing Derrick with the salty smell of their cunts that lay one on top of the other. His mouth watered. He drew closer. Fit himself at the drizzling founts of their sex. Sampled Eva's musky pussy, licked her, pulled the long petaled lips into his mouth, slid his tongue into her hole, fucking her gently as she gasped in surprise, then pleasure.

His fingers delved into Nuria's pussy just beneath, teasing her with what he could do with his tongue. Would do. Both women gasped. Moaned. And Derrick felt himself getting hard against the sheets even after his second cum, wanting them again. Ready for them. Again.

"Are you sure I can't fuck you?"

Eva's mouth opened and frantically sucked air. Her neck bent back as Nuria fucked her with quick fingers, two fingers plumbing into the dripping cunt, the thumb floating across Eva's clit with practiced skill. Nuria was sweating, too, her lips parted, tongue darting out to catch the sweat around her mouth. Her eyes focused solely on the taut, gasping, sweating body under her hands.

Behind her, Derrick felt like a spare. His dick lay soft, his own sweat drying, the condom drooped and full, its outer skin wet from Nuria's pussy from where she'd abandoned it and Derrick's dick moments before to lean farther into Eva, to focus more on making the other woman cum. Moments before, he had been clutched in a small heaven. His cock buried inside Nuria's sweating heat as she rode his, twisting like a snake in his lap, mesmerizing him, calling up fire and heat and fulfillment, his balls aching to come, her back and ass whirling as he barely held on, barely caught a breath as she, incredibly, fucked him, riding his dick like a rodeo pro, her hair flashing across her back as she leaned toward Eva, fucking her, too, with lightning-quick fingers, paying attention to both her lovers with equal generosity. Her juice dripped down Derrick's dick. The muscles of his belly and chest stood out in thick relief as pleasure shuddered through him.

Now it was Eva's turn. Her pussy eagerly swallowed Nuria's fingers, slick and slurping, her hard stomach vibrating with the force of her breaths. Her breasts shuddered as Nuria reached up to caress and squeeze the dark nipples. Derrick licked his lips at the sight.

"More," Eva hissed, splaying her legs wider. "More!"

Nuria gave her what she wanted. And as soon as she was done, as soon as the orgasm rocketed through her, Eva leapt on Nuria to feed on her breasts, cunt, and ass, waving her drenched pussy in the air in front of Derrick's face. What else could he do? He buried his face in it, diving into the hot banquet of flesh like a starving man at his last meal. The wet pussy slid under his tongue, flooded his mouth and chin. Her hole swallowed Derrick's tongue, clutched hotly around it until his dick stirred in response. Their moans were like music.

It was nighttime when they finished fucking. Darkness had descended on the room that smelled thickly of sex and satisfaction. The noise of late-evening traffic, a lulling wave of sound that threatened to put Derrick to sleep, came through the windows. He stirred from leaning back against the headboard and looked at Nuria sprawled in his lap.

"Hey," she murmured, blinking up at him.

Nuria seemed comatose in the aftermath of her pleasure, body limp, eyes unfocused, muscles now only twitching occasionally.

"Hey, yourself," Derrick said. He stretched his back, feeling the kinks release themselves as well as the beginnings of tiny aches that he would feel more in the morning. Nuria's hair slid through his fingers as he brushed it away from her face.

"You really care for her." From the foot of the bed, Eva's voice thrummed low in surprise.

Derrick looked at the woman. "Of course. Why are you surprised?"

"You better ask her that." Eva gestured with her chin to Nuria before slowly getting up from the bed to disappear through a door that Derrick only just then noticed.

"What did she mean by that?"

"Nothing." She blinked again and sat up in the bed.

Against his will, Derrick's eyes followed the movements of her naked body, even though he'd been feasting on it with his mouth and hands for hours. He dropped his head back against the wall to force himself to look in her eyes.

"Was this some sort of a test? Did you just call me here to see if I would do this?" he asked.

"No." She stood up, sweat limned and beautiful, and headed for the door Eva just disappeared through. "I called you here because I *wanted* you to do this." Nuria closed the door behind her.

When she returned from the bathroom, she was even calmer. Smelling clean but like someone else, she silently put her clothes on, keeping her back to Derrick.

"You can take a shower here if you like," Eva offered.

But Derrick shook his head. "Thanks for the offer, but I can clean up at home." He was already dressed and waiting for

Nuria. "Drop me off at my car," he said when she had all her clothes on. Derrick's mouth twisted when he saw her exchange a quick look with Eva. "I'm sure it won't take long," he added.

It felt strange to have her dressed again and by his side as they walked into the humid evening. The coyly cuffed jeans, ballet flats, and even the white blouse with its innocent sensuality seemed as if they belonged to a different time. Before tonight. Before the raw nakedness they had shared with the other woman.

Derrick put his hands, smelling like Eva and Nuria, in his pockets. "Are you going back to Eva's?"

At first, Nuria was silent. Only their footsteps sounded as they walked through the nearly empty parking lot behind Eva's condo. Then she stopped and turned to him.

"When you came to my house last time, you played me." Her eyes watched him carefully. "In that bed—*my* bed—I was someone I didn't think I could be. Weak. Under your control. Today was about getting that control back." She turned away, releasing him from her eyes. "And, yes, I'll probably go back to Eva's after you go back to your bourgie girl and pretend to be an honorable man. Maybe she'll keep on buying that and the rest of your bullshit."

Derrick clenched his teeth against her words. Trish wasn't in the picture anymore. He'd told her that things weren't working out for him. That he needed a break. But if Nuria didn't want him, there was no point in revealing that.

They climbed into her little white car for a silent ride back to his Lexus in the parking lot of the Bay Diner. Derrick opened the door.

"This is the last time I'll say it," Nuria said as her hands clutched the wheel. "I don't want to see you again. Don't call me. And I won't call you. This thing with us is poison. It's bad for me."

Derrick slammed the door shut and walked toward his car without uttering a word. There was nothing for him to say.

13

His skin didn't feel like his own anymore. It missed hers. Always felt stretched, like it was reaching across the miles toward her. Derrick ached. He didn't know what to do with the agony. Out of habit, he called Tori. The update to his sad story was finished by the time his clothes were a jumbled heap on the bedroom floor and the whisky rubbed hot against his palm through the glass. He stood at his kitchen table peering out at the inky quiet of his backyard.

"Did you think that she was just going to let you back into her bed like nothing happened?" Victoria asked.

From the distance of her voice, he could tell she had put him on speaker phone. She was making dinner in the house that she and Dez shared since renting out her little cottage. The hiss of something hitting hot oil, then a knife against the cutting board.

"I'm surprised she didn't cut off your balls and feed them to you. A woman sexually manipulated, especially a woman like Nuria, is not one to take lightly. You should know that."

"I never manipulated her." Derrick suppressed the rising whine in his voice. "I just showed her what it could like between us if she kept seeing me. That's it. There's nothing devious in that."

"But you knew that it could never be like that between you all the time. You were giving her a false, very false, impression of how it would be to be with you. And Trish." Tori laughed. Then sobered. "Sorry. I'm surprised she didn't offer to make it a threesome with you, her, and Trish just to get things out in the open."

"Me too." He'd actually imagined, especially as he'd lain there in the afterglow of their evening with Eva, perhaps he could talk Trish into something like that. But the thought had quickly been crushed in the wake of reality. Derrick sighed. "I actually miss her."

"Who, Nuria or Trish?"

There was no question. Although he'd broken it off with Trish after spending that last day in Nuria's bed, it was the volatile Dominican woman he would miss. That pouting smile. The fragrant sway of her hair when she laughed, rocking back and forth with mirth. The way she made worlds appear for him in the same moment that she destroyed his old one. Derrick raised the glass of whiskey to his lips and took a long sip.

"Who do you think?" he finally asked. "Who would you miss if you were in my shoes?"

Tori laughed. "You know I like bad girls. . . ."

When they finally got off the phone nearly an hour later, Derrick's skin was still hungry. The bottle of whiskey on the counter stood nearly empty, and he was close to feeling empty himself. He turned away from the counter, but the phone trilled and pulled him back.

On the other end of the line, a choked voice caught him by surprise. "Wasn't I good enough to have on your arm in front of your boss and all your friends?"

The whiskey congealed in his belly. "It's not like that."

"But you can't tell me what it's really like, can you?" Before he could speak, Nuria continued. "I could have loved you. I could have been your everything." The phone clicked and the dial tone dropped in his ear.

Derrick swallowed, staring down at the telephone with his fist wrapped tightly around it. The muscles in his jaw ached as he swallowed. Clenched his teeth. *He could have loved her, too.*

SEXUAL SATISFACTION

Ten years as a sex slave in a Turkish brothel left Lord Valentin Sokorvsky with an insatiable appetite for sex. Now the time has come for him to marry, but finding a woman who can satisfy his lustful desires proves a challenge . . . until he meets Sara and all he can think about is having her lie under his rock-hard body, begging him to taste and touch her. . . .

SENSUAL SEDUCTION

Sara Harrison knows she should be shocked and scandalized by Lord Sokorvsky's bold advances, but instead she is secretly aroused by this sensual, seductive man. For beneath her calm and composed manner is a wanton woman who longs for a man's intimate caress. She is most willing to be educated in the art of sensuality, to receive and give pleasure and to succumb to the wild desire that knows no limits. . . .

**Please turn the page for an exciting sneak peek of
Kate Pearce's
SIMPLY SEXUAL
coming next month from Aphrodisia!**

1

Sara pressed her fingers to her mouth to stop from gasping as she watched the man and woman writhe together on the tangled bedsheets. Daisy's plump thighs were locked around the hips of the man who pushed relentlessly inside her. The violent rhythm of his thrusts made the iron bedstead creak as Daisy moaned and cried out his name.

Sara knew she should move away from the half-open door. But she couldn't take her gaze away from the frenzied activity on the bed. Her skin prickled, and her heart thumped hard against her breasts.

When Daisy screeched and convulsed as if she were suffering a fit, a small sound escaped Sara's lips. To her horror, the man on top of Daisy reared back as though he'd heard something. He turned his head, and his eyes locked with hers. Sara spun away, gathered her shawl around her shoulders, and stumbled back along the corridor. She had her hand on the landing door when footsteps behind her made her pause.

"Did you enjoy that?"

Lord Valentin Sokorvsky's amused voice halted Sara's hurried retreat. Reluctantly she turned to face him. He strolled toward her, tucking his white shirt into his unfastened breeches. His discarded coat, waistcoat, and cravat hung over his arm. A thin glow of perspiration covered his tanned skin, a testament to his recent exertions.

Sara drew herself up to her full height. "The question of enjoyment did not arise, my lord. I merely confirmed my suspicions that you are not a fit mate for my youngest sister."

Lord Valentin was close enough now for Sara to stare into his violet eyes. He was the most beautiful man she had ever seen. His body was as graceful as a Greek sculpture, and he moved like a trained dancer. Although she mistrusted him, she yearned to reach out and stroke his lush lower lip just to see if he was real. His hair was a rich chestnut brown, held back from his face with a black silk ribbon. An unfashionable style, but it suited him.

He arched one eyebrow. Every movement he made was so polished, she suspected he practiced each one in the mirror until he perfected it. His open-necked shirt revealed half a bronzed coin strung on a strand of leather and hinted at the thickness of the hair on his chest.

"Men have . . . needs, Miss Harrison. I'm sure your sister is aware of that."

As he moved closer, Sara tried to take shallow breaths. His citrus scent was underscored by another more powerful and elusive smell that she realized must be sex. She'd never imagined lovemaking had a particular scent. She'd always thought procreation would be a quiet orderly affair in the privacy of a marriage bed, not the primitive, noisy, exuberant mating she'd just witnessed.

"My sister is a lady, Lord Sokorvsky. What would she know of men's desires?"

"Enough to know that a man looks for heirs and obedience from his wife and pleasure from his mistress."

She felt a rush of anger on her sister's behalf. "Perhaps she deserves more. Personally, I cannot think of anything worse than being trapped in a marriage like that."

His extraordinary eyes sparked with interest as he appeared to notice her nightclothes and bare feet for the first time. Sara edged back toward the door. He angled his body to block her exit.

"Is that why you frequent the servants wing in the dead of night? Have you decided to risk all for the love of a common man?"

Sara blushed and clutched her shawl tightly to her breasts. "I came to see if what my maid told me was true."

"Ah." He glanced back down the corridor. "Daisy is your maid?" He swept her an elegant bow. "Consider me well and truly compromised. What do you intend to do? Insist I marry her? Go and tell tales to your father?"

She glared at him. How could she tell her father that the man he regarded as a protégé was a licentious rake? And then there was the matter of Lord Sokorvsky's immense wealth. Her father's seafaring enterprises had not faired well in recent years.

She licked her lips. His interested gaze followed the movement of her tongue. "My father thinks very highly of you. He was delighted when you offered to marry one of his daughters."

He leaned his shoulder against the wall and considered her, his expression serious. "I owe your father my life. I would marry all three of you if such a thing were allowed in this country."

"Fortunately for you, it is not," Sara snapped. His face resumed the lazy, taunting expression she had come to dread. "As to my purpose, I thought to appeal to your better nature. I wanted to ask you not to dishonor my sister by taking a mistress after you wed and to remain true to your vows."

He stared at her for a long moment and then began to laugh. "You expect me to remain faithful to your sister forever?" His eyes darkened to reveal a hint of steel. "In return for what?"

"I won't tell my father about your dishonorable behavior tonight. He would be so disappointed in you."

His smile disappeared. He stepped so close his booted feet nudged Sara's bare toes. "That's blackmail. And there's no way in hell you would ever know whether I kept my word or not."

Sara managed a small triumphant smile. "You do not keep your promises, then? You are a man without honor?"

He put his fingers under her chin and jerked her head up to meet his gaze. She found it difficult to breathe as she gazed into his amazing eyes. Why hadn't she realized that beneath his exquisite exterior lay a deadly iron will?

"I can assure you, I keep my promises."

Sara found her voice. "Charlotte is only seventeen. She knows little of the world. I am only trying to protect her."

He released her chin and slid his fingers down the side of her throat to her shoulder. To her relief, his air of contained violence dissipated.

"Why didn't your parents put you forward to marry me? You are the oldest, are you not?"

She glanced pointedly at his hand, which still rested on her shoulder. "I'm twenty-six. I had my chance to catch a husband. I had a Season in London and failed to capitalize on it."

He curled a lock of her black hair around his finger. She shivered. His rapt expression intensified.

"Charlotte is the most beautiful and biddable of my sisters. She deserves a chance to become a rich man's wife."

His soft laugh startled her, and his warm breath fanned her neck. "Like me, you mean?"

Sara stared boldly into his eyes. "Yes, although . . ." She frowned, distracted by his nearness. "Emily might be a better match for you. She is more impressed by wealth and status than Charlotte."

"You possess something neither of your sisters has."

Sara bit her lip. "You don't need to remind me. Apparently I am impulsive and too direct for most men's taste."

He tugged lightly on the curl of her hair. "Not all men. I have been known to admire a woman with drive and determination."

She lifted her gaze and met his eyes. Something urgent sparked between them. She fought a desire to lean closer and rub her cheek against his muscular chest. "I think I will make a far better spinster aunt than a wife. At least I will be able to be myself."

His lazy smile was as intimate as a caress. "But what about the joys of the marriage bed? Might you regret not sampling those?"

She gave a disdainful sniff. "If what I have just seen is an example of those 'joys,' perhaps I am well rid of them."

His fingers tightened in her hair. "You didn't enjoy watching me fuck your maid?"

Sara gaped at him.

His smile widened. He extended his index finger and gently closed her mouth. "Not only are you a prude, Miss Harrison, but you are also a liar."

Heat flooded her cheeks. Sara wanted to cross her arms over her breasts. She trembled when he stepped back and studied her.

"Your skin is flushed, and I can see your nipples through your nightgown. If I slid my hand between your legs, I wager you'd be wet and ready for me."

Sara's fingers twitched in an instinctive impulse to slap his handsome face. She waited for a rush of anger to fuel her courage, but nothing happened. Only a strange sense of waiting, of tension, of need—as if her body knew something her mind hadn't yet understood. She let him look at her, tempted to take his hand and press it to her breast. Somehow she knew he would assuage the pulsing ache that flooded her senses.

As if he'd read her thoughts, he reached out and circled the tight bud of her nipple. Sara closed her eyes as a pang of need shot straight to her womb.

"Sara . . ."

His low voice broke the spell. She covered herself with her shawl and backed away. As soon as she managed to wrench the door open, she ran. His laughter pursued her down the stairwell.

Valentin stared after Sara Harrison as his shaft thickened and grew against his unbuttoned breeches. He absentmindedly set himself to rights and considered her reaction to him. She needed a man inside her whether she realized it or not. Perhaps he should reconsider his plan to marry the young and oh-so-biddable Charlotte.

His smile faded as he followed Sara down the stairs. John Harrison had a special bond with his eldest daughter. Knowing Valentin's sordid history, would John allow him to marry his favorite child? It was interesting that she hadn't been offered to him as a potential bride to begin with.

He strolled down one flight of stairs and made his way back along the darkened corridor to his bedroom. There was no sign of Sara.

Valentin surveyed his empty bed and imagined Sara lying naked in the center, her long black hair spread on the pillows, her arms open wide to welcome him. He frowned as his cock throbbed with need. Sara Harrison would not be a complacent wife. To lay the ghosts of his past, he needed to settle down with a conventional woman who would present him with children and leave him to his own devices.

Before leaving town, he'd spent an uproarious evening with his friends and current mistress, composing a list of the qualities a man required in a society wife. One of her sisters would definitely be a better choice. He suspected Sara would be a challenge.

Her frank curiosity stirred his senses. He'd wanted to part her lips and take her mouth to see how she tasted. He'd forgotten how erotic a first kiss could be, having moved onto more interesting territory a long time ago. Her innocence and underlying sensuality deserved to be explored. Wasn't that what he truly craved?

He stripped off his clothes and let them drop to the floor. The meager fire had gone out, and coldness crept through the ill-fitting windows and door. At least he had a few days' grace before he needed to make his decision. John Harrison was not due to return to his family until Friday night. Valentin climbed into bed. His brief, interrupted tryst with the enthusiastic Daisy had done little to slake his desire.

Valentin tried to ignore the unpleasant smell of damp and mildewed sheets as he closed his fist around his erection and stroked himself toward a climax. Imagining it was Sara who touched him made him want to come quickly. He didn't allow her image to destroy the sensual buildup of sexual anticipation that burned through his aroused body.

He pictured her startled face as she'd watched him fuck Daisy. Had she wanted to touch him herself? The thought made him shudder. His body jerked as he climaxed. He closed his eyes, and a vision of Sara's passionate face flooded his senses.

His last thought as sleep claimed him was of her coming under him as he took his release deep inside her again and again.

2

Sara glanced over her shoulder as Charlotte's girlish giggle rang out again. Whatever Lord Sokorvsky had said was obviously highly amusing. She resisted an urge to frown at the engrossed couple. She'd asked him to pay more attention to Charlotte and had no right to feel disappointed because he'd heeded her words. In truth, she should be delighted. She took a savage swipe at a buttercup in the grass with her parasol and decapitated it.

Daisy, her maid, had been ecstatic about Lord Sokorvsky's prowess in bed. Apparently he was the best lover Daisy had ever had. She'd gone on and on about the size of his cock and exactly what he could do with it until Sara begged her to stop.

Surely a true gentleman would make love to a woman with more gentleness and civility? Lord Sokorvsky reminded her of a swaggering pirate. Even his skin was tanned like a commoner. And the way he'd rutted with Daisy . . . She ignored the subtle throb of desire she experienced low in her stomach every time she pictured that rude coupling.

She sighed as she reckoned the distance to the ruins of the

medieval castle on the hilltop above them. Her mother had arranged the outing in the hopes of furthering Charlotte's acquaintance with Lord Sokorvsky. To Sara's surprise, her plan appeared to have worked.

She lifted the hem of her olive-green calico skirt and set off up the last part of the hill. Someone touched her elbow. She turned to find Lord Sokorvsky at her side.

"Good afternoon, Miss Harrison. Are you enjoying the view?"

Sara favored him with a cool smile, aware of the heat of his gloved fingers on her bare skin. "Good afternoon, my lord. The view was delightful until you obscured it. Please feel free to find another, less able lady to assist up the hill."

His fingers tightened on her arm. "But I wish to walk with you. You left me in a devil of a quandary last night."

She shot him a suspicious glance. "I am glad you have reconsidered your options and that I was able to guide you."

He looked politely confused and then gave her a slow smile that screamed danger. "I'm not talking about your little moral lecture but something far more important that kept me up"— he glanced down at his breeches "and awake for most of the night."

Sara kept her gaze on the ragged yellow grass in front of her. Did he think she was naive enough to ask him to explain himself?

"You are far too modest, my dear. Would you not like to know what I am referring to?"

Sara counted each torturous step and tried to control her ragged breathing. Her temper smoldered as the slope grew steeper. "No."

"I was thinking about your breasts."

He glanced at her averted profile. "If I might be even more specific, I spent several hours wondering what color your nipples are. Some women's nipples match the color of their lips, others are a surprise. Now, your lips are a deep rose pink. Are your nipples the same shade?"

To her annoyance, her nipples hardened into two tight buds as if they enjoyed being discussed. She continued to slog up the hill, refusing to join in such an insulting conversation. An urge to shove her outrageous companion in the chest and watch him roll merrily down the hill threatened to overcome her.

Lord Sokorvsky laughed softly as they reached the outer ring of fallen stones. "Silent, my dear Miss Harrison? That seems so unlike you. Perhaps you are breathless after our steep climb."

She stepped back and planted the tip of her parasol in the center of his chest. She met his amused violet eyes, a challenge in her gaze. Before she could apply any real force, Lord Sokorvsky brought his hand up and yanked the parasol from her grasp.

"Oh, no, you don't."

Deprived of her weapon, Sara cried out as she lost her footing and fell forward. He caught her in his arms and deliberately pulled her flush to his chest. The strength of his muscled grip surprised her. His heart thumped against her cheek as she struggled to right herself.

"Are you all right, Sara?"

Charlotte's anxious question made Sara jerk herself free. Lord Sokorvsky's triumphant grin disappeared as he turned to speak to her sister.

"All is well, Miss Charlotte. Your dear sister felt unwell after her exertions." He bowed to Sara, a picture of concern, and placed his hand over his heart. "I am simply glad that I was available to help a beautiful damsel in distress."

Sara straightened her bonnet. "You, sir, are no knight," she hissed as soon as her sister's back was turned.

His eyebrow rose in a slow arc. "I never said I was. And if you choose to challenge me, don't expect to be treated like a lady."

She swung on her heel and stomped off across the grassy mound of the ruined bailey to find better company. This was the second time Lord Sokorvsky had bested her in a fight. Should she ignore him for the duration of his visit and hope he made the right decision about Charlotte or continue to try to influence him? She couldn't decide.

She glanced sideways at him and found he was still watching her. His gaze settled on her breasts. Blast the man—all she could think about was him coupling with Daisy. He winked. Sara resisted an urge to button her pelisse.

A dense heat shuddered through her belly. He unsettled her in ways she didn't quite understand. Part of her, the wild, dangerous part she tried to suppress, was drawn to him; the rest wanted to run back to the safety of her boring life and hide. With all the determination she could muster, she began to talk to her sister Emily.

Sara spared a smile for her dinner companion as she rose from the table at her mother's signal. Sir Rodney Foster was an entertaining and clever man. He treated her like an intelligent woman. It was a shame he was already married. She stifled a yawn as her mother shepherded the ladies into the drawing room. Thick red velvet curtains blotted out all the natural light and created shadows in the overfurnished, fussy room.

Tea awaited them, with the prospect of a little musical entertainment and a lot of idle gossip. Sara often wondered what it would be like to stay with the men and discuss matters of real importance over a glass of port. As she matured, she'd begun to understand why men avoided coming in to see the ladies until they were foxed.

Sometimes she felt so trapped she wanted to run out of the stuffy drawing room and never return. She often dreamed that her mother and sisters stood over her, their faces full of love as they slowly suffocated her beneath a growing pile of petticoats.

Despite her considerable abilities, she had begun to understand that her choices had narrowed to spinsterhood or marriage.

She glanced across at Charlotte. Her sister had appeared in her room again last night, her face flooded with tears. Charlotte claimed Lord Sokorvsky frightened her and that he made her feel stupid. If it wasn't for her mother's objections, Sara knew Charlotte would already be married to her childhood sweetheart, the local curate, rather than chasing a man of Lord Sokorvsky's exalted rank.

Charlotte gave her a watery smile. Sara felt a familiar surge of exasperated affection. Why couldn't she simply say no to their mother and do what she wanted instead? Surely Lord Sokorvsky wouldn't want a wife who'd been forced into marrying him?

After an hour of insufferable boredom, Sara was even glad to see Lord Sokorvsky enter the drawing room. He was dressed in a simple blue coat and white breeches, which clung to his muscled thighs. His thick, dark hair was confined at the nape of his neck with a narrow black ribbon.

Exactly how long was his hair? Sara's fingers twitched to untie the ribbon and touch his luxuriant locks. She imagined it unbound, curling onto those broad shoulders. She folded her hands in her lap and stared down at them as Lord Sokorvsky came closer.

"May I get you some tea, Miss Harrison?"

Sara looked up, which gave her a perfect view of the bulging front panel of Lord Sokorvsky's tight-fitting pantaloons and his flat stomach.

"No, thank you, my lord."

He continued to study her. "You look well in that gown, Miss Harrison. With your strong coloring, you are wise to avoid the pale colors debutantes often prefer."

She glanced down at her rose-red gown and suddenly felt

naked. "I'm no debutante, but thank you, my lord. I didn't realize you were an expert on fashion as well."

Without asking for permission, he sat beside her. "When you've helped as many women as I have out of their clothes and back into them, you form some opinions."

Sara opened her fan with a snap. She must stop baiting him. Every time she tried, he trumped her efforts with the skill of a professional card shark. The sound of a harp being tuned saved her the necessity of replying.

To her consternation, Lord Sokorvsky continued to sit by her side as several young ladies performed with varying success on the harpsichord and harp. He stretched out his legs, and his long thigh touched hers. There was no space for her to move away, so she suffered the intimacy in silence.

Sara applauded Charlotte's dutiful if uninspired performance and glanced over at her mother. Surely it was time to end the dreadful evening? Lord Sokorvsky caught her hand as she attempted to rise.

"Miss Harrison, are you going to perform for us? How delightful." He linked his arm through hers and towed her inexorably toward the harpsichord. Sara's mother frowned and shook her head.

He sorted through the music and placed a double sheet in front of her. "If you are unsure of the notes, Miss Harrison, I'll sing along and try to drown you out."

Her mother sat down again, a false smile pinned to her lips. Sara began to play and immediately lost herself in the music. To her delight, Lord Sokorvsky had a pleasing baritone voice that blended well with her husky contralto.

A smattering of applause brought her back to the present and the realization that Lord Sokorvsky was smiling at her. Well, not exactly at her—his gaze had dropped to the low lace-edged bodice of her gown.

"Damnation," he murmured, "pink or red? I'm still not sure. . . ."

Sara tried to stand, but he handed her another piece of music. "Play this for me. I'm sure it's well within your capabilities."

She glanced at the Mozart concerto and began to play. The storm of applause that greeted her performance made her blush and hurry to her feet. She avoided her mother's eye as she gathered up the music. The chattering guests drifted out of the drawing room, leaving her alone with Lord Sokorvsky.

He took the pile of music away from her and stacked it neatly on the table. "You play like an angel. Why does your mother disapprove?"

Sara covered the harpsichord and blew out the candles. "Because she believes I play too well, and that is not ladylike."

"She's a fool. With your talent, you might perform professionally."

She gave him a guarded smile, aware that they were the last people in the room. "Ladies do not do that. I was quite disappointed when my mother told me I couldn't continue my studies abroad. Even when I begged my father, he refused to agree with me."

He laid her hand on his sleeve and led her toward the double doors into the hall. "I should imagine you were more than a little disappointed. You probably made your displeasure known for weeks and drove your father to distraction. You strike me as a little spoiled."

Sara laughed to disguise her annoyance. "I really can't remember how I felt, my lord. It seems so long ago." She attempted to disengage her arm as they approached the doorway. Before she could manage it, he pulled her behind the door. He pressed her against the wall; his body covered hers completely.

She bit back a scream as he stared down at her, his vibrant eyes full of heat. Every inch of his lithe, hard body was pressed firmly against hers. His mouth feathered her lips, and his tongue sought admittance. He kissed her slowly until she learned to kiss him back. When he drew away, Sara opened her mouth to speak.

"Sssh." He stroked his index finger across her full lower lip and continued the movement down her throat. She swallowed hard as his finger came to rest on her ruffled bodice.

She closed her eyes as he delved beneath the warm silk and exposed the tip of her breast. The rush of cold air on her heated flesh felt like ice on fire. His finger circled the tight bud of her nipple, and she shivered.

"Ah . . . deep rose pink. Like raspberries and cream." His approving murmur made her want to touch him, to beg him to touch her. In the hallway behind them, she could hear her mother exchanging pleasantries with one of the departing guests. He leaned closer, and she opened her eyes to find herself viewing the top of his head.

He cupped her breast through her bodice, forcing her rounded flesh to overflow her corset, and licked her exposed nipple. Sara bit down hard on her lip. Who would have known that such a small thing could bring such pleasure? He did it again, more strongly, and then sucked her nipple into his mouth.

Instinctively Sara arched her back and tried to give him more. She kept her hands fisted at her sides in a desperate attempt not to grab hold of his head and hold him there forever. His teeth grazed her, and she couldn't hold back a whimper of pure need. This wasn't right, but it felt so good. From the moment she'd watched him with Daisy, she'd wanted him like this.

He brought his head up and stared at her. He dragged down the other side of her bodice to reveal her other breast. "Spoiled and possibly shameless. If you were mine, I'd sit you on my lap every morning. I'd fondle and suck your breasts until you begged me to stop, until they were swollen and sensitive with need."

He returned to torment her until it felt as if she would explode. When he lifted his head, his breathing was ragged.

He studied her taut nipples. "Imagine how they'd feel against the lace of your gown and your corset. All day long, every time you took a breath, you'd remember my mouth on you." He slid his knee between her legs and pressed against the silk of her dress. "By the time I came to your bed, you'd be desperate for me to finish what I'd started. You'd be begging me to fill you with my cock."

Sara forgot about her mother and the servants. She could barely remember her own name. She shamelessly rubbed herself against the firm pressure of Lord Sokorvsky's knee wedged between her thighs. Somehow it seemed to relieve the ache that had built there since she'd caught him with Daisy. As she moved, another more frantic sensation grew instead. Her body was poised on the edge of something, but she didn't know what.

Lord Sokorvsky rolled her nipples between his fingers and thumbs. "If you looked at me like that, Miss Harrison, I might have to visit you during the day and fuck you on the dining table. Would you enjoy that? Would you like my cock filling every inch of you?"

His casual crudity made her stare intently at his face. Was he punishing her for interfering in his courtship of her sister? He ground his hips against hers, and she forgot all about her family. Her body warmed to his touch; her nipples ached from his attentions. She wanted to climb inside his clothes and lick his skin.

He dragged her hand down to his groin. "Can you feel what you do to me?"

The thick rod of his erection stirred under her hand. She wanted to unbutton his breeches. She wanted him to stop tormenting her and give her whatever it was she needed. He spread his hand over her buttocks and lifted her until she fitted against him. His mouth returned to plunder hers. Then he abruptly stopped.

Sara pushed him away and scrambled to pull up her bodice. She'd completely forgotten Lord Sokorvsky was expected to propose to her sister tomorrow. How could she have behaved so brazenly? He was her sister's intended. She still wasn't even sure if she really liked him!

"My father is due back tonight. Do you intend to inform him of your decision then?"

Lord Sokorvsky helped rearrange her bodice. His knuckles constantly brushed her sensitive flesh. "My decision?"

Considering her tumultuous state, Sara was amazed she sounded so calm. She drew in a deep, steadying breath. Damnit, he was right about the delicious friction of her aroused flesh against the fabric of her gown. "About marrying Charlotte. I'm sure he will be delighted."

He drew back and offered her his arm as they moved out from behind the door. "As to that, Miss Harrison, I haven't quite made up my mind about Miss Charlotte."

A familiar dry voice rang out from the hall and startled Sara. "I'm glad to hear it, Lord Sokorvsky, because if that is the case, you seem to be displaying an interest in the wrong sister."

She ran forward to hug her father, who waited at the bottom of the stairs in the deserted hall. He looked tired, and his greeting to her was distracted. Sara resisted the temptation to pat her flushed cheeks and check her bodice. Did her father know what she and Lord Sokorvsky had been doing?

"Sir, it is good to see you again." Lord Sokorvsky strode forward and offered his hand to Sara's father.

"Valentin, my boy, come into my study and share a glass of brandy with me." He turned to Sara. "Go to bed, my dear. And a word of advice; try to avoid being left alone with young men until you are suitably married."

Sara smiled at her father and kissed his cheek. He understood her so much better than her mother did. She curtsied to Lord Sokorvsky, who bowed. Her last sight of them was as her father firmly closed the study door.

Valentin took the glass of brandy from John Harrison and cradled it in his hands. Thank goodness he'd heard the carriage approach or he might have been discovered doing something far too intimate with his host's eldest daughter. There was no denying that Sara stirred his blood. He glanced down and hoped John hadn't seen the extent of his arousal as he approached him in the hall.

He waited until John took the chair opposite him. His old friend looked tired and drained. His once-abundant hair was thinning, his eyes sunken.

Valentin raised his glass to his host. "Thank you for inviting me to your home."

John grimaced as if the brandy tasted spoiled. "You know why I asked you here."

Valentin hid his hurt beneath another smile. He'd never been invited to meet John's family before. He was considered too dangerous. "Of course. You want me to marry one of your daughters. Preferably the youngest, if I recall."

"You've done well for yourself, Valentin. Your shipping business prospers."

"With Peter's help."

John drained his brandy glass. "You should rid yourself of Peter Howard, my boy. He does nothing to help your reputation."

Valentin smiled again, although the effort this time was greater. It was an old argument, one he grew weary of discussing. "I owe Peter the same debt of gratitude I owe you. Without him, I wouldn't have survived." Images of the lush, repellant brothel he and Peter had escaped threatened to flood his mind. With the ease of long practice, he pushed them aside.

"I did not offer Sara to you as a bride, yet you seem taken with her." John hesitated. "Sara is exceptional. Yet I fear she wants too much from the world."

"Because she is a woman?" It irritated him to hear John belittle his daughter. It was not surprising Sara felt stifled. Needing something to do, Valentin got up and added more brandy to both glasses.

John nodded. "She would've made a fine boy. All that intelligence and drive, wasted on a female. I admit I am to blame for her lack of docility. I allowed her too much freedom as a child. I encouraged her to pursue her studies in both music and arithmetic." He drank from his glass. "My wife insists I have made Sara discontented and unwilling to behave like a proper young lady."

"She seemed perfectly ladylike to me, sir."

"Sara will require careful handling. I see her marrying a much older man who is willing to tolerate her eccentricities."

Valentin drew in a breath. "Am I too young and repulsive for Sara, then? Or do you fear my 'interesting' past will taint her innocence and make her worse?"

John flinched and avoided Valentin's gaze. "You are a good man, Valentin, but . . ."

"After what you know of me, you don't want me to marry your favorite daughter." Valentin shot to his feet. "Well, I regret to inform you that she is the only one who interests me. If I can't have her, I'll pay off my debt to you in another way."

He left the study before he said something he might regret. The brandy burned a hole in his stomach. John Harrison had rescued him and Peter from a life of erotic slavery in a distant barbaric country. To his credit, John had never revealed to another soul exactly where he had found the two young Englishmen. His being enslaved for seven years was enough for most people to consider Valentin an oddity. Twelve years had passed since his rescue, and yet he felt as sick and vulnerable as his eighteen-year-old self.

It was obvious that the man he'd admired for over a decade didn't consider him fit to mate with his favorite daughter. He knew just how desperate John's financial state must be if he'd even considered him suitable for the other girls. The man hadn't quite masked his disgust at the thought of Valentin touching one of his precious children, although, to his credit, he had tried.

Valentin loosened the knot of his cravat. Christ, he wanted a bath, but it was far too late to disturb the servants. He paused at the bottom of the stairs and considered saddling his horse and disappearing into the night forever.

Turning, he walked back through the deserted kitchen and let himself out into the back garden. He fumbled in his pocket for a cigar and lit it. Should he abandon his visit? The cloying scent of honeysuckle invaded his nostrils and clashed with the smell of brandy and cigar smoke on his breath. He'd always hated strong fragrances. They reminded him of the lush per-fumed bodies of the customers he'd serviced, willingly and un-willingly.

In the distance, the lap of the sea against the shore stirred his overwrought senses. He moved sharply away from the long brick wall that bordered the garden. Would he ever be able to shrug off the rumors and innuendo about his life with Peter in a Turkish bordello?

For a brief while after his rescue by John Harrison, he and Peter had become reluctant celebrities. The release of two Eng-lish boys after years of captivity had fascinated the nation. To his annoyance, the newspapers still found it necessary to allude to his scandalous past whenever they mentioned his commercial success. Thank God they didn't know the full story, or he and Peter would be considered social pariahs.

After finishing his cigar, he turned back to the crumbling stone manor house. Perhaps John was right. Sara deserved a better husband. He pictured her slender figure in her rose-pink gown, her black hair braided high on her head in a shining coronet. He'd sensed her frustration, her desire to be free, and had deliberately offered her one way to relieve some of that tension.

Her eager response to his touch had unmanned him. Even now, a wave of lust shuddered through him. She didn't have the sexual experience to realize how strongly he was attracted to her.

Perhaps it was just as well.

A single tallow candle illuminated the somber grandeur of his bedchamber. Valentin strode to the window and drew the thick brocade curtains. A moth flew out of the fabric, drawn by the flickering candlelight. From the ramshackle state of the house, it was obvious that John needed money. The family lacked sufficient servants, and he'd noticed Sara and her sisters wore unfashionable, well-mended gowns. He was also convinced that Charlotte had no desire to marry him at all. Was she being forced into considering him by her rather overbearing mother?

He frowned. Was it possible that John was in danger of losing everything? If so, his desire to protect Sara from Valentin might cost him dearly.

Valentin caught the circling moth between his finger and thumb and pinched hard. Damnation, he'd leave a draft from his bank that should see John through the worst of his debts. He'd also try and forget his ridiculous notion that he was capable of sustaining a marriage.